NEST

ESTHER EHRLICH

A Yearling Book

Text copyright © 2014 by Esther Ehrlich
Cover and interior art copyright © 2014 by Teagan White

Visit us on the Web! randomhousekids.com

Educators and librarians, for a variety of teaching tools, visit us at RHTeachersLibrarians.com

The Library of Congress has cataloged the hardcover edition of this work as follows:
Ehrlich, Esther.
Nest / by Esther Ehrlich. — First edition.
pages cm
Summary: On Cape Cod in 1972, eleven-year-old Naomi, known as Chirp for her love of birds, gets help from neighbor Joey as she struggles to cope with her mother's multiple sclerosis and its effect on her father and sister.
ISBN 978-0-385-38607-4 (trade) — ISBN 978-0-385-38608-1 (lib. bdg.) — ISBN 978-0-385-38609-8 (ebook) [1. Family life—Massachusetts—Cape Cod—Fiction. 2. Multiple sclerosis—Fiction. 3. Sick—Fiction. 4. Schools—Fiction. 5. Bird watching—Fiction. 6. Cape Cod (Mass.)—History—20th century—Fiction.] I. Title.
PZ7.E332Nes 2014
[Fic]—dc23
2013036245

ISBN 978-0-385-38610-4 (pbk.)

Printed in the United States of America
10 9 8 7 6 5 4 3 2 1
First Yearling Edition 2016

FOR MY NEAL

PART ONE

CHAPTER ONE

I SHOULD HAVE TAKEN THE shortcut home from my bird-watching spot at the salt marsh, because then I wouldn't have to walk past Joey Morell, whipping rocks against the telephone pole in front of his house as the sun goes down. I try to sneak around him, pushing so hard against the scrub oaks on our side of the road that the branches scratch my bare legs, but he sees me.

"Hey," he says, holding a rock and taking a step toward me. He doesn't have a shirt on; it's been broiling all week.

"Hey," I say, real friendly, like I'm not thinking about the fact that I'm a girl and he's a boy who might pop me with a rock, since he comes from a family that Dad says has *significant issues*. The Morells have only lived across Salt Marsh Lane from us since early spring, but that's long enough to know that his two brothers are tough guys, and Joey, he goes hot and cold.

"It's getting kind of dark for you to be wandering around all by yourself," he says, tossing the rock up and catching it with one hand.

"I know."

"Things can happen to girls outside in the dark on summer nights," Joey says, smacking the rock into the palm of his other hand.

"I know."

"So where were you?" Joey asks, like it's his right to know.

"Nowhere."

"How was nowhere?"

"Just like somewhere," I say.

He looks at me, real serious, and then he smiles and drops the rock.

I don't smile back, since he might be trying to trick me, which is what tough guys do.

"How's your arm?" he says.

"My arm?"

"You know, do you throw like a girl?"

"I *am* a girl."

"Here," Joey says. He picks up some rocks and holds one out to me.

I don't take it, but I don't run away, either.

"Let me see you throw," Joey says. "You don't even have to wind up." His voice sounds gentler now, so

I take one baby step closer to him. His blond hair is as dried out and tangly-looking as a song sparrow's nest. I can just hear our teacher from last year, Mrs. McHenry, saying, "A comb, young man. Do you not know the *function* of a comb?" if he had ever dared to show up in class like that.

"Stupid mosquitoes!" Joey says, slapping his cheek. He's got three bites on his forehead and too many bites on the rest of him for me to count without him asking what the heck I'm staring at, like maybe I'm interested in his skinny, suntanned chest. His bites look like hot-pink polka dots, which means he's been scratching, scratching, scratching.

"Why don't you go get some bug dope to keep the mosquitoes off you?" I ask.

"'Cuz I can't go in."

"Why can't you go in?"

"'Cuz I'm locked out."

"But the lights are on," I say. "It looks like someone's home."

"They're all home," Joey says. "They're having dessert. Chocolate pudding. But I'm locked out." I want to ask Joey what he did wrong, but I don't want to make him feel worse.

He throws a rock against the telephone pole. *Bam.* "Your turn."

I grab a rock from the ground and take a few giant steps so I'm a whole lot closer to the telephone pole than Joey. Too close to miss.

Bam.

"Not bad," Joey says. He comes and stands next to me. He smells like the lime Dad cuts up for his gin and tonic before dinner.

Joey's turn. *Bam.*

My turn. *Bam.*

His turn. *Bam.*

My turn. *Bam.*

"Crap," he says.

"Crap," I say.

"Double crap."

"Triple crap." Dad says swearing is *inappropriate* and not what he expects to hear from either of his daughters. I don't know if *crap* is officially a swear, but I do know there are lots of more polite words in the English language.

Joey picks up a whole handful of rocks. He throws them into the air, and they smash down on the road.

"Is your mom's leg okay?" he asks.

"Not really."

"That sucks."

"Yeah, it sucks." My heart is pounding.

"I *love* chocolate pudding," Joey says.

I pick up more rocks and hand them over to Joey. He throws them up really, really high, and we run out of the way to make sure they don't crash down on us.

"When will they let you in?" I ask.

"When they're good and ready," he says, flapping at the mosquitoes near his face.

"Want me to go get you some bug dope?" I ask.

"Nah." He bends down to get more rocks. When he stands up, he looks right in my eyes. His are gray-blue, like the water in our inlet on a stormy winter day.

"You're not gonna tell anyone that—"

"Don't worry," I say.

"I guess you'd better get home."

"Yeah."

"Catch you on the flip side," Joey says. I feel him watching me. It's like a light shining on my back as I walk away.

"Joey?" I stop and turn around.

"What?"

I want to ask him when he was paying so much attention that he noticed Mom's left leg.

"Nothing."

"Whatever you say, Milky Way." He starts whipping rocks again. *Bam bam bam* follows me across our road, up six stairs, and home.

⚏

Rachel and I are in the middle of Salt Marsh Lane, singing louder than the rain that gushes down on us and smacks the asphalt like a zillion tiny drumbeats while we twist and shout in our matching green bikinis. Finally the sky's opened up after way too many days of the 3 *h*'s—hazy, hot, and humid.

"Well, shake it up, baby, now . . ."

We sing so loud that I bet Mom can hear us, even though she's sitting on the porch in her watching chair and not dancing with us, since her left leg isn't strong enough these days to carry her down our six stairs, let alone do the Twist. She's not dancing with us, but her laugh is here. It makes me laugh and Rachel shimmy like she *has* something to shimmy, but she really doesn't have much. I have even less, being two years younger.

"Hey, Chirp," Rachel says, slowing down her shaking shoulders, "let's do it for Mom. Can you?"

"Can *you*?" I answer.

"Of course, we cancan!" we shout at the exact same time. We stop twisting. The cancan isn't exactly the coolest dance to be doing in 1972, but Mom loves it. I slither my wet arm around my sister's wet waist. She slides her arm, warm, around me. Now we're kicking our legs high, flinging streaks of cool water into the steamy air. Little streams land on Rachel's tanned, blackberry-scratched legs. *Good, strong girl-legs,* Mom calls them. When we're sure Mom's watching, we do our special reverse formation, taking tiny steps backward, legs straight, chins up, just like she taught us. My bikini bottom's slipping down in all our kicky wetness. I yank it up, hoping Mom doesn't notice. I don't want to wreck our show. I don't want Mom to feel disappointed. I want to be a success like

Mom was when she used to dance in contests in New York for the grand prize. Most of all, I want Mom to keep on laughing, *heeee heeee hee hee hee,* like some kind of bird I'm trying to identify by its happy sound.

We're gearing up for our finale. I'm crouched down low in the sandy dirt by the side of the road, facing Rachel, who's still in the middle of the road. My job is to splash through the puddles and spring into my sister's arms. *One, two, three* and I'm running fast on my girl-legs. Does Mom see how strong they are? *Light as air, soft as a feather, light as air, soft as a feather.* I fly up toward Rachel's arms just as there's the biggest flash and then the loudest crash. The scrub oaks glow with light. *"Whoaaa!"* Rach yells, and hits the deck, scared. Without her arms to catch me, I land, hard, on top of her. My arm scrapes the road, and I wonder if there's blood. With my ear on Rachel's chest, I can hear her heart beating.

"Okay?" I ask, but I know she's fine. We're tough as nails, is what Mom tells us. What I really want to know is if Mom's all right. Did the thunder and lightning scare her? Is her laughing squeezed down so deep that I'll have to wait a long time again to hear it? I lift my head off Rachel and make myself look through the rain at our front porch. Dad's hovering over Mom. She's peeking around him like she's trying to check on us, but he moves his body in the way. I bet he's talking to her in his psychiatrist voice, explaining what's what. He puts his arm around her shoulder and steers her inside like she just might get lost, even though she's lived in this house since before I was born.

"Don't worry. We're okay!" I shout after them, but the screen door has already bumped closed.

Time to get up. If Joey and his brothers look out their window and see me lying on top of my sister, they'll call us lezzies and try to dunk us the next time we go swimming in Heron Pond. They might try to dunk us anyway, because we're Jews and they're not, but I don't want to give them more ammunition.

"Let's go," Rachel says, just as I'm rolling off her and pulling her to her feet. I check my arm. No blood, just trickles of water.

"Let's go see if Mom liked our dance," I say, flinging my wet hair out of my eyes.

"She and Dad are probably talking," Rachel says. "We should give them privacy."

"But I want to find out if she liked our cancan."

"Dad told us at lunch that they're worried about Mom's leg. It's been more than a week now that it's been hurting her. Just leave them alone." Rachel's heading for the stairs.

"That's not what he said." He said they were *terribly preoccupied,* which I'm pretty sure is psychiatrist secret code for *Don't you dare bother us,* but I hate admitting that maybe Rachel's right and I shouldn't go check on Mom.

"What *did* he say, then?" Rachel asks from halfway up the stairs.

"I'm singin' in the rain!" I belt out, ignoring her. She sits in Mom's watching chair on the porch while I take big, swaying steps down the middle of our road, like I'm Gene Kelly in the movie and there's nothing that's worrying me, nothing at all, since there's nothing in the world but a sky crammed with dark clouds and these fat, beautiful drops of rain.

⇌

My favorite bird in August is the red-throated loon, and my favorite time to see the loons is now, when the rest of the family is still sleeping. I need to move fast so that I'm up and at 'em before Dad wakes up. He has an early patient four days a week, so the odds are good that this is one of those days. I wouldn't want to be him and listen to people talk about their problems when the day is just beginning and nod *uh-huh, uh-huh, uh-huh,* like I understand everything about everything.

I slept in my green bikini, so all I need to do is pull on my jean cutoffs. I've got my knapsack pre-packed with my birthday binoculars, notebook, pen, and pennywhistle, and I grab it off the hook on the back of my door. I slide down the banister so I can avoid the stairs' squeaks. Breakfast is important for clear thinking, but I don't need to think clearly when I'm looking for loons, so I skip it. Anyway, there's a blackberry patch with ripe berries on the way to the salt marsh. I leave a note that says, "Back before long. Love, Chirp," in case anyone notices that I'm gone.

The air's already thick and warm, even though the sun's still just a spritz of light in the pitch pines and scrub oaks and not a hot, round ball bouncing on the top of my head, like it will be soon. On the path behind our house, bunny tracks in damp sand, wet spiderwebs, mourning doves, chickadees, a couple of crabby starlings, and the *thwop-thwop, thwop-thwop* of my blue flip-flops. No delivery trucks yet racing down Route 6. In class last year, Mrs. McHenry taught us that Harriet the Spy is good at what she does because she's observant and that careful observation is a skill all of us should develop while we're young, so I'm working on it.

If I take the biggest steps I can from the beech tree, I'll be at the fork in the path in thirty-eight steps, unless my legs grew a lot since last Thursday. This time I'll try to hop the whole way, no counting. Anyone seeing my tracks will think I have just one leg, like Timmy Mahoney, who was just honorably discharged from Vietnam and hangs out in the town square smoking cigarettes with his pant leg neatly folded up and safety-pinned. But if they observe the ground closely, like they're supposed to, they'll wonder why there's no sign of crutches. It'll be a mystery, solved only by a team of searchers with magnifying glasses and sniffer dogs. And at the end of the investigation? Just me, an almost-sixth-grade girl who hopped on one foot on her way to look for red-throated loons.

Red-throated loons can't walk on land, because their feet are too far back on their bodies, but they can use their feet to kind of shove themselves along on their bellies. Underwater, it's a whole different story: they're fast and graceful and do all kinds of cool stuff, like dive super deep down to catch fish and flap their wings when they really want to put the pedal to the metal. When Dad first met Mom, she was scared of the water, since she grew up in the Bronx, where there aren't any ponds or lakes. I guess there might be swimming pools, but her parents were too poor and busy to teach her how to swim, since they were immigrants from the old country, and even put her in the Hebrew Orphan Asylum for two years when she was really little because they didn't think they could afford to keep her. Dad, on the other hand, was a very patient teacher, and now Mom can swim okay, even when it hurts to walk. We found that out yesterday morning when we all went to Heron Pond to try our experiment.

The pond wasn't crowded, because all of the summer people were scared off by the storm clouds. In general, summer people only like blue-sky days for swimming, and they leave the not-blue-sky days to locals like us and the Morells and go play miniature golf and eat soft ice cream at Windee's Dairy Breeze.

"Now, don't push yourself, Hannah," Dad said, but Mom was already walking toward the water with her long, slow dancer steps and her dark, twisty dancer bun.

"Here I go," she said, dipping in before Dad could catch her and finish his lecture. She swam underwater all the way to the rope at the other side of the shallow area and then started doing laps.

"Bravo!" Dad yelled from shore.

"Bravo!" Rachel and I yelled, but Dad shushed us and said that Mom preferred not to draw attention to herself.

"But, Dad," I said, "you're the one who—" But he wasn't listening, because he was already sprinting toward Mom, just in case her leg decided to give her more of that new nasty business.

Rachel had her fake smile on, which means she's upset but won't admit it.

"I think Mom would like us to cheer. Don't you, Rach?" I asked, standing close enough to her that I could smell lemon shampoo and see the goose bumps on her arm. Rachel shook her head and wouldn't look at me, like I'd done something wrong.

"Go, Mom, go," I whispered, jumping with my legs bent up behind me like a cheerleader.

"Stop it, Chirp," Rachel said. "You're being a baby.

Dad knows what Mom wants better than you do." Then she folded her arms and stared out at the water like she was having deep thoughts. I looked at her hard to get her to look back at me. What I observed was that her hair is wavy-curly, not corkscrew-curly like mine, and her eyes aren't green with different colors sprinkled in. She's got Mom's eyes, nice dark brown ones like wet dirt.

"Fine," I said when she still wouldn't look at me, and I dove into the water just like Mom. I skimmed my belly along the sand until my lungs ached and I had to pop up. I figured it was about a minute, which is the average time that my red-throated loons stay under.

The truth is, I've only seen a few in my whole life. They're not easy to find, like cormorants and herring gulls. The encyclopedia says that the red-throated loon population is declining, due to the fact that we're messing up their habitat with oil spills and garbage. I'd like today to be my lucky day, but that might mean lying low and watching for hours, and my stomach's already grumbling, since I forgot to load up at the blackberry bushes. Being hungry won't kill me, but dehydration is a real possibility in the summer heat, which is why Dad says Rachel and I must always take responsibility to bring our own canteens, filled up, when we go on family nature walks, and he really shouldn't have to remind us since Rachel is no longer a child but in adolescence and I'm not far behind.

No one's here to remind me what I am and what I'm not, which is a good thing, like this spot under the pitch pine that has a perfect view of the water, and my birthday binocs, which turn the sun sparks on the water into big bursts of light, and the air that's so salty and warm I open my mouth, again and again, and gulp it into me—not sweet like blackberries but almost as satisfying.

⚓

"Oh, oh," Mom says, fluttering her hands like butterflies around my face, "you, my girl, are the loveliest creature on all of Cape Cod, the prettiest one on land or sea." We're sitting together at the kitchen table, and Mom's pulled my curly hair into a twisty bun and tied her purple silk scarf around my neck. Dad would *not* approve of a hairbrush on the kitchen table, but Dad isn't here. Just me and Mom. Just Mom and me. I turn up Herb Alpert & the Tijuana Brass.

Mom smiles at me. Her leg hurts a lot less today, and she thinks that maybe whatever ugly beast grabbed hold of it has let go. As Dad was walking out the door to go to his office this morning, I heard him say to Mom, "Promise me that you'll lie low on your alone night with Chirp and read a book or just take a bath," but now she's reaching for me, swaying and bending like dune grass in the wind.

"C'mon, Snap Pea," she says, twirling in front of

me. She turns the record player up even louder. I take her hand and she leads me to the middle of the kitchen. At first, she closes her eyes and just rocks back and forth in time to the beat. I rock, too, but my eyes are wide open. I could watch Mom all night, with her eyes closed tight and her quiet, pretty smile and her rocking. I like how the wavy hair by her ears ticks back and forth, like our metronome. Her neck is long and skinny, like the necks of the Modigliani ladies in the art book at school. She's wearing her really short sleeveless dress that's green like the bay leaves she drops into spaghetti sauce, and her arms and legs and even her feet look strong—not like a muscleman looks strong, but more like pictures I've seen of tigers running. A trumpet shouts and Mom's eyes pop wide open. "C'mon, baby!" She's dipping and diving like the craziest bird. I'm laughing so hard my ears feel hot. "Show me your stuff!" So I do my lowest limbo and my highest leap while Mom claps her hands. She grabs me around the waist, and we whirl together in a tight circle. Lavender, sweat, lemons. We spin until the song stops, but still we don't let go. Mom's heartbeat is all over my body. When she sniffs the top of my head, I feel a cool puff of air.

"You know how much I loved to dance when I was your age, right, honey?" Mom asks, turning off the record player and sitting down at the table. She dances every day, practicing in the studio on her own or rehearsing with the Saltwater Dance Brigade, not counting the last while, when she hasn't been able to dance at all.

I nod, hoping she'll tell me the story anyway.

"When I was in fourth grade at P.S. 16, a modern-dance troupe from another school did a performance at assembly. I'd never seen anything like it. All of those beautiful, strong girls dancing their hearts out. 'That's me! That's me!' I said to myself. I was so excited watching those girls that I could barely stay in my seat." Mom taps her fingers fast, *tip, tip, tip,* on the table.

"I raced home after school and ran into the kitchen, where my mother was chopping onions. Isn't it funny that I still remember that—the stained wooden cutting board, the pile of onions, the way my mother held that big knife?" I nod, but Mom isn't really asking me.

"'Mama,' I said, running up to her, 'I'm a dancer!'

"She didn't even look up from her onions. 'No, you're not,' she said. 'You're just a silly little girl who doesn't know anything about anything.'

"I felt like I'd been slapped. Here I was with this amazing discovery, this fantastic news. And my mother didn't even want to hear it.

"'Mama,' I tried again. 'There were dancers who came to school, and they did a show for us, and—'

"And do you know what she said to me? 'And I suppose if you saw the circus, you'd be telling me you're an elephant. Now go change out of your school clothes and pull the laundry in off the line.'"

Mom shakes her head slowly. She sighs. "My mother was a *chaleria*. That's Yiddish for 'a very difficult woman.' She sure didn't give me an easy ride." Now Mom's all drifty and sad. She's talking to me, but I'm not sure she really sees me. I think she's seeing that gloomy old apartment in the Bronx and her mean mother, who I don't even have a name for, since she died four days before I was born; and maybe she sees the gray walls and gray floors of the orphanage where her parents dumped her when she was only three years old and picked her up two years later and never even said they were sorry. She had to stand in a long line of girls and have her head checked for lice by a lady who was probably as awful as Miss Minchin in *A Little Princess.* Poor little-girl Mom.

I touch her arm. She looks up, startled. "Mom," I say, "so tell me about how you learned to dance *anyway.*"

"Oh, honey," she says. Her voice is different now. Wiped out. Washed out. Done. "You already know the story. I took lessons in secret. Mr. Blumenstein, from the temple, paid for my classes. You've heard all of this before."

I take the record off the stereo and hold it carefully by the edges. Mom doesn't even open up the jacket for me.

"Mom?"

First she rubs her face. Then she looks around. Then she rubs her face again. It takes forever before she opens up the jacket. I slip the record in. On the album cover is a lady with whipped cream all over her body and a blob of whipped cream on her head. Mom and I look and look together. We're careful observers.

Finally Mom smiles. *"Mmmm-mmm,"* she says. "Whipped cream."

"Mmmm-mmm," I say, smiling, too. While it's still just the two of us, just us and no one else, we turn off the downstairs lights. We flick the porch light on and sit together in the living room on the gold velour couch in the almost-dark and cricket-quiet.

CHAPTER TWO

DAD BELIEVES IT'S CRUCIAL that a family bonds together, so that means lots of talking, like right now at the dinner table, when I'd rather just look out the window and watch the tree swallows swoop down and catch horseflies while I eat my mashed potatoes.

"Naomi?" he asks again, and Mom looks at me like *Honey, please,* so I answer him that, yes, it's a little hard that there are only two weeks left of summer vacation.

"And how are you feeling about the start of school?"

"Okay."

Dad sighs and runs his hand through his wavy dark hair.

"Anything you're particularly looking forward to?"

"Not really."

Dad scrunches up his eyebrows. He's probably

trying to decide how much he should push me to express myself, which he thinks is an important thing for me to learn to do better. On our last alone night, he bought me an ice cream sundae at Benson's and asked a ton of questions, like *What is it about having just turned eleven that's special?* and *Why do you like to watch birds?* I just wanted to eat my chocolate ice cream with hot fudge and whipped cream, but I made myself answer all of Dad's questions. My answers weren't long enough or deep enough, though, because I noticed Dad's forehead all wrinkly with disappointment.

Rachel's leaning forward in her chair, looking right at Dad and smiling. She reminds me of Sally, who always raises her hand in class and never blurts out, even when it's a hard math problem and she's the only one with the answer.

Once when I asked Rachel what she and Dad did on their alone night, she looked at me like it was the craziest question.

"We *discussed* things, Chirp," she said. "*Important* things. That's what Daddy and I always do."

Now Dad asks, "What about you, Rachel? How are you feeling about the start of school?"

"Well," Rachel says, setting down her fork and taking an excited breath, "it's been a great summer so far, but there's a lot about starting eighth grade that I'm looking forward to. I expect that I'll learn all kinds of new things about—"

Dad reaches for his glass of red wine, sits back in his chair, and smiles.

I'm off the hook, and just in time. Two swallows dive-bomb for the same snack. I watch them shoot toward the ground, then do a U-turn, *urrrreeeeech,* like in the cartoons, and disappear into the purple-dark sky. Mom watches me watching them. I think she gives me the teeniest wink.

⇌

"Ready for our expedition?" Mom asks. She's wearing her floppy orange sunhat and—just like me—her black one-piece bathing suit under her jean cutoffs.

"Ready," I say. Every year Mom and I celebrate the end of summer by going for a hike on the Wood Thrush Trail, just a few minutes' drive up Route 6. But this year Mom's leg isn't quite up to it. Our expedition today was my idea, which Mom says is proof that she can always count on me for creative solutions.

I've already schlepped the duffel bags with the fold-up kayak, my backpack with my binocs, and a canvas bag that Mom packed with hard-boiled eggs, cheese, Wheat Thins, and watermelon out to the car. Joey Morell watched me from his front porch. He's always just sitting out there by himself. "Moving out?" he said, but I pretended not to hear him, because even though he didn't throw rocks at me the other night and actually was pretty nice, he chose Sean O'Keefe as his best friend, and Sean is definitely rough around the edges. Also, Joey has two nasty brothers, and you never know when they'll rub off on him. Dad says that the Morells aren't fully intact as a family, which probably means that they don't have long discussions at the dinner table or take nature walks together. I think the Morells think Dad's the one who's missing some marbles, since he's a Jewish headshrinker who doesn't just vacation here in August, like all the others, but actually lives here year-round and doesn't boat or fish or drink beer in cans and last month offered to pay Vinnie Morell to fix our broken porch step instead of just doing it himself.

"Let's go, my girl," Mom says, and tugs on the end of my braid. "Dragonflies, here we come!"

Today Mom can walk down the front stairs, but she has to hold on to the banister. "I'm still just a little wobbly," she says, "but soon I'll be leaping down these stairs. I can feel it in my bones." I want to sing *"Weebles wobble but they don't fall down!"* like in the commercial, which I think Mom will think is funny, but just in case she doesn't, I don't. Mom manages okay walking across the front yard to the car; she's just kind of slow.

The door handle on the car is hot, even though it's still early. "Whew," Mom says, "it's going to be a scorcher!"

"Three *h*'s," I say in my radio voice.

"Hazy, hot, and humid," Mom says in her radio voice.

"The mother and the daughter roll down all of the car windows in an attempt to cool off the car before entering," I say.

"Then, fearless and brave, they enter the car—"

"—hot as it is, and head off on their adventure!"

"Stay tuned for—"

"—the next installment of—"

Mom looks at me, giggling. "Umm . . . help me out here, honey."

"Overheated Mama and Her Daughter, Toasty Roasty!"

Mom laughs. "Perfect."

She pulls out onto Route 6. Since it's summer, there's plenty of traffic. The warm wind swirls around us. Mom's smiling. I'm smiling. Mom turns on the radio. *I feel the earth move under my feet. . . .* I sing along, really loud. Mom shimmies her shoulders and hums off-key. I wish we could drive all the way to Hyannis. Or maybe we could keep on going right over the Sagamore Bridge to Boston. We could take a ride on the swan boats, like we did the last time we were there. We could eat a picnic in the Boston Public Garden. We could send a postcard home to Dad and Rachel: *Sorry for the short notice, but we've always wanted to see Canada, where the geese come from and men who don't want to be drafted to Vietnam can go and live in freedom. Don't worry. Chirp will learn*

25

tons on the road. We'll try to be home for the High Holi-
days. If not, please forgive us. All our love, Hannah/
Mom, Chirp

Mom pulls off Route 6 onto a paved road that
turns into a dirt road that turns into a bumpy sandy
road that most summer people aren't brave enough
to drive on. Mom looks nervous, biting on her bottom lip, but I know she's determined that we'll have
our expedition, since her achy leg already messed
up our tradition of hiking on the Wood Thrush Trail
and Mom is a big believer in traditions. "Here we go,"
she says every time we hit a new bump or a blackberry bramble swipes our window. Even though Mom
knows exactly where we are, this looks like the kind
of road you could get lost on. Mom hates getting
lost. Last Thanksgiving when we were going to visit
Grandma and Grandpa, we took a wrong turn on the
highway and Mom and Dad got in a fight right in front
of us and Dad said, "You have *got* to work out this
ancient fear, Hannah, because it's absolutely impossible!" and Mom yelled, "I'm doing just fine, Mr. Privi-
leged Childhood!" and Dad yelled, "Well, *this* is a good
way to begin the visit with my parents!" and Mom
yelled, "At least you *have* parents to visit!" because
both of her parents have been dead for years. Rachel
whispered to me, "Mom hates getting lost because of
the orphanage," which I still don't really understand.

"Mom, is the reason you hate getting lost—"

"Shah, Chirp. I'm concentrating here," she says,

just as the road gets wider and ends, right in front of Dragonfly Pond. "Ta-da! I knew it!" She pulls over and parks the car.

We get out, take off our cutoffs, throw them on the seat, and walk right over to the edge of the pond. The water is tons of shades of blue and green. It ripples and dances, shooting off more sun sparks than I've ever seen.

"Wow," Mom says. She takes my hand and we walk a few steps into the water. The sand is soft. The water bumps, warm, around our ankles.

"It's a mystery, Chirp," Mom says. "Magic. A scorcher in August and we have this whole sweet pond to ourselves!" Her voice is peaceful and excited at the same time, like she's blessing the Shabbos candles. Even though she gave up most of her family's Orthodox Jewish traditions when she left home at sixteen to study dance, she still thinks Shabbos is a special time that should be passed down through the generations, and so we always light the candles and say the blessings. I'm about to ask Mom if we can just sit in the shallow water and watch stuff for a while when she reaches for my hand.

"Let's just sit for a while," she says. She puts her arm around me. We watch two bright blue damselflies zip and dip and chase each other. We watch a bunch of minnows swim right up to our toes, then dart away. We watch a pickerel, like a dark green flute, floating around in the reeds. My plan was to put the kayak together and paddle us around the pond, but right now right here is just right.

"Whew, hot, hot, hot." Mom slowly leans back until she's stretched out in the water. "Ahhh," she says, and when she laughs, her belly makes ripples. I lie down, too, warm water filling my ears. I hear my breath. I hear my heartbeat. The sky throbs, as bright blue as the damselflies. A flash of yellow. Goldfinches! Mom grabs my hand and squeezes. *Yes! Yes!* I squeeze back.

⇋

"Naomi Eva—"

Everyone giggles.

"—Orenstein?"

"Here."

That's the way it works. You always giggle at everyone's middle name when it's read out loud during attendance on the first day of school. I turn around in my seat and try to look mad, which is what I'm supposed to do. Actually, I like my middle name, because it belonged to my great-grandmother on Mom's side, who was one smart Russian lady who knew enough to hide out in a field from the Cossacks for three days and nights with her two daughters and just one little bit of cheese and a piece of bread so they wouldn't be picked on and maybe even killed for being Jews. After today, Miss Gallagher will skip our middle names. And by the end of the week, she'll skip our last names, too, except for the Lisas, who'll get an initial, since there are two of them. Lisa R. and Lisa B.

Miss Gallagher tells us that she assigned the lockers boy-girl, boy-girl because she assumes that we know how to treat each other respectfully now that we're in sixth grade, which means, of course, no hair-pulling or name-calling or trying to see underpants, like we did when we were little. I think she's brave to even say the word *underpants* on the first day of school, or maybe because she's a new teacher she just doesn't get it. Sean O'Keefe starts laughing, and Joey Morell whispers, "Where, oh, where's the underwear?" which makes Sean laugh so hard he starts to slide out of his seat, and they both get sent out to stand in the hallway and think about whether this is really the way they want to begin sixth grade.

"Let's talk a bit about our summers," Miss Gallagher says, but she's still shuffling papers on her desk and not looking at us, so everyone keeps talking.

"Hey, Chirp"—Dawn Barker leans over—"are you taking the bus home?" which she's asked me, I swear, every day since first grade. Mom says maybe it's like a nervous tic and Dawn can't really help herself. I always take the bus home, since there's no other way to get home. And I always sit next to Dawn, who is pale and skinny and mostly still reads picture books, because there's something not quite right with her brain.

"Yup. Do you want to sit together?" I ask.

"Yeah," Dawn says, smiling, and hands me a green SweeTART.

"ONE, TWO, THREE," Miss Gallagher starts counting, and since she forgot to tell us what number she's counting to or what the consequence will be, we all quiet down out of surprise.

"Of course, I know we'll have a terrific year together," Miss Gallagher says, but her eyes are flitty, and I don't think she's convinced. I try to show her with my eyes that I'm paying attention, because most of the other kids aren't and I'm already feeling sorry for her. The end of the school year is a long, long time from now.

In the middle of her speech about how we're all part of the classroom community and need to follow the same class rules so we can work well together and benefit from the opportunities that learning offers us, Joey and Sean must be getting bored out in the hall, because they start making peace signs in the window in the door and Lori Paganelli and Debbie Leland crack up, because they think everything Joey and Sean do is hysterical, period. Then the boys bump against the door, *wham,* but Miss Gallagher must have bad hearing, because she doesn't do anything.

"Shouldn't they be in here listening to the rules?"

Claire DeLuca asks in her breathy voice. Lori and Debbie glare at her, and I know she'll be sitting by herself at lunch. Just as I'm picturing her at the picnic table all red-faced and nervous, nibbling on her ham-and-pickle sandwich and trying to ignore Lori and Debbie, who will sit really close and touch each other's hair and trade Fritos for potato chips, she mouths *Lunch?* to me from across the room. I hold up my book.

"Is there something you'd like to share with the rest of the class, Naomi?" Miss Gallagher asks.

"Uh, no thanks," I say.

"If you're not planning to share your book with all of us, perhaps I should—"

She's coming at me with her hand out, but I'm already shoving my book onto the wire shelf under my chair.

Sally gives me a thumbs-up, because she's the biggest bookworm in the world and understands how important reading is to me. Claire gives me a thumbs-down, because she's mad that I'm going to read during lunch instead of saving her from Lori and Debbie. Meanwhile, Dawn is humming the chorus to "I Woke Up in Love This Morning" by the Partridge Family over and over so quietly it sounds like the buzz of the lights on the ceiling but much worse. First day of school, and it's not even halfway over.

⇔

"Doesn't sound like you were in the best hands today, kiddo," Mom says when I tell her about underpants and peace signs and almost getting *The Burgess Bird Book* snatched away by Miss Gallagher. She buzzes around and I follow her while she pulls on her black leg warmers, puts up her hair, and grabs an apple.

"Maybe she was just having beginner's bad luck," Mom says. "I bet she'll get the hang of it soon. Don't you think, Chirp?" She touches my cheek with her warm fingers. Her fingers are always warm. "Change out of your school clothes. I've got to hurry to rehearsal. I'm still taking it a bit easy, so I'll be home soon, definitely in time to make dinner." She's so happy to be rehearsing again. The Saltwater Dance Brigade is having a show soon to protest the war in Vietnam, and Mom's a dead soldier. She choreographed the dance, which is something she hasn't done since before we were born. I watch her purple dance bag bonk against her hip as she walks down the front steps.

"Mom?" I yell.

She turns around.

"Nothing!" I yell. She gets in the car and slams the door. "Be well," I whisper.

Now it's my turn to buzz. I eat four Fig Newtons, change into my jeans, grab my knapsack, and head out. There's no time for hopping or counting steps, since it will be dark before too long and darkness isn't where I'm supposed to be when I'm alone. Last week I tried to find out what could happen to me in the dark. Mom and I were reading together on the porch when I saw an eastern wood-pewee flap by. I jumped up and told Mom I wanted to follow it for as long as I could.

"I understand that twilight is the best time for watching birds, but I don't want you out alone in the dark," Mom said.

"But—"

"Absolutely not," Mom said.

"But what will happen to me in the dark?" I asked.

Mom sighed, hugged me, shook her head, looked sad, looked worried, but didn't answer my question. Sex is usually what it's about when grown-ups don't answer questions, but I'm not sure which neighbor would be outside doing sex in the dark, since everyone has bedrooms, which is a lot more private. If I catch Rachel in the right mood, I'll ask her and she'll tell me. In the wrong mood, she'll look at me and shake her head and say *That's an inappropriate question for a girl your age,* and I'll want to knock her block off, since *inappropriate* is one of Dad's words and it makes me mad when she copies him instead of just being a normal thirteen-year-old sister who tells me what I need to know.

Right now what I know is that I'd better start watching if I want enough watching time, even though I'm not in my pitch-pine perfect spot yet. I pull out my binocs and keep walking. I see a red-winged blackbird pecking dried-out blueberries off a bush. I see some fishing line wrapped around a cattail. I see a seagull standing so still by the edge of the water it looks like a windup toy that needs to be wound up. I check out the sky, and it's still daytime blue with no purple dusk swirled in. I check out the seagull, and it still needs winding. Up, blue sky. Down, stuck seagull. Blue sky. Stuck seagull. Blue sky. Stuck seagull. My careful observing makes me dizzy. I let the binocs dangle from the strap around my neck and just look with my eyes. And then I see him. A little man in a lumpy green jacket, sitting right in my perfect spot. His back's against my tree.

Without my binocs, I can only tell what he isn't. He isn't a fisherman, because he doesn't have buckets and boxes. He isn't a landscape painter, because he doesn't have an easel. He isn't a hippie singer, because he doesn't have a guitar.

With my binocs, he's a she. She's rubbing her face, and her hands are wrinkly and her hair is snarly and dried-out and really needs conditioner. Mom thinks conditioner is an unnecessary expense, but Dad says that she's being overly influenced by the deprivation in her past and he would like his daughters to be freed up from that pain, which means that my hair is extra soft and shiny and smells like coconuts right after I've showered. The lady's jacket is too big, and she's kind of snuggled down inside it. Her eyes are closed, but she's thinking, not sleeping. I can tell by the way her mouth twitches and her forehead is all scrunched up. She doesn't look upset, but she doesn't look peaceful, either. I guess she looks like she's trying to figure something out.

She's got half a sandwich sitting on top of a plastic bag on the ground next to her. She must not be from around here, or she'd know that if you leave a sandwich out, the black ants call a party. Maybe her family all died and now she's wandering around the country trying to find a new home with decent people who will love her. Or maybe she's the one who's sick and she ran away so that she wouldn't be a burden to her family.

I could sneak out food and blankets to her and help her make a home in the woods out of branches woven together with dune grass. Sometimes in the summer Rachel and I sleep outside in the woods or in the sand at the edge of the salt marsh, and if you remember that the crunchy night sounds are just chipmunks and birds, it's really peaceful. I could let the lady stay in our toolshed with the snow shovels and flowerpots when it gets too cold. I'll lend her my sleeping bag and old copies of *National Geographic* so she won't feel too lonely at night, and I'll bring her hot soup in a thermos when it snows. Mom's been teaching me how to make soup, and so far I can make mushroom barley by myself, which is a good winter soup. The lady probably isn't Jewish, but if she is, I'll show her how to make a menorah by poking holes in a raw potato and sticking the candles in, so that she can keep her tradition alive and feel connected to her ancestors. Dad says that it's important for people to feel connected to where they've come from and to understand their past so they can make sense of their present, which is what his work as a psychiatrist is all about.

Now the lady's standing up and waving a stick so I'm sure to see her.

"Hello!" I shout, waving back. Maybe she got disoriented in the sun and needs me to give her directions out to Route 6. Before she goes, I could let her borrow my binocs so she can check out the birds.

I start walking toward her. She's waving the stick harder.

"I'm coming!" I yell. "I'll be right there."

She's waving her other hand above her head, too. She must be in some kind of a hurry.

Like a speed walker, I take long steps and swing my arms until I'm right in front of her.

"Hi," I say, nice and gentle, like I'm talking to a lost dog.

She doesn't say anything, just keeps on shaking the stick and shaking her hand.

Maybe she's hard of hearing. Maybe she only speaks Portuguese, like some of the early inhabitants of Provincetown that we learned about last year in social studies.

"Hi," I say again, nice and loud and slow. "Do you need me to show you how to get to Route 6?"

"You know what I need?" Her voice is soft and raspy. She might be crying a little, or maybe it's just that she's gotten too much wind and sun and salt spray in her eyes. "I need you to just leave me alone. I'm sorry, but I really need some peace and quiet."

She wasn't signaling me over with her stick; she was waving me away! She was shooing me from my own special spot. I'm a kid and she's a grown-up, so I have to listen to her. I want to smile a big smile to show her I'm just fine, thank you, but my chin is trembly and my lips feel scrunched up, like I've just sucked a lime fished out of Dad's empty gin and tonic glass. My eyes are watery, and it's not from wind or sun or salt spray.

"Have a good day, lady," I whisper.

As I walk away I hear her mumbling, "Just a little peace and quiet. Peace and quiet, that's all I want." When I know she can't see me, I start running down the path. I'm Pocahontas, racing through the woods without making a sound. No thuds. No twig snaps. Just peace and quiet. Quiet and peace. I'm the fastest, quietest runner in the world. I run so fast that even the wind can't keep up with me. I run so quietly that even the ants can't hear my footsteps.

Take the left fork in the path. *Peace and quiet. Quiet and peace.* Running this fast, I'll be home in a flash, a milli-flash, which is one thousandth of a flash. No one will be there yet, so I'll have four more Fig Newtons and then I'll feel better. I'm at the beech tree. There must be a speeder on Route 6, because I hear a siren, messing up my peace and quiet. No, it's not the police on Route 6. It's an ambulance with flashing lights on Salt Marsh Lane. An ambulance with flashing lights in front of our house. There's an ambulance with flashing lights in front of our house.

"Mom!" Rachel screams from the front porch as the ambulance drives away. White lights flashing, and the awful red wail of that siren.

CHAPTER THREE

"**D**O I HAVE TO flip them over?" I ask Rachel.

"What does the box say?"

I'm making fish sticks while she makes a salad. I've never made fish sticks. I keep checking on them, because the last thing we need tonight is burnt-black fish sticks thrown into the trash.

"It doesn't say."

"Then you shouldn't flip them," Rachel says.

"Okay."

I don't know how Rachel knows that I shouldn't flip them when the instructions don't say that, but I don't want to fight. She's working really hard to peel the cuke for the salad just like Mom does, sliding the peeler toward herself instead of away. There are little flecks of green all up and down the cuke.

"I don't mind a little skin, you know. It's got extra nutrition," I say.

Rachel gives me a tired smile and shakes her head. "I can do this," she says to herself. "I can do this."

I like the smack of heat when I open the oven door. I'm shivery-bone cold, even though I just took a long, hot shower. Rachel stayed in the bathroom with me the whole time, because we wanted to have a good alibi if Mrs. Morell knocked on the front door and tried to make us come over to her house to eat supper even though we have Dad's permission to stay here by ourselves until he and Mom come home from the hospital later.

"Oh, really? We didn't hear you knock," we'll say if Mrs. Morell ever questions us, which probably won't happen, since, based on my observations, she never leaves her house. Anyway, just in case, we won't be lying, which is something you don't do to an adult, even one who has three lousy boys and a yelling husband you can hear through the closed windows, and even when you have a good excuse, like you were shooed away from your special spot and your mother got rushed to the hospital when you thought she was at dance rehearsal.

"What happened to Mom?" I asked Rachel after the ambulance was gone and we were in the front hall with the door closed and no more siren.

"You're shivering and it's warm out," she said. "You should go take a hot shower."

"First you have to tell me what happened to Mom.

You have to tell me that right now." My body wouldn't stop shaking with scared shivers.

Rachel stared at me like she was trying to figure out what my words meant. She looked like a troll doll with her bugged-out eyes.

"Rachel!" I yelled. She blinked her eyes and started talking super fast.

"Mom forgot her boom box, so she came back home to get it and was walking down the stairs to go back to rehearsal. I saw her fall. All the way to the bottom step. I was just getting home from school. 'I couldn't help it,' she said. She told me to call an ambulance, and they came and they checked her. 'I can't feel my left side,' she said, and they put her on a stretcher and then into the ambulance. They called Dad, and he said that he'd meet them in the emergency room in Hyannis and that we had his permission to stay here, and then you came home with the shivers."

"Were they nice to Mom? Was she scared? Was she crying?" I asked.

Rachel looked at me. She took a big breath. First her eyes got wet with tears, and then her tears spilled over. She sobbed and sobbed, so I took her hand and walked her to the couch. I held on to her and rubbed her head and said, "You don't have to worry" and "You don't have to talk," and because of that she hasn't told me anything else, not while I showered, not while we've been making dinner, so I still don't know if Mom was scared and crying.

Fish sticks used to be for when we had babysitters, but clearly our babysitter days are over, because we're doing a very good job taking care of ourselves. The fish sticks look perfect, golden brown. And if you ignore a couple of green spots on the cukes, the salad looks just like Mom's, with lettuce and slices of tomatoes and capers. Mom believes in salads every night, because she says they're the closest thing to eating spring.

"Wash up?" my sister says, and we stand together at the kitchen sink and wash our hands with Palmolive and dry them on the dish towel.

"Time—" she says.

"—for dinner," I say, and my sister and I sit down at the kitchen table that we've already set with two plates and two cups and two forks and two knives and two napkins so we can eat our perfect fish sticks and our almost-perfect salad.

I have the privilege of reading in the reading corner, since I proved to Miss Gallagher that I understand how the Pilgrims and Indians helped each other out, by getting all of my multiple choices on the worksheet right.

"Your pick, Naomi," Miss Gallagher said, smiling,

and now I'm sitting by myself on a puffy red pillow on the floor, trying to decide. I'd like to read *The Burgess Bird Book,* but the rule is only reading-corner books, since Miss Gallagher specifically selected them to improve our reading skills.

"Ten more minutes to finish up your worksheets," Miss Gallagher says, which means I only have ten more minutes in the reading corner. I'd better get cracking.

I want to read the book about the girl who runs away and hides out with her brother in the Metropolitan Museum of Art and sleeps in the fancy beds, but then I can't read the one about the girl who wants to be a writer. And there are two other books that sound just as good, and that's not even counting the poetry book about birds and bugs.

I try spreading the books out in front of me on the rug, closing my eyes, and pointing, but the trouble is that I remember which book is where, and so it's the same as picking one and I just can't.

"Naomi," Miss Gallagher says from her desk at the front of the room, "I hope you're using this privilege well. It doesn't look like you're reading."

My heart's beating fast.

I make myself pick up the poetry book and open to the first page. I try to read, but the words are blurry, and when I blink, the tears spill down. They're coming faster and faster. I've got to wipe them away quick, before anyone notices. I don't know why I'm crying, but I can't stop. Now my shoulders are shaking, and Miss Gallagher notices.

She's not at her desk, as usual, where she can keep an eye on all of us and make sure we're behaving respectfully. She's standing here above just me and whispering, "Really, Naomi, it's nothing to cry about," but it's a scold whisper, and everyone hears her and turns and looks. I'm not a crybaby. I'm tough as nails. That's what Mom always says, but Mom and Dad didn't come home from the hospital last night like I thought they would, and Rachel and I had to get ourselves ready for school with no parents at all, and now I'm not tough as nails; I'm crying like a big fat baby right in front of everyone.

On the bus ride home, Dawn hands me a whole pack of SweeTARTS. We're not allowed to eat candy on the bus, but I do anyway. Sean sits behind me and says, *"Waah waah waah,"* and Joey smacks him in the arm and says, "Shut up about stuff you don't understand," which makes me think that maybe he wouldn't have dunked us in Heron Pond after all.

When the bus pulls up at our corner, Joey and I get out and I run ahead of him, because I see Mom's car, so I figure she's home before I remember that it was the ambulance that drove her to the hospital and her car being parked out front means nothing. I cross my fingers and hold my breath and fly up the stairs and open the front door. She's lying on the couch with a quilt up to her chin.

"Snap Pea," she says, but her voice is soft and creaky, and she doesn't sound like her.

I'm walking so I can close the terrible space between us when Dad shows up and stands in the way.

"Your mother's tired," he says. "Let's let her rest."

Mom's eyes are fluttering closed. Dad puts his arm around me. He twitches like he's nervous, but he doesn't let me go.

"Honey, I know that this is hard for you. I'm sure you're feeling helpless," Dad says.

I'm not sure how I'm feeling.

"That's a natural reaction right now."

I wish Dad would be quiet.

"If you want to talk about your feelings, of course, I'm here."

What I want is for Dad to stop talking. Just me and Mom. Just Mom and me.

But Dad doesn't stop. He talks about *trauma*. He talks about *pain*. Then he starts walking, and since his arm is still around me, I have to walk, too. I have no choice but to walk away and leave Mom with something wrong with her alone in the room.

⇌

We're going to watch TV together while we eat our dinner, which isn't something we ever do, because there are better ways to occupy ourselves, which makes us people with richer lives. Tonight, I guess, we don't need richer lives. We just need to get through dinner, which is Dad heating up canned tomato soup and Rachel and me making open-face cheese melts in the toaster oven and then carrying it all on a tray into the living room, where Mom is stretched out on the couch, pretending to be interested in *Get Smart*.

"Pretty funny, kiddos," she says, but she can't fool me. She doesn't think the show is funny, and she doesn't think the way her left leg drags along the ground when she walks is funny. Nothing funny at all about two days and nights stuck on the couch so that she's close to the bathroom. And I bet she really doesn't think it's funny that the doctors have no idea what's wrong with her, even though they did a bunch of tests in the hospital and then just told her to take it easy and not to worry and they'll know more if new symptoms show up and she feels like a ticking time bomb, a damn ticking time bomb, which is what she told Dad yesterday when he brought her a bunch of brownish-pink hydrangeas from the garden to cheer her up and they thought I was loading the dishwasher but I was actually spying on Mom.

"Very clever," Dad says, staring at the screen. "I'm actually quite impressed."

"Yes," Rachel says. "It's really impressive."

"The dialogue is well written and certainly holds its own," Dad says.

"Yes," Rachel says, "it really does."

I want to yell, *MOM, I KNOW YOU DON'T FEEL LIKE LAUGHING,* but she's trying so hard to be a good sport, nodding and giggling and holding Dad's hand, so I just touch her hand and smile.

"My bird girl," she says, looking away from the TV for a second and right at me with her dark brown eyes, and suddenly I want to tell her about the marsh lady and her shooing stick. Then I see the purple circles under her eyes and I know it isn't right to say anything. Mom is sick and I am fine.

Dad says, "This is terrific, watching TV together. Isn't it?"

So I laugh when Agent 86 takes off his shoe and uses it as a phone, and I laugh when the Cone of Silence comes down on Agent 86 and Chief and they start yelling secret things at the top of their lungs for everyone to hear. I fill the room up with my *haaaa* so there's no room for anything else.

When Rachel and I are upstairs in the bathroom brushing our teeth, she says, "You know, Mom will die if she has to give up dancing."

"No, she won't!" I say. "Take it back."

"It's just an expression. Don't you know that?"

"Take it back anyway."

"No," she says. "Don't be stupid."

"Just take it back!" But she shakes her head, all

stuck-up and stubborn, so I elbow her in the ribs and she spills water all over the front of her yellow nightgown, which makes what she's got on her chest totally obvious.

"You're *such* a baby. Look what you did!" she yells.

"Girls!" Dad shouts up from downstairs.

"Sorry, Daddy!" Rachel shouts back.

We're both red ashamed, because Mom and Dad need our fighting right now like a hole in the head. But still Rachel doesn't take it back. She rubs her nightgown really carefully with a towel, like she thinks that what she's got might disappear, and stomps off to her room. And I go to bed without saying good night.

⚎

Miss Gallagher has pink lipstick on. She's put Dixie cups filled with Hawaiian Punch and a plate of store-bought sugar cookies on Claire's desk and is saying, "Please, everyone, make yourselves at home, have a cookie, and then we'll get started." Mom could make herself at home much better if there was a couch she could stretch out on, like in our living room, and if everyone wasn't staring at her, trying to figure out if there's anything else wrong with her, *poor thing,* besides her draggy leg.

Yesterday in assembly our principal, Mrs. Mitchell, said that it's a bold new adventure to invite students to accompany their parents to back-to-school night, and she's sure it will be a worthwhile experience for us all. I'm not so sure. For example, Tommy is wearing a white button-down shirt and a navy-blue tie that must be strangling him, because he keeps pulling at the knot, even though Mr. Gale glares at him and whispers, "Cut it out, boy." Joey doesn't have a parent problem, because his parents didn't even show up. He's sitting by himself with at least five sugar cookies stacked up neatly on a napkin on his lap, but no one says anything to him, since he's probably allowed to have extras to make up for the fact that he's all alone. I don't know how he got here, but if Mom and Dad offer him a ride home, I'll say *Race you to the car* and I'll get a head start so he'll chase me and he won't end up walking behind Mom and having extra time to see her draggy leg. My final example is Dawn, who's circling the classroom with her parents following her. She's trying to find some of her work to show them. The trouble is, none of her work is pinned up, because she hasn't finished one single thing since school started over three weeks ago.

"Over here?" Mrs. Barker asks, pointing.

"Nope," Dawn says.

"Over here?" Mr. Barker asks.

"Nope," Dawn says. Round and round while the rest of us sit here, waiting for Miss Gallagher to get started.

Finally Miss Gallagher says, "Pilgrims and—?" We're supposed to say "Indians!" to show that we're paying attention, but this doesn't feel like school, since we're sitting with our parents, so we don't say anything.

"PILGRIMS AND—?" She tries again, louder.

"INDIANS!!!" Dawn yells, and her parents smile and rub her back.

"Welcome," Miss Gallagher says. "Let's begin by having the adults introduce themselves and say one thing that they're looking forward to in this new school year."

Maybe no one told her that in the off-season this is a tiny town and all of us kids have been in school together since kindergarten, except Joey, and the parents are always bumping into each other at Flanagan's Market and at the Savings and Loan. Claire's dad, Mr. DeLuca, even took Debbie's mom, Mrs. Leland, out for a fancy dinner at the Oyster Bar and Grille, and they clinked wineglasses and touched each other's hands, because they didn't think anyone would see them at such a snazzy place on a Tuesday night a few miles out of town, but somebody did. Lots of families have lived here for *generations,* which is why Mom and Dad say it's a hard community to break into and maybe they would have given up and headed back to New York if Dad hadn't absolutely fallen in love with the Cape way back when he was an intern at the Thorne Clinic and dreamed of meeting a woman who'd love it like he did. Then he met Mom at a party in Boston and brought her to the dunes in Truro on their third date and she did love it; she loved it so much.

Mrs. Barker says, "I'm Gloria Barker, Dawn's mother, and I'm looking forward to Dawn improving her reading skills and really, well, reading," and Mr. Barker says, "Ditto," and most of the moms and a couple of the dads smile and nod, and if I were Dawn, I'd be embarrassed, but she waves her hand above her head, all happy.

Joey's sitting next to Dawn, and there's a long silence and no grown-ups jump in to save him, so he says, "Joey Morell. Field trips, like to the P-town lighthouse. My brother dropped me off tonight, because my parents couldn't come. He just got his license."

Then Lisa B.'s parents. Then Lisa R.'s parents.

Mr. Paganelli says, "I'll leave this to my wife," and Mrs. Paganelli starts a speech about how pleased she is that Miss Gallagher has joined our community and how we all wish her great success in leading our children forward in their educational pursuits. Whenever Mrs. Paganelli decides to wrap it up is when it will be Mom's turn, so I look over at her next to me and her eye is flicking side to side, like she's reading at supersonic speed. I don't think she notices. She's just looking calmly at Mrs. Paganelli with her other eye. I don't know what to do. I poke Dad, and I guess I look scared, so he leans in front of me and sees what's going on. He whispers in Mom's ear, and she covers her supersonic eye with her hand. Then Dad says, "Excuse me. I hate to interrupt, but we need to leave right now." When we stand up, our chairs squeak, *eeeeeee,* and Mom wobbles, so Dad holds one arm and I hold the elbow of the arm with the hand that's covering her supersonic eye. Joey jumps up, *eeeeeee,* like he wants to help, but Dad and I, we've got it covered, and that's the end of back-to-school night for us.

⇌

Twinkies, Yodels, Ring Dings, potato chips, and Screaming Yellow Zonkers! At Sally's house, you can just open up the cabinet next to the stove and dig in.

"We're well stocked today, honey. Help yourself," Mrs. Trowbridge says, grabbing a pink can of Tab from the fridge and heading back to the sofa in the den to catch the end of *As the World Turns,* her favorite soap opera.

I'm crouched in front of the open cabinet, staring.

"C'mon, Chirp, let's go to the basement and work on our dance routine," Sally says, biting into her Ring Ding.

"Hold on," I say. I love looking at the pictures on the boxes. I love reading the descriptions: "Frosted Creme-Filled Devil's Food Cakes." "Sweet Glazed Crispy-Light Popcorn Snack."

"You can always come back for more."

I've been playing at Sally's house since I was little,

but I still can't quite believe that the treats won't disappear, *poof,* as soon as I walk away.

"Chirp!" Sally's tugging on my shoulder.

I grab a Ring Ding and a Yodel and another Ring Ding and follow Sally down the steep wooden steps into the basement. By the time my feet hit the green shag rug, I've eaten all of the first Ring Ding and half of the Yodel.

"Don't your parents feed you?" Sally laughs, shaking her head so her wavy blond hair bounces around.

"Yeah," I say, "a strict diet of Fig Newtons with a few Oreos thrown in."

"You're *too much,* Chirp. *Too much,*" Sally says, which cracks me up, since she sounds exactly like her grandma, who I see every year at Sally's birthday party.

Sally walks over to the record player. "What part of our routine should we work on?" she asks.

"I don't know. I can barely remember what we came up with last time."

We've been choreographing a dance to "Help!" by the Beatles since we were in third grade. Our bad habit is that we let too much time go by between practice sessions, and then when we finally get together, we've forgotten the routine or it feels babyish.

"I have an idea," I say. "How about if we have a dance party instead?"

"But we should finish—"

"I could *really* use a dance party."

Sally opens her mouth like she's about to argue with me, but then I see in her eyes that she remembers Mom and back-to-school night last week, though I know she won't say anything. Sally doesn't talk much, especially about hard stuff. When we get together, we eat and dance. Dance and eat.

"Party!" Sally shouts, plugging in the lava lamp on the Formica bar top.

"Party!" I drag the beanbag chairs out of the middle of the room.

You can stack six 45s on Sally's record player and they'll play in a row, which is perfect for a party. Sally chooses our tunes.

"Let the *r-r-r*-records *r-r-r*-roll!" I yell.

"For our first song, let's see you get down and dirty to Stevie Wonder's 'Signed, Sealed, Delivered'!" Sally says, like she's a DJ.

I start out calm enough, but soon the thumping of the music sneaks inside me and settles in my feet. I'm stomping, stomping, stomping, and Sally is, too. Faster! Louder! We're teenagers in the high school gym, stomping on the metal bleachers, cheering for our basketball team.

"Jump!" Sally yells, and now we're jumping up and down with our arms above our heads.

"Twist!" I yell. We twist and jump like wild rabbits getting their kinks out.

When I start whirling in circles, Sally copies me. Our hair's whipping around and the room's spinning.

We're bonking into the beanbag chairs. Watch out! We're shiny silver balls in a pinball machine! Sally takes the hem of her T-shirt and sticks it through the collar and yanks it down so it turns into a T-shirt bikini top. I turn my shirt into a bikini top, too, and now our bellies are out. Our bellies are out and we're wiggling them. We're wiggling our bellies and we're wiggling our hips and we're wet with sweat, and when David Cassidy sings *"I think I love you,"* we know he's singing to us. He's got to be singing to us, because we're just so filled up with everything good and bright and shiny that how can he not be crazy in love with us?

⇌

It's almost twilight, which means I shouldn't be heading to the salt marsh by myself, but I don't care and I don't think anyone else does, either. I didn't even bother leaving a note. Dad's still working, Mom's still napping, and Rachel's probably at her new best friend Genevieve's house, and I bet she'll end up staying there for dinner again, because Genevieve's family is *so cool* and *totally on the right wavelength* and *wicked interesting.*

No hopping, no counting, just my strong legs and this almost-twilight chilly air that feels sharp to breathe in, like eating mints. I've got my binocs, a wool sweater, and some cheddar cheese in my knapsack, in case I get hungry. I'm not scared, even though the branches of the pitch pines are already making spooky shadows. I'm not scared.

I run past the dead beech tree. I run past the fork in the path. I run and run until I see my perfect spot, loud and clear. I pick up a big stick, which might be *her* stick.

"Listen, lady," I whisper. It's hard to talk into the purple swirl, darking up the sky. It's hard to talk into the bird squawks, cricket chirps, water slaps. I take a deep breath. "Listen, you," I say again, louder. "This is *my* tree. This is *my* spot. You had no right to shoo me away." I stop. I wait. Nothing happens.

"How would you like it if you were just wanting to watch birds in your special spot and a lady shook a stick at you? Do you think you're the only one who has had bad things happen to her? You don't even know what the doctor said."

I smack the ground with my stick. I'm not allowed to say mean things. "You must be a stupid lady. A really stupid lady who doesn't know anything. You don't even know that the doctor said today that Mom might have multiple sclerosis, because first her leg had weird burning and then her left side went numb and then her leg dragged and then her eye started jerking and you only need three unrelated symptoms to diagnose multiple sclerosis and Mom has already had four. It will be definite when the doctor says it's definite, so Mom still feels like she's waiting for the sky to fall, which is what she told her friend Clara on the phone. She just lies around and feels bad, and the Saltwater Dance Brigade is going to have to replace her in the show with another dancer, because there's no way she'll be able to be a dead soldier in time when she's got so many symptoms."

Something dark swoops down above my head. It might be a bat. It might be a bird. But I'm not ready to take out my binocs and watch.

"So just leave me alone. I'm going to come here and I'm going to look for loons and you can't stop me. If you behave yourself, I don't mind if you're here, too. You have my permission to come here and do whatever you were doing. But leave me alone. No more sticks. No more shooing."

I take my stick and toss it like a spear at the water. It gets stuck in the sea lavender. I take a handful of sand, pitch it, and watch the grains drift down.

"And by the way, if you leave your sandwich out, the ants will get it. Next time, keep it in the bag."

Finally I'm calm enough to take out my binocs and lean against my tree. The water's so dark that the white bellies of the herring gulls stand out. The double-crested cormorants have got to be out there, but with their black feathers, black feet, and black bills, I can't see them at all. In the sky, it's mostly swallows swooping, but there are a few bats sprinkled in. Everybody's hunting flies. I watch until it's dark enough that I can't tell birds from bats. Then I eat my cheese, put on my wool sweater, and start my slow walk home.

Mom's still lying on the couch. "Oh, good," she says when she hears me open the door, "let's make supper together." I walk into the living room. Her hair's tangly. Her face looks puffy. She's not getting up.

I sit down next to her. She opens her eyes and smiles.

"C'mon, Chirp, let's go," she says, like I'm the one holding up the show.

I stand up.

Slowly, Mom slides her body around so she's sitting. She rubs her left leg with her hands.

"Maybe something simple tonight?" she says. "Scrambled eggs and toast?"

"Sounds good," I say. Last night was fried-egg sandwiches.

"Give me a hand here, honey," Mom says. She reaches out her hands and I pull. When she's standing up, she puts her arm around my shoulders. "Mmmm, you smell like fresh air. You smell like stars." Her voice sounds far away, even though she's whispering right in my ear. She's leaning on me, hard, as we walk into the kitchen. Her draggy leg weighs us down.

"Why don't I be the supervisor, you be the cook?" Mom asks, like we're playing a fun game. I walk her to the chair, and she sits down heavy, *oy*.

"Rachel's going to eat at Genevieve's tonight," Mom says. "Dad should be home soon, but we can go ahead and get started."

I get out the margarine. I get out a pan.

"Two eggs each," Mom says.

I get four eggs. Dad likes his dinner hot. I'll cook for him later. When I'm ready to chop the onions, Mom says, "Tell me about your day, honey."

I can't think of one thing to tell her. Not one single thing. My heart starts to race. Mom needs a story.

"How about a poem?" I ask, and start right in on *Tyger, tyger, burning bright, in the forests of the night,* which is one of our favorites, especially the part where the stars throw down their spears and water heaven with their tears. Mom closes her eyes while I chop onions and ask so many questions:

> *What the hammer? what the chain?*
> *In what furnace was thy brain?*
> *What the anvil? what dread grasp*
> *Dare its deadly terrors clasp?*

And when I get to the end, I wish my eyes had been closed, too, because the onions have been stinging me for too long.

"Oh, sweetie love," Mom says when she opens her eyes and sees the onion tears streaming down my face, "it's awful, just awful." Mom slides her chair back and opens up her arms for me, and since I'm

59

scared to get in her lap because of her leg symptoms, I kneel in front of her and wrap my arms around her stomach.

"I can't believe this is happening to me, to us," she says. "I can't believe that I might have MS and my body is falling apart." She's crying into my hair and now my onion tears are real tears.

"I can't believe this," she says.

"It's okay, Mom," I cry into her stomach.

"No, Chirp, it's *not* okay," she says, and suddenly her voice sounds mad. She pushes me back by my shoulders so she can look right in my face. I'm glad her eye stopped being supersonic yesterday. Her face is wet, but her tears are over.

"When you were born, I swore that you'd have an easier path than me. My mother caused me so much pain, and sometimes I still feel like it's swallowing me up. I swore that, for you, it would be different. And now . . ." Mom takes a breath. "And now . . ." She slowly pushes each word out, like it's stuck in her mouth. "You—have—a—sick—mother." She folds me back into her arms. My cheek's against her stomach. She's moaning now, a sweet, quiet sound like a mourning dove. I hold Mom tighter. I *cooooo* my own soft bird sound. What else does Mom want me to do?

CHAPTER FOUR

ISS GALLAGHER THINKS IT would be *nifty* if we made our own Halloween masks. She thinks a lot of things are *nifty,* like the electric pencil sharpener that Mr. Simpkins, the gym teacher, brought her on the second day of class, and the fact that I'm Jewish and stayed home from school on the High Holidays, and her latest discovery, which is that I make my own lunch. She found that out yesterday when she was carrying a box from her car in the parking lot back to the classroom. I was watching from my lunch rock and saw her short red skirt get shorter and shorter, because the box was hiking it up. I was scared that she was going to start showing her underpants, which would be about the worst thing that could happen to a teacher.

"Miss Gallagher!" I yelled, and waved. I had to tell her.

"Naomi," she yelled, all cheery. Then she shifted the box to her hip so she could wave back to me, which made her skirt problem a definite emergency. She walked over to me on her tippy high heels. I looked away, because I was scared that I would see what I really didn't want to. But then she put the box down, so I was safe.

"Wow, Naomi," she said, hovering over me and peeking in my lunch box. Her blond hair was like a silk scarf blowing in my face. "Your mom sure packs you a healthy lunch. Apple. Carrot sticks. Cheese sandwich on wheat bread."

"I make my lunch."

"Really? Every single day?" She backed up and looked right in my face with her eyebrows up. I could see her green eye shadow. I could see squiggly black lines under her eyes.

I nodded.

"Nifty!" she said. "Your mom is a very lucky lady to have such a responsible girl. You tell your mom I said that she's one lucky, lucky lady."

I nodded, but I haven't said anything to Mom. She's been feeling lots of things lately, but lucky is definitely not one of them.

Now Miss Gallagher says, "Okay, children, let's see the artists in you come alive," but first we have to tear a lot of strips of newspaper and mix up paste out of flour and water. "There's no limit to our imaginations," she says as she hands out one balloon per student to blow up and use as a mold for the mask. So far, everyone is doing a pretty good job of cooperating and not playing balloon volleyball or whacking each other with rolled-up newspaper, since Miss Gallagher told us during class meeting this morning that our Halloween party on Friday is a privilege, not a right, and she will happily enjoy the treats herself while we sit with our heads down on our desks if we choose to act like hooligans, which is, she's afraid, becoming our bad habit, just like some people choose to smoke cigarettes.

While we work, Miss Gallagher reads us a story about a girl who sees a glowing light in the swamp near her house at midnight on Halloween and sets off by herself to investigate the mystery. She's scared of everything—the dark, the birds, the shadows, the bats—so I don't understand why she doesn't just stay home under the covers, relax, and forget about it.

"*Now* what do I do?" Dawn whispers to me after she has a pile of newspaper strips, a milk carton of paste, and a blown-up balloon.

"Take one strip. Dip it in the paste like this. Press it on the balloon."

Dawn nods and smiles.

The girl's flashlight wimps out when she's in the middle of the swamp. It's the blackest night. The very darkest night of the year. *"Whooooooo,"* Sean says, but I guess Lori and Debbie are too scared to laugh. Joey looks at me and rolls his eyes.

"Make sure you only cover half of the balloon," I whisper to Dawn. "Otherwise you won't be able to get the balloon out and you won't have a mask."

"I know that already," Dawn says.

Rachel told me at breakfast that she might not trick-or-treat with me this year. She says that Genevieve's parents are having a Halloween party and she and Genevieve might hang out with the grown-ups, because they're really laid-back and fun to be with.

"But, Rach," I said, "we *always* trick-or-treat together. It's our tradition."

"Well, traditions change. Everything changes. Case in point." She waved her hand at Mom's empty place at the table.

"As soon as she's feeling better, she'll start coming to breakfast," I said.

"C'mon, Chirp. She's not going to be feeling better. Only worse. That's how MS works."

"She might not have MS. We don't know for sure."

"Fine," Rachel said. "You keep living in your fantasy world. Meanwhile, I'm going to go to a really cool party."

Before I could ask her who she thought I'd trick-or-treat with then, since there are no other kids on our road except the Morell boys, she jumped up from the table.

"Rachel!" I yelled.

"Shhh," she said, "you'll wake up Mom. A little

consideration, Chirp." Then she pulled on her penny loafers, grabbed her books, and headed out the door.

I want to be a seagull. With a bright yellow beak. And a red dot on the beak. I'm going to make cardboard wings and just keep my fingers crossed that it won't rain.

Last year Rachel was a hula girl and nearly froze to death because she wore a pink tube top and a grass skirt made out of torn-up brown paper bags, and Mom said that she absolutely had to wear a jacket and no point in trying to argue, so Rachel walked out of the house in her peacoat but then stashed it under the first pitch pine. I was toasty because I was a coconut. I wore Dad's brown down jacket with a belt around the bottom and stuffed it with towels to round me out, and Mom put brown face paint on my face.

"Aloha, my tropical beauties," Mom said when we came home, and if she noticed Rachel's chattering teeth, she didn't show it. Then Dad said, "Show us your loot," and Mom said, "Any chocolate for the parent who loves you best?" and Dad said, "Chocolate, shmocolate. If you love me, you'll turn over the Sugar Babies," and Mom laughed and hugged him while we dumped our loot out on the living room floor. The four of us sat in a circle and ate candy until it was way past my bedtime and we just couldn't eat any more.

Miss Gallagher is still reading. Now the girl is lost. Even though the swamp is practically in her backyard and she supposedly plays there all the time, she has no idea how to get home. She's scared, and lost, and danger is lurking, and there's no one to lend her a hand.

"Uh-oh," Dawn says. "Uh-oh, uh-oh." I think she's uh-ohing about the girl, but then I see that she's covered her whole balloon with newspaper.

Suddenly I'm so tired I think my head might crash down on my desk. I raise my hand and ask for permission to go to the girls' room. I splash my face with cold water and then go into a stall, lock the door, sit down on the toilet, and close my eyes. *Once there was a curly-haired Jewish girl who went into the girls' room a few days before Halloween and never came out. People searched high and low—neighbors, the kids in her class, detectives with fingerprint powder and sniffer dogs—but she seemed to have just vanished into thin air. Poof.*

When I walk past Joey on my way back to my seat, he whispers, "What are you going to be for Halloween?"

"Poof!" I whisper.

"Wacko," he whispers, smiling.

Maybe, actually, it wouldn't be so bad if he wanted to trick-or-treat together. If he asks me what I think, I guess I'll tell him that I'll put it in my pipe and smoke it.

"I've got to be able to flap. Otherwise, what's the point?"

I made my wings myself out of cardboard from a Sears box in the basement, but Rachel's helping me attach them to my arms. With just one strap of cloth per wing, they slip when I flap.

"You're flapping too hard," Rachel says.

"No, I'm not. I just need more straps to hold the wings on," I say.

"Why can't you be something easy, like a cowgirl or a clown?" Rachel mumbles, but she's reaching for the ragbag so she can cut me some more strips to make into straps.

"Are you sure you won't come with me tomorrow night, Rach?" I ask. "You can have all the SweeTARTS and Bit-O-Honeys. I might even split the chocolate with you."

"Genevieve's dad makes poison potion, and he told me that he'd give me a sip, even though it's for the grown-ups. And Ned—that's her dad—reads from *Frankenstein* with all the lights off except this weird red one that they use every year. Anyway, I'm kind of old to trick-or-treat."

"So what am I supposed to do? Most kids just go with whoever's on their street, but we've only got the Morell boys. Dawn said I could go with her family, but they start before it's even dark, since Trent's only four. And Sally always goes to her grandma's in Barnstable."

"And I guess you don't want to go with Mom and Dad. Or just Dad?"

"Rach, we haven't trick-or-treated with them since we were tiny!"

Rachel pokes two holes near the top of each wing and threads the strips of cloth in. She pokes two holes near the bottom of each wing and does the same thing. Then she ties the wings to my arms.

"Flap," she says.

I start off slow, like I'm standing on wet sand and just warming up for takeoff. Flap-flap-flap-flap.

"So far, so good," Rachel says.

"So good, so far," I say.

"Try faster," she says.

I speed up, like I'm about to take off, faster and faster, then *whoosh,* I'm off. I flap around the living room, where Mom is stretched out on the couch, talking with her friend Annie, and out into the hall.

"Oh, birdie!" Rachel yells. "Here, birdie, birdie!"

I flap up the stairs, with Rachel right behind me. I'm running and flapping and flying and laughing, and Rachel's laughing, too. I fly down the stairs. I fly right out the front door. It's a bright, chilly morning, a great day for flying. I fly around the hydrangea bush. I fly in a huge circle in the front yard.

"Here, birdie, birdie!" Rachel yells. "Seagull want a cracker?" I turn around, cock my head, and fly right toward my sister. Before she can catch me, I swoop away with my wings spread wide. Now I'm soaring.

I soar down the driveway, up the front walkway, around the house.

I slow down a little so Rachel can catch up. Her cheeks are pink. Her hair is wild.

"You soar, too," I say.

For a split second she stares at me like I'm crazy. Then she sticks her arms out and she is, she's soaring, too! We soar around the house two times. We soar single-file down the sand path, because it's not wide enough for side-by-side soaring.

"Wow, look how tiny our house is from way up here," I say.

"Just a speck of a house," Rachel says.

"Just a speck of a town," I say.

"Ocean? What ocean?" she says. "Oh, it must be that teeny blue spot down there."

"Hello, Miss Gallagher! I know you're down there somewhere, but you're microscopic!"

"Hello, my stupid junior high school! You're not even a blip on my radar screen. Too bad for you!"

"Yeah, too bad for you!"

We soar together until my arms start to throb.

"Coming in for a landing," I tell Rachel. One flap, two flaps, three flaps, and I'm down, in front of the dead beech tree.

"Landing gear down," Rachel yells, and she flaps a few times, too, and plops down next to me in the sandy dirt.

"It's hard work, being a bird," I say. My heart's

pounding. My T-shirt's wet with sweat, even though this is definitely jacket weather and I'm not wearing one.

"Hard work," Rachel agrees. She looks at me and shakes her head, her dark wavy hair bouncing around. "You're a nut-job," she says, but for the first time in a while, her eyes are really, really happy.

I guess this is a cool party, but it's all grown-ups and too dark and really loud and everyone's just sitting around and talking, except for a pirate and the Queen of Hearts, who are dancing in the corner near the blue lava lamp. Not dancing, really, just holding on to each other. I don't know how Genevieve's parents know so many people, since they just moved here two years ago, but it's crowded, too crowded for me to fly. I barely recognize anyone, which is strange, since the summer people left in September and I know practically everyone in town. Maybe Genevieve's parents have secret party friends they import from P-town and Hyannis.

"Hey, Chirp," Genevieve says, "do you want to help me pass around the appetizers?" She's a fairy in a miniskirt and sparkly top. I think she's the prettiest girl I've ever seen. Her hair is long and wavy, and I bet she can sit on it. Her eyes are blue-green, like the bay when there's no seaweed churned up in the water.

I follow her into the kitchen, and her mom, who's a cat in a black bodysuit, says, "Hey, little bird, I think we need to clip your wings if you want to be a waitress like my lovely daughter," and a man in a rubbery President Nixon mask, who's helping her open wine bottles, starts laughing like that's the funniest thing he's ever heard. Genevieve's mom says, "Just call me Debsy," and unties my straps, takes off my wings, and sticks them behind a bookcase. She's holding a plate with rolled-up bacon and white bread stuck with toothpicks. "At this joint, we pay in bacon roll-ups." She winks at Nixon, who puts his hands on her hips and squeezes. "Payday," she says, and holds the plate in front of me.

"No thanks," I say. I've never eaten bacon or ham before, since Mom doesn't feel comfortable with them. We don't officially keep kosher, but bacon and ham just aren't on Mom's radar. She loves clam strips, though. And steamers. And quahogs. Mr. Pialetti at the liquor store calls me Missy Quahog, since Dad came into his store on the night I was born to buy a bottle of champagne, so he knows that I'm a Cape Cod native, and all Cape Cod natives are nicknamed quahogs and know to say it "co-hogs."

"Hard to find good help these days," Nixon chuckles, and I think he's making fun of me. My face turns hot.

"Leave the girl alone, Mr. President," Debsy says, but she's giggling while she gulps red wine. She hands me the plate of bacon roll-ups and a stack of little napkins with ghosts on them that say "Have a boo-tiful night." She gives Genevieve a plate loaded up with Ritz crackers with cream cheese and green olives. "Go get 'em, girls!" she says, and kisses the top of Genevieve's head.

Everyone either pretty much ignores us or tries to guess our costumes, which is tricky in my case, since my wings were clipped and I took my papier-mâché mask off because it was too hot. I just look like a curly-haired girl in a white Danskin top and gray Danskin pants and pink sneakers, because seagulls have pink feet.

"Wow, what a beautiful fairy princess!" Prince Charming, who works at the hardware store, says to Genevieve. He has a deep voice and arm muscles and a silky purple cape, and he's not a teenager but he's not quite a real grown-up yet, either. He reaches out and runs his fingers slowly through Genevieve's hair. She blushes and smiles. I feel kind of dorky just standing there, so I keep passing the plate, solo, until it's empty, and then I go look for Rachel.

She's not in the living room, and she's not in the dining room, and she's not in the kitchen. Upstairs, all of the doors are closed. I put my ear to one. I hear flushing. A devil comes out. I think she works at Flanagan's. "Your turn, sweetie," she says. I wait until she goes downstairs, and then I press my ear against the next door. Lots of laughing and talking. I put my hand on the doorknob and slowly turn it. Like a good detective, I push the door open carefully, carefully, without a sound.

A bunch of grown-ups are sitting in a circle on a bed with a green Indian-print bedspread in what must be Debsy and Genevieve's dad's room. Rachel is standing at the foot of the bed.

"Hey, Little Sister," some guy in a sailor hat says. "Come on in and close the door."

"Hey, Chirp," Rachel says. "Come on in and close the door," and everyone laughs. The room's smoky. It smells like burnt-black popcorn.

"Does Little Sister belong to you?" Mr. Sailorman asks Rachel. She nods and smiles.

"My name's Chirp. Rachel, I want to go home."

"Home?" Mr. Sailorman says. "But the party's just getting started, Little Sister."

"We just got here, Chirp," Rachel says. "We haven't even heard *Frankenstein* yet."

"I want to go home," I say. "I want to trick-or-treat." Something feels funny, like they're all on one team and I'm on the other.

"We have a trick we could show you right here," a pirate says.

"Hey, good idea," says a lady with a black witch's hat. "Do you want to see a trick, Chirp?"

I shake my head, because the only thing I want

is for Rachel to leave this stupid party with me. If we move fast, we can probably trick-or-treat at a few houses before everyone turns their porch lights off.

Mr. Pirate lights up a cigarette. He sucks on it and slowly blows smoke into Miss Witchy's face. Her eyes are closed. She gulps the smoke in like she's eating food. Then she opens her eyes and blows a wimpy little ring into the smoky air that's swirling all around her head. Mr. Sailorman claps, but I think it's just about the dumbest thing I've ever seen.

"Can we go now?" I ask Rachel.

"We'll be reading *Frankenstein* really soon," Miss Witchy says.

"Hang out for a while, Chirp," Rachel says. "It's a cool party. We can listen to *Frankenstein*. It'll be better than trick-or-treating."

"Much better," Mr. Sailorman says.

"We can walk home together later," Rachel says, but I'm already out the door, and I don't close it like I opened it, carefully, without a sound. *Wham.* I'm not a detective. I'm a girl at a grown-up party on Halloween with only half of a seagull costume on. I go to the kitchen and get my wings from behind the bookshelf. I go to Genevieve's room and get my mask off of her dresser. Even though the polite thing is to say *Thank you very much for having me,* I don't feel like talking to the wine-gulping cat woman, so I wave to Genevieve, who's now dancing with Prince Charming, grab my jacket, and start my around-the-corner-down-Starling-Lane-left-on-Quonset-Neck-Road-right-on-Salt-Marsh-Lane walk home.

It's cold and dark, and there are hardly any trick-or-treaters still out, only a few older kids with pillowcases and no-good costumes, like just a straw hat or just a blond wig. It's hard to walk fast when you're carrying cardboard seagull wings. It's hard not to think about ghosts and vampires and men with dripping blood when it's Halloween night and you're a gull with clipped wings walking home all alone and the moon is glowing green behind a fat cloud. What I really want is to be on Salt Marsh Lane, almost done trick-or-treating, with Rachel next to me and a big bag of loot that I'm schlepping and about to dump out on the living room floor, with Mom and Dad asking me for chocolate and Sugar Babies. If Rachel were here with me instead of at that stupid party, she'd sing *You can't always get what you waa-ant,* and I'd sing *You can't always get what you waa-ant,* and we'd sing together to the end of the chorus, finishing with a nice, loud *waaaaahhhh!* and before I knew it I'd be home, instead of on Quonset Neck Road by myself and needing to pee.

It's not a good night for peeing behind a bush. It's not a good night for pulling my pants down outside. Mom says it's important for girls to move through the world with a sense of purpose so that they're not easy targets. *Swing your arms. Take up space. Show that you're a strong girl.* Mrs. Newlon, on the corner, is bringing her pumpkin in off of the porch. I give her a strong wave and a strong shout—"Hello, Mrs. Newlon!"—but I guess she doesn't hear me, because she closes her door and turns her porch light off.

The Graysons. The Bonazolis. Home. I'm just about home. There are people standing in the road. Joey and his two brothers, lit up by the moonlight.

"What's up?" Vinnie says, and starts walking toward me. He's wearing a beat-up leather jacket. He's got something behind his back.

"What's shakin'?" Donny says. He's got something, too. Joey's following them, looking down.

"Happy Halloween, Tweety Bird," Vinnie says. He's the oldest one. He jerks his chin up to get his stringy blond hair out of his eyes.

"How's Dr. Dad, the headshrinker?" Donny asks. His face is all pimply, and he always looks mad, even when he's pretending to be friendly. "Has he been shrinking your head lately?"

"I think I see something there on her neck." Vinnie takes a step closer to me, stares hard. He smells like cigarette smoke. "Yeah, I definitely see a little round thing on her neck. Must be her head."

He laughs. Donny laughs. Joey's quiet, staring at the ground.

"Think fast, bro," Vinnie says, and he tosses an egg, gently, to Joey. Joey catches it. "Maybe Chirp would like to play ball, Joey. Why don't you throw it to her?" He winks at his brother.

"Nah," Joey says, and he tosses the egg back to Vinnie.

"Aw, that's not very nice of you, leaving the girl out," Donny says. He takes an egg from behind his back. "I bet the nice girl wants to play ball. Don't you want to play ball, nice little Jewish girl?"

I shake my head. I start walking backward.

"I think she does," Vinnie says.

"I'm sure she does," Donny says.

"It's the windup," Vinnie says.

Donny winds up.

I don't want to cry. I don't want to pee. I don't want to run back into the dark, away from home.

"It's the—"

"Wait!" Joey says. "I thought we were on a mission. Leave her alone. Her mom's really sick. I'll catch up to you guys. Meet you in front of the you-know-what."

"Hey," Vinnie says, "it looks like Joey's got a girl-friend."

"Oh, Joey, you're my hero," Donny says in a squeaky high voice, but he lowers his pitching arm.

"Oh, Joey, you're just the cutest little *freak*!" Vinnie says, cracking up.

They're laughing their heads off. They walk away. I can't help it. I'm crying. Joey's looking at me. He's shaking his head. He doesn't say anything.

"Sorry," I say. "Thanks for helping me."

"*You're* sorry? You didn't do anything. Jerks." He kicks the ground.

"It's just that this has been the worst Halloween ever," I say. I hand Joey a wing. I throw mine down in the sand by the side of the road and sit on it. Joey watches his brothers walking away. Then he gently puts his wing down. He looks at it and nudges it with his sneaker a few times, like he's trying to get it lined up just right, but with what, I can't tell. Then he sighs, dusts the wing off with his hand, wipes his hand on his pant leg, and sits down.

"What I wanted was to go trick-or-treating with Rachel, like I always do, and come home and share candy with my mom and dad, but she convinced me to go with her to this stupid party." Words keep filling up my mouth and spilling out. I tell Joey about the cat woman and Nixon and the bacon roll-ups. I tell him about the grown-ups sitting around blowing smoke. I'm not even sure if he's listening, because I'm not looking at his face, but I don't care. I can't stop talking. I'm about to tell Joey about my walk home when he interrupts me.

"Wait," he says, "I have an idea. Give me a head start, and then come over to my house. Make it quick, 'cuz I've got to go meet my brothers," and he tears off across the street.

I walk into our backyard and pee behind our rhododendron bush, because I'll pee in my pants if I wait one second longer, and then I run back to Joey's house, since I don't want him to be late for his brothers and have them punch his arm or throw an egg at him. I ring the doorbell. Joey opens the door. I stand there, waiting for him to tell me his idea. He looks at me. I look at him. I hear a TV upstairs. I hear his father yell, "It's pretty damn late for the doorbell, Joseph!" Joey just stands there.

Finally he says, "C'mon, Chirp."

"C'mon, what?"

"Well, what do you say?" Joey says, and lifts his eyebrows up.

Finally I get it.

"Trick or treat!"

Joey smiles. He grabs a bowl of Hershey's Kisses and SweeTARTS and Dots.

I put out my hands and he tips the bowl and dumps a big old pile in.

"Happy Halloween," he says, and punches me in the arm one, two, three times, so gently it's like he's patting me. I'm a good dog and he's patting me. Then he pulls the door closed behind us.

"Stay out of trouble," he says.

"Woof," I say.

Then he runs off to meet his brothers in front of the you-know-what.

Our porch light is on. Our pumpkin isn't out anymore. Mom and Dad's bedroom light is on. I bet they're lying in bed, talking. Maybe Mom's saying *Wow, Katie Henderson was a pretty snazzy daisy with that homemade costume,* and Dad is saying *Yes, she looked sweet, but what I really wonder is what's going on with the older brother. Did you see how much candy he took? He just reached in, and when I told him to take one of each, he acted like he didn't hear me, which suggests that he's dealing with issues of boundaries and . . .*

I open the front door. The full candy bowl is sitting on top of the wicker sweater chest. Mom and Dad said that they would pass out candy. Dad stood right here in the front hall when Rachel was tying on my seagull wings and said, "Don't worry, honey. We'll man the fort. Candy in every bag!" and Mom nodded from the couch and said, "Of course we will. Of course. It's Halloween," and I could tell she was trying hard to make her voice sound excited. But Mom and Dad didn't pass any candy out.

When no one answers the door on Halloween, it means that the people hate kids or someone is very, very sick and can't even manage to hold out a bowl of candy and say *Help yourselves,* or they might actually be stone-cold dead.

I know that I should knock on Mom and Dad's bedroom door and say I'm home, safe and sound. But I don't feel safe, and I'm not sure what *sound* means. Somehow I bet I'm not feeling that, either. I'm cold and quivery, like someone dumped ice water down my back, so I creep up the stairs, quiet, quiet, and into my room, where I pile up my blankets in the middle of my bed, the warm, snuggy red one and the fluffy white quilt and the yellow Therma-Weave that I've had since I was a baby. I put a Hershey's Kiss in my mouth. I'm burrowing under and curling up tight in my nest with just a little air tunnel so that I can breathe. With my eyes closed, there's only the sweet taste of chocolate and the quiet ocean rumble of Mom and Dad's voices through my wall.

⇔

"I'm sure you're already aware that this is important, since we never call family meetings," Dad says, the next day after dinner. He's standing in front of the fireplace, and his face looks worried, even though he's talking in his calm, slow voice and nodding, like he's happily agreeing with something. It must be an emergency, since we weren't even supposed to clear the table or put the leftover spinach lasagna in the fridge. Just come follow Mom and Dad right into the living room.

What I'm hoping is that maybe Dad found out about the smoke at Genevieve's house. I want him to give us a speech about appropriate behavior and then say that we're not allowed at Genevieve's house if grown-ups are blowing smoke in each other's faces. And I wouldn't mind at all if he finished up by saying that he *really* would have expected that Rachel would have walked me home so I wasn't at the mercy of hoodlums on Halloween and he's a bit *disappointed* and thinks it might be a good idea for Rachel to say she's sorry. Maybe he'll even say that *he's* sorry for forgetting to hand out the Halloween candy.

I can't tell what Rachel's hoping for, since I can't see her face, because I'm sitting in the green chair and she's sitting on the floor, playing with the fringe on her bell-bottoms. Mom's stretched out on the couch.

"Well—" Dad says, and Rachel interrupts.

"You know, I have a ton of homework that I really need to do," and Dad looks at Mom like *Honey, can you give me a hand here?* but Mom's staring into space, like she's a zombie.

Dad puts his hands on his hips. "Mom and I got disappointing news yesterday evening," he says. "We heard from the neurologist that a diagnosis of multiple sclerosis has been confirmed."

Rachel mumbles, "See, I knew it," and Dad says, "I didn't hear that, Rachel. What did you say?" but she just shakes her head and waves her hand near her ear like she's swatting a mosquito.

"Of course, I'm aware that this is a lot to absorb. The doctor said that usually it takes longer to diagnose MS, but in this case they're quite certain," Dad says. Mom looks pale. I want to hold her hand, but I'm scared that it will feel cold and clammy. Mom is the least cold and clammy person I know, but maybe her MS has already changed that.

"Your mother and I are open to any questions that you may have," Dad says. I don't think he's noticed that Mom's closed up shop. That's what she always says when she's tired and needs us to leave her alone for a while. *Kiddos, I'm closing up shop now. You need to give me a little break here.*

"First, I'd like to explain a bit about the disease," Dad says. "And then I'd like to hear about what you're feeling. Does that sound good?" He doesn't wait for an answer. Rachel is pulling threads out of her fringe. She's piling up little white strings on her knee.

"For our bodies to work properly," Dad says, "our nerves send out signals, telling our bodies what to do. Our nerves are protected by a coating, called myelin. In the case of MS, the myelin sheath deteriorates, and it affects the way the signals get through to the body."

Tears run down Mom's face and drip off her chin. She's not wiping them away. She's not making a sound.

"Remember how we always take the subway when we visit Boston?" Dad asks. Last time we were there, Mom and I rode the swan boats in the Boston Public Garden while Dad and Rachel walked down Newbury Street. Mom yelled *Yahoo!* when the boat took off, so I yelled *Yahoo, too!* and the man pedaling the boat, who reminded me of Bert in *Mary Poppins* because of his good-looking dark hair and the sparks in his green eyes, started laughing, and he gave us an extra-long ride because it was a slow day due to a nip in the air and a blowy wind and there was only one other passenger, an old lady, who was reading her book and not even looking around. Mom and I had our hair down, and the wind stirred it all up. A bunch of mallards followed us the whole way. When the ride was over, Mom did a fancy twirl and a really low curtsy for the driver and he said, "You must be a dancer," and I said, "You should see her," and he said, "Ah, if only I could," and Mom smiled and turned pink, and the driver said, "Come back and visit me sometime." Then Mom and I held hands, crisscrossed like ice dancers, and sashayed up the dock.

"Remember the pull cord you yank to signal to the conductor that he should stop the train at the next station?" Dad asks.

Rachel nods. I nod.

"Well, think of the nerve as the wire of the pull cord. The myelin sheath is like the plastic coating that protects the wire."

"And I'm the damn train wreck," Mom says in a quiet, hard voice.

"Hannah!" Dad starts to walk toward her.

"Don't." Mom's zombie eyes are gone. She glares at Dad, and he stops walking.

There's a long silence. On and on and on. I see

Joey's porch light flick on. I hear a car drive by. Then Rachel says, "Is it okay if I get started on my biology project now?" and she gets up and walks out of the room.

Dad's got his face in his hands. I wait to see if Mom will open up shop. I watch her face. Finally she feels me watching, and she gives me a sad smile. When I touch Mom's hand, it's cold and clammy, and that's how I know that everything's changed.

CHAPTER FIVE

CE-BLUE QUIET SMACKS ME when I open the front door after school. It's been this way every day since the diagnosis, six days ago.

"Hi, Mom, I'm home!" I yell into the loud quiet, but I know she won't answer me.

She's curled up on her side on the couch. She's still wearing her pink flannel nightgown and green wool sweater. Her eyes are wide open, but she doesn't look like she's seeing anything. There's a bowl of tomato soup with a spoon in it on the coffee table. Soggy pieces of saltine crackers float in the cold orange soup.

"Mommy," I say, and crouch down next to her. I rub her head really gently, just the way she likes.

"Chirp," she says in the littlest voice. Her breath smells like something that needs to be cleaned out of the fridge.

She doesn't ask me how my day was. She doesn't tell me to change out of my school clothes and into my play clothes. She just lies there with her eyes open.

"Do you need anything?" I ask.

"No," she says.

"I'll go change into my play clothes and put my school clothes in the hamper," I say.

"Okay," she says.

"And then I'll come right back."

"Okay," she says.

"Have you eaten anything?"

"Uh-huh," she says.

She's my mother, so I'm supposed to believe her. What I know is that she's barely been eating all week, because she's so depressed, and Dad's really worried. Last night he made her *kasha varnishkes,* which is food from her childhood, and she promised that she'd eat it, but she just pushed the kasha and bow-tie noodles around on her plate like a little kid.

I take a deep breath and hold it while I climb the stairs. I hold it while I walk to my room. I hold it while I jump, *one, two, three,* on my bed. I hold it three more jumps, just to be safe.

If I can take off my skirt, turtleneck, tights, and shoes before I count to fifteen, everything will be okay. If I can toss my clothes into the hamper without having anything fall on the floor, everything will be okay. *Okay.* I pull on my purple corduroy bell-bottoms. They're the color of blackberries. I pull on my Saltwater Dance Brigade sweatshirt and then change my mind, since being reminded of the dead-soldier dance might make Mom even sadder. Should I wear a nice bright color to cheer her up? Or would it be easier on her if I were a little gloomy, too? According to Miss Gallagher, white isn't its own color but all of the colors mixed together, so I guess it isn't cheery or gloomy. I pull on my white turtleneck.

"Coming, Mom!" I yell. "I'll be right there!" As if she's called me, as if she's waiting.

"I'm so sorry," Mom says when I walk into the living room. "I'm so, so sorry." That's pretty much all Mom says these days. I'm not exactly sure what she's apologizing for. I've tried to ask her, but she just says, "Oh, Chirp," and shakes her head.

"Okay, Mom," I say, "time for the show. C'mon. You have to sit up so you can see."

Mom doesn't move.

"You have a front-row seat, Mom. You have the best seat in the house. Sit up, Mom. You don't want to miss it."

Mom slowly uncurls herself. She rolls onto her back. She just lies there, staring up at the ceiling, like she's forgotten what she was doing.

"Mom." I reach my hands out to her. I pull her up and tuck a pillow behind her back. Now she's sitting.

"Two minutes to showtime," I say. I run to the kitchen and grab the record player. I run up to Rachel's room and grab her pink plastic box of 45s.

When I get back to the living room, Mom's head is bent forward so her chin is resting on her chest. Dad says she's been having a terrible time falling asleep, because she's feeling so down. He gives her sleeping pills, since he can get a prescription because he's a psychiatrist, but the medicine doesn't help her.

I put the record on.

"And now, for your entertainment, Lily of the Valley will spin and dive, twist and jive, to the lovely strains of 'Build Me Up, Buttercup'!" I say in my radio voice.

Mom lifts her head, but she looks sorrowful. *Sorrowful* means "full of sorrow," and that's exactly what Mom is. I start off with my eyes closed, just tapping my foot. By the time I'm done, she might be smiling. *Why do you build me up, build me up, buttercup, baby . . .* I shimmy my shoulders. I wiggle my hips. I twist my way over to the corner of the room so that I'll have space to do my leaps. First I do a simple side leap. Mom taught me how to do them when I was really little. Now here's the tricky switch leap. It's a fake-out where it looks like I'm going to leap with my right leg but actually I bend my right leg and kick it back while I leap forward on my left leg. Three leaps. Three nailed landings. *Pah pah pah.* An attitude leap is the hardest. Mom showed me how to do them at the beginning of the summer at Heron Pond in water up to my armpits. She picked me up so that I could practice the positions underwater. "Okay, Snap Pea. Right leg stretched out long and strong in front of you, left leg lifted high and bent behind you, back arched, chin up. There you go. That's it! That's my dancing girl!" Then I tried the leap over and over again in shallow water, because the soft, wet sand makes for a nice, easy landing.

"And now for some attitude," I say. I wonder if it's called an attitude leap because a perfect one can change your attitude. I really want Mom's to change, because I can't see any sparks left in her eyes and she doesn't even answer the phone when she's home all day alone, which her friend Clara says is disturbing behavior, since everyone in the Saltwater Dance Brigade adores her and wants to help her pull through this tough time and she can lead a good life with MS but they can't help if she won't let them and would I please encourage Mom to pick up the phone herself the next time since Clara, of course, is always happy to hear my sweet voice but it's not really me who she's worried about and I do understand, don't I?

The music's building up right before it's going to fade out at the end. *I—I—I—I need you-ou-ou, more than anyone, darlin'*. I twirl twice, and then I spring into the air. My back leg's bent just the way it's supposed to be, front leg straight and strong. I arch my back. I'm flying through the air. I land right in front of the couch. I look at Mom to check on her attitude, to see if she's smiling.

Her face is buried in her hands. She's rocking back and forth. She's mumbling to herself. Maybe she's doing her own version of what Zayde, Mom's father, did when he visited us when I was five. Every morning he bowed and swayed and chanted in a beautiful box of sunlight in front of the window in Rachel's room. Rachel explained to me that her window faced Jerusalem. Zayde was praying to God.

⇔

"This should fill you with a sense of wonder," Miss Gallagher says, pointing to the gray rock stuck behind a metal fence that's stuck behind some fancy white columns. I'm still too full of bus sickness to be filled with wonder.

"It's just a gray rock," Joey mumbles.

"With a crack in it," Lisa B. says.

Miss Gallagher starts in on her Plymouth Rock speech, which is pretty much like Mrs. McHenry's Plymouth Rock speech from this exact same field trip last year.

"I think it shrinked," Sean whispers, loud enough for everyone to hear.

"It did not," Dawn says, all huffy. "It was just this little last year, too."

"Enough!" Miss Gallagher says. "This rock is a significant part of our nation's history, and it deserves our respect. With Thanksgiving approaching, we should be thinking about the great gift of—"

"Turkey!" Sean shouts, all excited, and everyone

cracks up. Miss Gallagher turns pink, grabs Sean's arm, and marches him away to sit by himself under a maple tree. When she comes back, she takes a deep breath and talks, talks, talks about the Pilgrims, like her words are acorns that she's whipping at us. I wish that I was sitting by myself under a maple tree and looking up through the branches at the bright leaves. I wish that while I was under my tree the wind would blow, *shhhhoooo,* and make the leaves drift down on me. I wish I was getting buried under red and orange and yellow leaves and I could just reach out and choose the prettiest ones to bring home to Mom, since she's missing fall because she won't go outside, not even to the front door to take a peek, not even when Dad, Rachel, and I all stand together with the door wide open and say things like *Wow, the Morells' maple looks like it's on fire* and *I've never seen our birch tree quite so yellow* to try to lure her over.

Claire raises her hand. Miss Gallagher points to her and says, "Claire, question?" and Claire nods. Miss Gallagher looks happy.

"When are we eating lunch?" Claire holds up her pink Barbie lunch box.

Miss Gallagher's shoulders droop. "When I'm done teaching you about the significance of Plymouth Rock." Now her words aren't acorns. They're thick and oozy, like the mud in the mudflats where the oysters and clams live.

I take the world's tiniest step backward. Dawn, on my left, doesn't notice, but Joey, on my right, does. He looks at me. I don't want him to get me in trouble, so I don't look back. I nod like I'm listening to Miss Gallagher while I take another tiny step backward. This time, Joey comes along. Leaves crunch on the pavement under his feet. He smells like lime. Joey takes the next step backward. I come along. I hold out my fingers, *one, two, three,* and we go together. We've got enough free space in front of us now that someone walking along might think that we're two brave runaways who left our unhappy homes and hatched a smart plan to listen in on school groups so that we can get some education and grow up to be important members of society. *One, two, three,* step back. *One, two, three,* step back. The trick is not to move too far too fast.

When Miss Gallagher finally says, "Okay, okay, lunchtime. Stay within sight and within shouting range," Joey starts running backward, lifting his knees up high and pumping his arms like he's in the cartoons, and he looks so funny that I start laughing, which makes it hard to keep up with him.

"Never weaken, matey!" he shouts at me, so I know that he's happy that I'm coming, too.

"Heck no, matey!" I yell, and we laugh and keep running backward, away from everybody, but they don't notice. The wind is tossing around Joey's hair.

It looks like a messy heap of straw. My ears ache on the inside, since I'm not wearing my purple hat. We run until we come to a bench right by the water.

"I wonder how good Miss Gallagher can see," Joey says.

"I wonder how loud she can yell," I say.

Joey smiles and plops down on the bench. He pulls his blue wool sweater off, spreads it out on the bench, and smoothes out the wrinkles with his hands. He reaches into his brown paper bag, pulls out a sandwich on white bread, and lays it down on the sweater. He reaches in again, pulls out another sandwich, and puts it down right next to the first one. Then he moves the first sandwich over and carefully puts a bag of potato chips in the space between the two sandwiches. He smoothes out the sweater wrinkles again.

"What are you doing?" I ask.

"I'm eating lunch," he says. "What does it look like I'm doing?"

It looks like he's doing a lot of nothing, just like he did with the wing by the side of the road on Halloween, but I don't say anything. I sit down, careful not to bump his sweater, pull out my cheese sandwich, and start eating. The sun keeps going in and out between the clouds and making cool shapes in the water.

"Lemon," Joey says, pointing to one of the shapes.

"Clarinet." I point to another.

Suddenly a puff of wind turns a bunch of dried leaves into a minicyclone. It spins on the pavement right in front of us. Joey puts down his sandwich and stands up. He sticks his arms out and just stands there, like a cross. Maybe it's a Catholic religious thing that you do when you see a minicyclone. Joey starts spinning, slowly at first, then faster and faster. He tips his head back and whirls around and it looks really fun, so I jump up. I don't stand still like a cross, because I don't think I'm supposed to, just like I'm not supposed to say *Jesus,* so I say *Cheez Whiz* when we sing Christmas carols at school, but spinning feels good, spinning feels really good, like jumping into Heron Pond and swimming underwater on a 3 *h*'s day.

"Free at last! Free at last! Great God Almighty, I'm free at last!" Joey shouts.

"Free at last! Free at last!" I shout.

"Cowabunga!" Joey yells.

"Bowacunga!" I yell. I open up my mouth, and cold air rushes in.

Now we're slowing down. Everything is mixed up and not at all like it usually is, and that feels exactly right. I'm a little sick and dizzy, but there's sweet in my throat, like I've just chewed a giant gumball.

"Joey?" I say, but I'm not sure what it is I want to ask him. He doesn't say anything, and when I look at him, his eyes are closed and he's swaying back and forth. Miss Gallagher is calling, "Children, it's time!"

"I can't hear her," Joey whispers.

"Me neither." I close my eyes. "I can't see her."

"Me neither," Joey says.

"I guess we're breaking the rules."

"And we're rude and noisy and lousy little turds," Joey says, opening his eyes. He looks at me and smiles. "Rude and noisy and lousy little turds! Rude and noisy and lousy little turds!" he chants, jumping up and down. "Sing it loud and sing it proud!" he yells. "Rude and noisy and lousy little turds! Rude and noisy and lousy little turds!" We jump together. We jump until our faces are red. We jump until our hearts are pounding. We jump until Miss Gallagher has called us two more times.

"Okay, okay, here we come," Joey whispers. He's taking loud breaths while he carefully packs his lunch back in his lunch bag, then shakes off his sweater and ties it around his waist. I pack up, too. We walk back slowly, even though we know we should be rushing, even though we might get in trouble.

"Hear that?" I say, grabbing Joey's arm.

"What?" He stops walking and freezes, just like I want him to.

"There!" I say. *"Ah-ooo, ah-ooo."*

Joey tips his head to the side. He closes his eyes.

"It's a common eider. A female," I whisper. "They make pillows and quilts out of their feathers."

We stand still together. Joey keeps his eyes closed, and I don't let go of his arm.

Ah-ooo. Ah-ooo. The duck calls even louder.

"Cool," Joey says, opening his eyes. He's smiling like he's really happy. Then he shakes his head hard and says, "Wait a second. How?"

"How what?"

"How do they do it? How do they get the feathers?" Suddenly he looks mad. He's staring at me like I've done something wrong.

I let go of his arm. "They don't hurt the ducks. They just collect the feathers from the nests after the ducklings have moved out."

"Cool," Joey says.

When we're back at the maple tree that Sean had to sit under, Joey smiles at me and says, "Say it, don't spray it!" Then he runs ahead to the bus, where everyone is lining up. I take my time and am the last one in line, which really doesn't matter at all, because Dawn always saves me a seat.

When I get home from school, something is different. I feel it when I open the front door. No ice-blue quiet. Just a crackling sound that I can't figure out. I walk into the living room and look on the couch. Mom's not there.

"Mom?"

No answer.

"Mommy?"

No answer.

I check the kitchen table to see if there's a note for me. No note.

I walk upstairs. The crackle is a little louder. I check Mom and Dad's bedroom, but it's empty. I knock on Rachel's closed door, even though she's supposed to be at chorus practice. She doesn't yell, "Come in!" The bathroom door is open just a crack. I push it with my foot. Rachel's sitting on the counter by the sink, staring at the mirror. She has something silver in her hand, and she's poking at her face with it. The radio's on, but it's just playing crackle. I guess she doesn't notice.

"Rach?"

"What?" She doesn't turn to look at me. She doesn't stop whatever she's doing.

I walk into the room and sit down on the toilet. Tweezers. She's pulling out her eyebrow hairs.

"What are you doing?" I ask.

"I'm plucking my eyebrows," she says. "Giving them some shape." She's humming to herself.

"What's up with the radio?" I ask.

"Oh," she says, "I forgot. I was trying to get this cool station that Genevieve and I listen to at her house, but I couldn't get it to tune in."

She plucks. I watch. The radio crackles.

"Where's Mom?" I ask.

"I'm supposed to be at chorus practice," she says.

"I know."

"Dad called my school and told them to tell me to come home so that you wouldn't be all by yourself." Rachel plucks a hair and squeezes her mouth tight like she's sucking on a SweeTART.

"Where's Mom?" I ask again. There's a cold rock in my chest. Rachel hasn't looked at me once.

Rachel shakes her head. She doesn't say anything.

"Rach," I say, "did she fall down again? Did her MS flare up? Did she have to go to the hospital?"

"Well . . ." Rachel puts down the tweezers. She turns off the radio. She runs her fingers through her hair. I can see her brown eyes, Mom's eyes, in the mirror. She's looking at herself, not at me. "Let's see. Number one, no. Number two, no. Number three, yes."

"She had to go to the hospital? Mom is in the hospital?" The rock in my chest makes it hard to breathe.

Rachel sighs. She swings her legs over the end of the counter so that she's facing me. She looks mad. Her mouth is short and straight, like a dash, which I just learned is what you use to connect two words together.

"Yes, Naomi," she says. "Mom's in the hospital. But not just any hospital. The loony bin. The nuthouse. Our mom is in the nuthouse in Boston." Rachel tips her head to the side and gives me the angriest fakey smile I've ever seen. "Any more questions?"

I shake my head no. The rock is so heavy inside

me that I can't stand up. I'm stuck here on the toilet, because I can't stand up.

"Do you want to know what I think?" Rachel says. Her hands are tight fists. She's kicking her feet against the cabinet. "I think this is friggin' unbelievable. I think this friggin' sucks." Then she jumps off the counter, storms out of the bathroom, and slams the door.

I wait and wait on the toilet for Rachel to come back and say that she's really sorry and being in adolescence is hard and everything is going to be okay and do I want to come into her room with her and dance on her orange rug to "Sugar Sugar" while we wait for Dad to call and tell us that Mom's fine now, her depression after getting her MS diagnosis has finally lifted. I want Rachel to tell me that Dad said they'll be coming home tomorrow and we'll have stuffed clams as a treat for dinner, but she doesn't.

It's cold out and even Dad's down coconut jacket doesn't keep me from shivering. There are two herring gulls standing by the edge of the water, and they look cold, too, all plumped up and huddled together. I didn't bring my binocs, since my hands will get too cold without gloves and Mom hasn't brought the winter clothes down from the attic yet and I sure as heck wasn't going to ask Rachel to help me find them up there, since she was still all mad when I finally left the bathroom.

I lean against my tree and look out at the water. It's nearly winter, so the water's gray.

I wonder how long a person stays in a nuthouse.

I wonder if a daughter can visit a mother in a nut-house.

Suddenly I have a good idea. I don't see anything but pitch pine and scrub oaks and cattails and dried-out sea lavender, but that doesn't mean she isn't here. A lady like her might be an expert hider, since she believes in peace and quiet.

"Hello? Lady? Any chance you're here?"

She doesn't answer.

"Listen, lady, I don't want to step on your privacy. I just have two important questions for you."

I look carefully to see if anything moves to give her away, like a branch or a clump of marsh grass. It's a little tricky, since there's a breeze, like always. It's hard to know what's what.

"I'm sure you'd like to help me if you can." I give her some time. I don't want to rush her. "I mean, after shooing me away from my own special spot."

I stand still. I wait, even though I'm freezing my head off.

I walk down to the water. I walk over to the lav-ender.

"Lady?"

Nothing.

On my way back to my tree, I see something on the ground right near the trunk. A nest. A red-winged blackbird nest. I can tell because it's woven really neatly, like a perfect basket, and lined with sandy mud. Usually the female hides her nest in the cattails or rushes to keep her babies safe. I pick the nest up. There are pieces of dry grass inside, even though this isn't nesting season. I poke my finger around in the grass.

"Look, lady. A red-winged blackbird nest. If you come closer, I'll show it to you. It can be our secret." I hold the nest out.

She doesn't say anything. She's too scared to come see.

"Okay then, listen. I'll leave the nest right here where I found it. And now I'm going to walk home. We're having some trouble in our family. You can come take a look at the nest at your earliest convenience." I put the nest back exactly where I found it. I slowly turn around in a circle, so that wherever she's hiding, she'll see me wave good-bye.

From the outside, our house looks warm and cozy. Rachel's turned on all of the downstairs lights, and they make the windows glow yellow.

"Hi, Rach!" I shout when I come in the back door, like everything's normal, but she can't hear me, since she's got Dad's stereo turned up really loud. The rule is that we're not allowed to use Dad's stereo unless we ask permission, but I guess the rules don't matter when Mom's in the nuthouse. The music's so loud I wonder if the Morells can hear it.

Rachel's sitting on the living room couch with scraps of fabric all around her and a pair of ratty old jeans on her lap. She looks up when I come in.

"I'll make us popcorn if you thread the needle," she yells. I nod, and she gets up and I sit down. I wonder if the Morells will call the police on us, like we did on them last April when Mr. and Mrs. Morell were out of town and Vinnie and Donny threw a party and Dad politely asked them to turn their music down since it was way past midnight and they said, "Of course, Doc," and then turned it up even louder and threw a beer can against our beech tree.

"We will not let ourselves be intimidated," Dad said, but I could tell he already was, because his hands were shaking just a little bit and he looked like he wanted to hide in the basement behind the furnace, which is my favorite spot for hide-and-seek.

If the police come to our door and discover that Rachel and I are here at night without our parents again and our music's too loud and our dinner is popcorn, maybe they'll wonder if we'd be better off in a foster home, and when Mom and Dad walk in the front door the house will be empty, because we've been carted away, and Mom will be absolutely beside herself with worry and heartache, and they'll have to turn right back around and return Mom to the nuthouse before she even takes off her coat.

I'm scared to turn the stereo down, because I really don't want Rachel mad at me, but I do it anyway. When she walks in, though, she just says, "Thanks, Chirpie," and puts a bowl of popcorn on the coffee table. She reaches her hand out for the threaded needle, but suddenly I don't want to give it to her. I didn't want her mad at me, but now I'm mad at her.

"Why did you stay in that smoky room with all of those weird grown-ups?" I ask.

"What?"

"I had to walk home by myself, and stuff can happen to girls alone at night, especially on Halloween, and you should know that!"

"Oh, Chirp," Rachel says, but I interrupt her before she can say anything else.

"Things can happen, and things *did* happen, and things are *still* happening!" I don't want to be, but I'm crying.

"You're right, Chirpie," Rachel says, sitting down really close to me on the couch. "Everything's all messed up." She's pulling the fabric scraps onto her lap, like they're fall leaves she wishes would bury her. I pull some onto my lap, too. Purple corduroy. Red-checked cotton. Soft velour the color of melted margarine. Neither of us says anything. We just sit until the record ends and the arm of the stereo lifts up and the turntable stops spinning.

"When's Mom coming home?" I ask.

My sister shrugs. The quiet between us makes the air feel thick, like someone's thrown a wool blanket over my head. Rachel grabs a pair of scissors off the coffee table and cuts a square out of some bright green paisley. I hand her the needle, but she puts it down on top of the paisley patch and says, "First, I want to teach you something." She gets up, takes the record off the stereo, and sticks a new record on.

"Listen to this," she says. "It tells you all you need to know about really digging a guy. I mean, like, actually *wanting* him." Dylan starts singing, *Lay, lady, lay, lay across my big brass bed,* all sweet and croaky, and Rachel closes her eyes, so I close my eyes, too. When the song is over, we open our eyes and eat popcorn with lots of salt while she sews the green paisley patch on some jeans for Bruce Clarkman, who is the boy I have to not ask too many questions about and promise not to tell anyone she really, really digs.

CHAPTER SIX

"I THINK THIS WILL HELP keep us on track until Mom comes home," Dad says. He's holding up a round piece of red poster board the size of a 45. Inside it a smaller circle's attached with *Naomi* and *Rachel* written on it in Magic Marker in Dad's very neat handwriting.

"It's a chore wheel. See?" Dad spins the inside circle and our names line up with a list of jobs like *Empty the dishwasher* and *Cook dinner Monday, Wednesday, Friday.* "If you girls rotate this every Sunday night and I stay on top of the food shopping and laundry, we should be in fine shape. And Clara's planning to organize Mom's friends from the Saltwater Dance Brigade to drop off dinners, too, sometimes, to help us out."

Dad smiles like he's really pleased, but his jaw keeps twitching, which is what happens when he's mad or nervous. My guess is both, since it's pouring rain out and the wind is smacking the branches around and this is our first weekend without Mom. And Rachel is still in her pajamas and hasn't been nice to him for days or said anything at all yet to him today, even after Dad sighed while we were eating our Rice Krispies and looked really sad and said, "Wow, this is so tough, having Mom away."

"Cool, Dad," I say, and reach out so that he hands me the chore wheel. I spin it and study it, since Dad is trying so hard and his job is to help people with their feelings and his own wife is in the nuthouse because she's developed feelings that she isn't able to manage without professional help and how can that not make him feel like he's some kind of loser?

"Maybe Rachel would like to take a look," Dad says, because Rachel is staring at the streams of water running down the kitchen window. She hasn't been paying attention to the chore wheel at all. Rachel shakes her head, but I keep holding it out to her until she kind of has no choice. She takes it from me like it has dog doo on it, just touching the edge and wrinkling up her nose.

"C'mon, Rach," Dad says.

"C'mon, Rach, what?" she says.

"How about a little effort here," he says.

"Fine," she says. Rachel drops the chore wheel on the table and leans over it. "Wow!" she says. "Fascinating! What an amazing piece of work."

Dad stares at her like he doesn't know her. Rachel takes a peek at him and then looks down at the chore wheel again.

"Unbelievably interesting," she mumbles.

Dad's frozen like a wild brown bunny when you surprise it on the sand path. His shoulders are hunched up. His mouth is open. He might not be breathing.

I watch the way the rain bounces back up when it hits the picnic table in the backyard. It's raining in two directions. When I look back at Dad, he's shaking his head like he's got some stuck parts that he wants to loosen up. Then he slowly walks out of the room.

"What?" Rachel says to me, even though I haven't said anything. She sounds as cranky as a little kid who needs to take a nap.

"Want to play water worms?" I ask.

"Maybe," Rachel says, but she's already pulling her chair right up to the window. I pull my chair up, too. We don't choose contestants. We just watch all the squiggles of water running down the glass.

"You know, Dad doesn't even know how long she'll be gone," Rachel says. "He just dumped her off at McLean Hospital and drove away. He's waiting for a phone call from the people there."

"He didn't just dump her off. He told us it was Mom's idea. He said that she wanted to go somewhere to rest and get better. They met with a nice doctor there. And there are apple trees."

"Oh, Chirp," Rachel says. She presses her nose up

to the window. I don't know why she's *Oh-Chirp*ing me. There's too much I don't know. I don't know why Mom can't just get better at home if we give her lots of peace and quiet and take turns dancing for her and cooking her chicken soup and mashed potatoes and, every once in a while, bringing her an ice cream sundae with hot fudge from Benson's. I don't know when we'll get to visit Mom in the nuthouse. I don't know why Rachel used to think everything Dad said was so great and now she won't listen to anything he has to say. I don't know what happened to the marsh lady to make her want to keep her distance from people, even a girl who talks extra gentle and shows her a red-winged blackbird nest.

"Listen, Chirp, let's ask if we can go see Mom for Thanksgiving, okay?" Rachel finally says. She puts her arm around me.

"We'll make her a pie," I say, pressing my nose against the glass, too.

"Lemon meringue," she says.

The glass is cold on my nose. Our breath makes fog.

Rachel backs up and draws tic-tac-toe with her finger on the window.

"You can go first, Chirpie," she says. I'm just about to put a fat *X* right in the middle square when Dad walks in.

"Listen," he says, "we need to talk."

I turn my chair around, but Rachel just sighs

really loud, like Dad's said we have to pick up every grain of sand on every beach on the Cape. She keeps staring out the window.

"Rachel!" Dad says. I've never heard Dad's voice sound so sharp.

"Oh, *all right*," she says, and makes a big deal out of dragging her chair around as if it weighs a ton.

"This is a tough time for all of us," Dad says, looking right at Rachel. "And I have room for a lot of things, but I don't have room for your disrespect. I understand that you have a range of feelings, some difficult, that you're contending with. But you simply have to do better. Do you understand?"

"Sure," Rachel says.

"And?" Dad asks.

"And, I'm sorry?"

"Is that a question or an apology?" Dad asks.

"I don't know," Rachel says, "but *this* is a question." She stands up. She walks right over to Dad. She pushes her face so close to his face that I bet he can smell her milk breath. "Are *you* sorry?" she says. Then she runs out of the room and up the stairs before Dad can answer.

"Okay," Dad mumbles. "Well, that didn't go well." He's pacing around the living room and looking down, like he's hoping to find an escape hatch in the wood floor that he can jump into and be transported to another land, where he doesn't have a wife in a nuthouse and an oldest daughter who has turned nasty. I think I hear Rachel crying upstairs, but it might just be a maple branch scraping against a window.

It's probably a good time to check out what the birds are up to in this downpour. I get all suited up and I'm standing by the front door in my yellow rain slicker with my yellow rain hat that's shaped like an astronaut's helmet and my brown rubbers when Dad comes over to me and crouches down.

"Hey, honey," he says, looking right in my eyes, "do you want to play water worms?"

I nod, because suddenly there are tears in my throat that will bubble up and spill out of my eyes if I try to talk. Daddy helps me unbuckle my slicker, like I'm a little girl. He lifts my rain hat off my head and hangs my slicker back up in the closet.

He takes my hand, leads me to the living room window, and points to a squiggle of water near the very top.

"This one's mine," he says. "Alfred, I'd like you to meet my daughter, Naomi."

I point to a squiggle right near Dad's. "This one's mine. Dad, Josephine. Josephine, Dad. On your mark, get set, go!"

I lean against Dad, and he doesn't move away. He smells good, like dry grass. We watch Alfred and Josephine race down the window. Our contestants take their sweet time, but Dad and I, there's nothing else we need to be doing right now. He doesn't have to go see if Mom needs a bite to eat or if she's warm enough on the couch or if she'd like him to read a short story to her from *The Best Short Stories of the Sixties*. Maybe once we see whether Alfred or Josephine is the winner, I'll ask Dad if he'll come with me to the kitchen. Maybe I'll have milk tea in a pink mug and a piece of rye toast with margarine. Maybe he'll have a cup of instant coffee and we'll sit at the kitchen table and watch the rain splash and just not talk about all of the things there are to talk about.

⇔

"Turkey, Corn, Sweet Potatoes, and Peas, one more time!" Miss Gallagher says.

"Do I have to be the turkey?" Joey asks. "I really, really, really don't want to be the turkey."

"Joey," Miss Gallagher says, "we've discussed this. We had a fair process. Everyone chose his or her role by pulling a slip of paper out of a bowl. And the turkey is a very important part of the Thanksgiving meal."

"I guess you don't have older brothers," Joey says under his breath.

Miss Gallagher thinks we *could* have a blockbuster of a Thanksgiving play, because she's added a creative element, which is having the meal dance around the Pilgrims and Indians before it settles on the table to be eaten, *if only* Peas (Dawn) and Corn (Lisa B.) and Sweet Potatoes (Tommy) and Turkey would add their own unique flavor and spice to the basic step so it doesn't just look like the Mexican hat dance.

I'm tired of sitting on the floor, waiting to bow my head and lead the other Pilgrims in saying grace before the meal, especially since I'm not even sure I should be saying it.

"Dancers, again!" Miss Gallagher says. Aside from Dawn, who really is trying, because she's got her cheeks puffed up with air and actually looks a little like a pea, the rest of the meal is just shuffling around.

"I bet Miss Gallagher got this idea from *Harriet the Spy*," Sally whispers.

I nod. Miss Gallagher is staring at us with her I'm-one-breath-away-from-yelling-at-you look.

I'm glad that Mom can't come to our performance, since she thinks dance is one of life's great joys and what's going on here feels like the opposite of joy. Joey looks all stiff, and suddenly I remember Plymouth Rock and the way he tipped his head back and whirled around with the minicyclone and the wind and his tangly hair all lit up in the sun, so when the music stops on the record player, I jump up and say, "Miss Gallagher, I'd really like to be the turkey. My mother is a dancer, and I've inherited her genes, so I think I could add some inspiration."

Everyone stares at me. Miss Gallagher smiles the kind of smile a grown-up makes when they think they understand you better than you understand yourself.

"That's a generous offer, Naomi," Miss Gallagher says, "but it wouldn't be fair to the other students, who are sticking with their designated roles."

I know that I should just sit down, but I keep standing, because I also know that life isn't always fair and is filled with things like mean older brothers and dancer mothers who can't dance.

"Does anybody mind if Joey and I switch parts?" I ask. "Not at all!" Sally shouts in her dance-party, not classroom, voice. I look around and everyone else is shaking their heads no, even Tommy, who would be the only boy left dancing if Joey became a Pilgrim.

Miss Gallagher walks over to me, still smiling, but I can tell she isn't happy. "Now, Naomi," she says, "I really don't think we can trust that this is a fair representation of your classmates' true feelings, given your current situation with your moth—"

"Hey, Miss Gallagher," Joey says. "I know all my lines. *Gobblegobblegobble!*" He starts flapping his arms. "I can fly, too." He's flying right at her. *"Gobblegobblegobble!"* He looks really mad.

Miss Gallagher gets red, scurries back to the record player, and says, "Let's take it from the top." She turns the music back on, louder.

Now I know that she thinks everyone feels sorry for me, which makes me want to run out of the room and slam the door. Instead, I sit back down and bow my head like a good Pilgrim until the end of class.

On the bus, Dawn leans in and stares at me. "Don't feel bad, Chirp," she says. I just shake my head. If I talk, I might cry, since all of my mad got pushed down inside me and now my throat aches.

"Anyway," she says, "I think it would be more fun to lead the prayer than be a turkey." When I don't say anything, she says, "Well, maybe you can be the turkey next year."

When the bus drops Joey and me off, I don't run ahead. Joey walks right next to me, kicking a rock.

"What's cookin'?" he says.

I shake my head.

"You know who the real turkey is, right?" Joey says.

I shrug.

"Knock-knock," Joey says.

"Who's there?" I whisper.

"A stupid turkey teacher."

I can't help smiling.

Joey kicks the rock to me, and I kick it back to him, and he kicks it back to me.

"Hey, you want to see something?" Joey says.

"Okay."

When we're in front of our houses, Joey says, "Get your bike and meet me back here."

There's no reason to go inside, because nobody's there and we don't have any Oreos since Dad didn't buy any because he doesn't know that I always have them as a snack with a glass of milk when I come home from school. I go out to the shed in the backyard, pull on my blue jeans that I keep hidden there, take off my skirt and stash it behind the snow shovels, and grab Bluebird. Joey's already in the road waiting for me, so he must not have had a snack, either.

Joey takes off and gets a good head start, but he doesn't just leave me in the dust, because Bluebird has three gears and I'm riding standing up. I'm pumping, pumping, pumping, and the cold air hurts when I breathe. The harder I pedal, the more my legs burn, and the more my legs burn, the less my throat aches.

"Joey!" I yell. Suddenly I want to ask him if it's true. Is everyone just being fake-nice to me because they feel sorry for me?

"Joey!" Do they know that Mom is at McLean's, which means she's at a nuthouse? Who told them, since I haven't said anything to anybody?

"Joey!" But he's just far enough ahead that he can't hear me.

He's taking the shortcut to Route 6. I'm not supposed to ride my bike, only walk it, on Route 6, but Mom isn't going to care, since Dad says her clinical administrator says she's taking a break from our day-to-day goings-on, and Dad isn't going to care, because he's so busy with his extra work and responsibilities that he says he's having a hard time keeping his head screwed on straight.

The cars on Route 6 whiz by and make Bluebird shake. I have to not get stuck in the patches of sand. I have to keep my wheel straight and not wiggle out toward the cars. I have to not worry when a truck comes and the sound is like an angry yell, trying to knock me and Bluebird over.

Up ahead, Joey stops.

"We have to cross here," he says.

"Joey?" I say.

"What?"

"Nothing."

He's breathing hard and his cheeks are pink, and he's definitely not a sad turkey anymore. I'm not a good Pilgrim, either, because I'm breaking an Orenstein family rule by crossing Route 6 on my bike. We wait until the coast is clear. When Joey starts screaming, "Go, Speed Racer! Go, Speed Racer! Go, Speed Racer, go-oh!" we race across.

Up and down a couple of little hills and now we're on Seaview Drive. Even though there are summer houses and bluffs and the dunes between here and the ocean, I can hear the waves washing in and out. I can smell the salt water. The air is thicker and colder here than bayside. The ocean has lots of gray in it.

"Turn here!" Joey yells. It's a dirt road with a sign that says PRIVATE. In our family, *private* means that if someone asks how Mom is, you stay polite but you don't really say anything, for example, *Thanks for asking. We're doing just fine.* *Private* means that when a teacher says something mean and stupid that makes you worry that everyone knows everything and what you want to do is scream *You don't know anything about anything,* you just sit down and bow your head like a good Pilgrim.

I can barely pedal, because the dirt is mostly sand and my tires keep digging in. Joey's weaving back and forth, trying to find the safe spots. There are handmade signs nailed to the trees where another dirt road branches off. I see plenty of plain old Cape Cod names, like Randall and Johnson and McIntyre, but there are Jewish names, too, like Goldberg and Leventhal and Blum, so I guess this is where some of the Jewish psychiatrists who come to the Cape in August stay. Everyone makes fun of them and calls them summer shrinks, like *Don't even try getting a parking space at the beach today, because the summer shrinks have hogged all the spaces with their Mercedes and Volvos.*

Joey's getting off his bike. He wheels it to the side of the road and pushes it down into the bramble. "Leave your bike here," he says, so I push Bluebird down next to Joey's bike. Joey walks a few steps and then says, "Follow me," and starts walking on a path that I never would have noticed, because the bayberry and bramble hide it. Branches hit my arms. Blackberry vines grab my ankles. Joey picks up a big stick. "On guard!" he says, and smacks everything that's in our way, which makes walking much, much easier, and I get a sweet feeling inside, like when Mom blows on my soup to cool it off for me or Dad rushes into my room to close my windows before a thunderstorm.

"We're almost there," Joey says.

"Almost where?" I ask, but he doesn't answer me, because he's too busy shouting, "Take *that*! And *that*! And *that*!" This might be using bad judgment, since I don't know where we're going and I don't know why we're here and nobody knows where I am. Mom says examples of bad judgment are hanging out in the town center after dark with kids who drink beer or being in a deserted place where bad people might lurk, and I wonder if there were bad people lurking in the orphanage when she was a kid, but I can't really ask her, because she almost never talks about that time and I don't want to make her think about it if she doesn't want to. Anyway, there's no beer here, and Joey is with me, so it's not deserted, so I guess everything is A-OK.

Joey stops at the end of the path and faces me. "Right this way," he says.

He holds back the bushes and lets me walk

through. It's a little house made of glass. The roof is glass and the sides are glass and the doors are glass. The wood in between the glass is rotten, and the glass is so dirty it looks black. The house is much smaller than a real house but a whole lot bigger than our toolshed.

"What is it?" I ask.

Joey shrugs.

"Whose is it?" I ask.

Joey shrugs. "It's nobody's."

"It's got to be somebody's."

"Shhhh," he says, and starts walking around the glass house. I follow him, even though the blackberry thorns scratch my ankles. There's an old metal garbage can filled with rusty water. There's a dried-out hose that's broken into pieces and looks like a heap of fat green spaghetti.

Joey stops and looks up. Just below the roof, there's a row of broken windows. Some parts of the glass are busted all the way out. Other parts are only partway busted, and they're beautiful, like the ice that freezes in the salt marsh when we have a wicked cold snap. "Mine," Joey says, pointing to the broken windows.

He picks up a rock, dusts it off on his jean-jacket sleeve, and keeps walking. When he gets to the opposite side of the house, he looks up again.

"Top row, middle window," he says. He backs up. "Get out of the way," he says.

"Wait," I say. "You're not supposed to break windows."

Joey laughs. "Well, you're not supposed to have stupid teachers. You're not supposed to have mean—" Joey looks at me. "Move!" he yells.

He's got his arm up.

I run out of the way.

Joey throws the rock and the glass explodes. Tiny splinters of light shoot out like glowing fireflies. The sound is prettier than any bird I've ever heard. Joey picks up another rock. He dusts it off. He whips the rock. The glass flies.

"This is where I come when I'm mad," he mumbles. "I mean, sometimes this is where I come when I'm mad."

I pick up a rock. It's cold and hard and feels good in my hand.

Joey looks at me. "You can have a window," he says.

I shake my head. I'm a good girl. I don't break windows.

"We came all the way out here," Joey says. "I've never shown this place to anybody."

I grip the rock tighter.

"This is my secret place. Don't be a baby." Joey kicks the ground.

"I'm not a baby."

"Wah," Joey says. *"Wah. Wah. Wah."*

"Stop it!"

"Make me!"

I don't know why he's being mean to me. I don't know why he brought me all the way to the glass house just to be mean to me when he could have been mean to me right in front of our houses, like his brothers.

"Why are you being mean to me?"

"Is the baby gonna cry?"

"Shut up!" I yell. Suddenly I'm so mad I could blow the whole stupid glass house down in one breath. "Leave me alone! You can't bring me all the way out here just to be mean to me. I tried to get you out of being the turkey. You think I wanted to be the stupid turkey? I was being nice to you! It's your fault that Miss Gallagher said what she did in front of everyone!" I want to pull his blond hair. I want to say things that are so mean his heart will stop beating.

I look down at the rock in my hand. I'm a good girl. I pull my arm back. I'm a good girl. I look around. No Mom. No Dad. No Miss Gallagher. Just Joey. My heart is pounding. I'm a good girl.

"Any window you want," Joey says. I throw the rock as hard as I can. When the glass explodes and the splinters scatter, I yell like a crazy lady. *"Yaaaaaaaaa!"* Now Joey's throwing, too.

"Crap!" he yells.

"Yaaaaaaaa!" I yell.

"Crap!"

"Yaaaaaaa!"

"Crap!"

"*Yaaaaaa!*"

All this breaking makes me feel like something's getting fixed inside me.

When Joey says, "Okay, stop now," I don't hassle him. I know he wants to save some glass for another day. I dump my rocks in a pile on the ground. Joey dumps his rocks next to my rocks. We ride all the way home without saying anything, not one word at all, just a long, cold, peaceful ride.

CHAPTER SEVEN

WE'VE FINISHED OUR SUGAR cookies and pink punch, and Dad is trying to steer us out of the classroom, but people keep getting in our way, like Mrs. Paganelli, Lori's mother, who just let us know that the world is full of things to be thankful for if we only keep our eyes open to God's glory.

"God bless you," she says to Dad with a huge smile. She looks like she's about to hug him, too, but Dad says, "Happy Thanksgiving," and walks away fast. *"Oy vey,"* he whispers to me and Rachel, and the three of us start giggling, because we're uncomfortable with the Christian talk, being the only Jews in the room, as always.

Now Miss Gallagher is walking toward us.

"Nice to see you, Dr. Orenstein," she says, reaching out and shaking Dad's hand. "I hope you enjoyed the play. What are your plans for the holiday?"

Dad says, "It was terrific. Thanks for all of your effort. We'll be visiting with family in Boston."

Miss Gallagher says, "Nice, nice," but she has a little weird smile that could be a sign that she knows *family in Boston* means *Mom in the nuthouse.* Could Dad have told her? Wouldn't he have said something to me if he had? Anyway, he says he's proud that we're managing just fine, the three of us. If we're managing just fine, why would he need to share our private problems with my teacher, who he barely knows?

We've got our coats on and we've thrown away our paper plates and we're almost at the door and Rachel's whispering, "Let's go, let's get out of here," when Mrs. Paganelli claps her hands and says, "I just had an inspiration. Before ending this lovely evening, why don't we gather around and take just a quick moment to share our words of thanks?" Her question sounds more like a command, and everyone starts moving into a circle. Dad looks at us and we look at Dad, and even though we really, really don't want to stay, it feels like there's a magnet pulling us into the circle with everyone else, and unless we want to be even more different than we already are, we'd better just give in.

"Of course, we won't call this prayer, but as this special holiday of Thanksgiving approaches, let us consider our numerous blessings and offer up our words of thanks." Mrs. Paganelli takes a loud breath. She closes her eyes. She opens her eyes. She still has that smile. "Who would like to begin the sharing? What are we thankful for?"

No one says anything for a really long time. I can hear Rachel breathing. I'm thinking that I'm thankful Joey was absent today, so he didn't have to get teased or maybe even beat up by his brothers for being a turkey, and I didn't mind being the turkey, because I got to demonstrate all three of my leaps and everyone clapped hard when I curtsied, and also I didn't have to fake-pray, but I don't know if what Mrs. Paganelli wants us to share is big things, like ending the war and having enough food to eat, and before I can decide if I should brave it and be the first thankful volunteer, Miss Gallagher jumps in and says, "I'm thankful for these wonderful children, who worked hard and did such a good job in the Thanksgiving play."

"Yes," Mrs. Barker says. "Bravo!" She pats Dawn on the back and Dawn takes a little bow, as if peas were the only food on the Thanksgiving table.

Mrs. Paganelli says, "I'm thankful for this wonderful community and for my health and the health and love of my family, and I could go on and on with my bounty of blessings, but I don't want to hog the show," and then she laughs all snorty, like she's watching the episode of *I Love Lucy* where Lucy and Ethel work in a chocolate factory and the conveyor belt is going way too fast and they start shoveling chocolates into their mouths and down their shirts and into their hats.

There's a really long silence again. Most of the kids are looking at their feet. Most of the parents are looking into space. I want someone to start talking so no one will remember that the last time we all went around the room and talked was at back-to-school night, when Mom had her supersonic eye.

I check out Dad and he's staring at Mrs. Paganelli with a really strange expression, and suddenly I realize that he's about to cry. I've never seen Dad cry before. He makes a snuffling sound in his nose and shakes his head hard, and just one tear slips out of his eye and down his cheek, which isn't enough for anyone to notice. I take Dad's hand and he grabs my hand back, hard. It's almost too hard, but I don't let go, because Dad needs me. Mom needs me, too, but there's nothing I can do for her right now, which is probably what Dad's thinking: *Hannah is all alone in this exact moment at McLean Hospital without Chirp's Thanksgiving play and without pink punch and sugar cookies and without Mrs. Paganelli's bounty of blessings and there's nothing, not one thing at all, I can do about it.*

"Okay," Rachel says, "now we're supposed to stir this frequently until it comes to a boil." Rachel's reading the recipe from the cookbook.

"How frequent is frequently?" I ask, starting to stir.

"I don't know," she says. "Just keep an eye on it. Make sure it doesn't burn. The lemony part is really important. I'll start cracking the eggs."

Mom's going to be surprised when we hand her the pie this afternoon. *Wow, my girls, lemon meringue! My favorite!*

"Do you think Mom will share the pie with her new friends?" I ask Rachel.

"Oh, c'mon, Chirp," she says, sounding irritated, but then she stops. She looks at me. She tips her head to the side and wrinkles her forehead like she's trying to figure something out. "Actually, I have no idea what to expect. I can't picture what it's like there." Rachel looks like a little girl in Mom's pink flannel nightgown. She keeps pushing up the sleeves, but they keep slipping back down. She's worn the nightgown every night since Mom left.

"You know, Dad says we shouldn't call it a nut-house," I say.

"Well, it *is* a nuthouse," Rachel says.

"Dad says there's a maple tree and a frog pond in the courtyard."

"And lots of nutbars inside."

"Mom isn't a nutbar."

"Exactly," Rachel says. "That's why she shouldn't

be there." Rachel scoops some of the hot lemony stuff out of the saucepan, dumps it into the beaten eggs, mixes it, and then pours it back into the saucepan.

"At least it's much, much better than the state hospital in Taunton," I say.

"You need to stir constantly now until it thickens," Rachel says.

"Dad said he absolutely never would have taken Mom to Taunton, even though McLean is expensive and he's having to work extra hard to keep our heads above water."

"Keep stirring," Rachel says.

"I *am*," I say.

Rachel cracks the eggs for the meringue. She turns the mixer on high, and we can't talk anymore. The lemony stuff is hot and bubbly. I stir and stir and stir. I think maybe we did something wrong, because it's not getting thick, and we don't have time to start over again, because Dad said we have to be out the door and on the road by nine o'clock sharp, because we might run into Thanksgiving traffic.

"Rach," I say, but she doesn't hear me because of the whiny mixer. The lemony stuff is the prettiest soft yellow, and it smells like summer, but it's thin, not thick and not thickening. "Rach!" I yell. She still doesn't hear me. If we don't bring Mom a lemon meringue pie, then her face won't light up and she won't say *Oh, my sweet chickens! You knew just what I wanted!*

I'm stirring so fast now that the lemony stuff is splashing on the sides of the saucepan and making smoke. My hand is aching and my heart is racing and Rachel can't hear me and I can't stop stirring to walk over to her, because then I'll ruin the pie. It might already be ruined. I don't want to bring Mom a ruined pie. I can't bring Mom a ruined pie.

"RACHEL!" I yell as loud as I can, just as she shuts off the mixer.

"What *is* it, Chirp?" she says, all cranky, but then she sees my face and rushes over. She puts her arm around me, and I start to cry.

"It's no good," I tell her.

"It's okay, Chirpie," she says. She takes the spoon from me. I push my face into her neck, and she smells just like the lemony stuff. "Look. You haven't done anything wrong." I hear her stirring. She says, "See, Chirpie. You did a really good job. It's getting thick, just the way it's supposed to." I peek into the saucepan. She's right. My sister keeps her arm tight around me while she takes the saucepan off the stove and pours the lemony stuff into the piecrust.

"Help me with this part, Chirp," Rachel says. We spoon the meringue onto the lemony stuff. It's white and frothy. We press our spoons into it and make perfect waves.

"Just like the ocean," Rachel says.

"Mom loves the ocean," I say.

"Yeah," Rachel says, "she does."

"She'll love our pie, right?"

"Just like the ocean," Rachel says. She takes the pie and slips it into the oven that we preheated to 350 degrees, just like we were supposed to. We need to keep an eye on it and take it out in approximately ten minutes or when it's a light golden brown.

"The man in the Volkswagen bus!" Rachel says.

"Yay! That's thirty-eight!" I say.

We've been playing peace since we left the house. What you do is make peace signs through the car windows and keep track of how many people peace you back. I don't understand how anyone could not be for peace, but Dad says it's more complicated than I understand and has to do with people's political views on Nixon and Vietnam and patriotism.

"See that lady in the blue car?" I say. "She won't look at me."

"Let's try the dancing trick," Rach says.

She squishes next to me, facing my window. *"This is the dawning of the Age of Aquarius, Age of Aquarius. . . ."* We sing really loud and bop our peace signs around to the beat. The lady looks at us and waves.

"Peace! Peace! Peace!" we say, pointing to each other's peace signs, but the lady just smiles at us and keeps waving.

We're almost to the Sagamore Bridge. On the other side is Friendly's, where Dad says we can stop to get hot chocolate. Once we're in Boston, we'll have Thanksgiving lunch, since Mom is going to have her meal at the hospital without us. Kids aren't allowed on the floors or in the dining room at McLean Hospital. That's a policy. But there's a coffee shop in the hospital where we can bring our lemon meringue pie and celebrate.

"Whipped cream, Dad?" I ask.

"What?" Dad says.

"Can we have whipped cream on our hot chocolate?"

"Yes, kiddo," Dad says. "You guys are troopers. I know this isn't the way we usually spend Thanksgiving."

"Troopers?" Rachel says, just loud enough for me to hear. "Great. Dad thinks we're in the army." She's shaking her head, like she can't believe she actually has to live on the same planet as him.

Usually for Thanksgiving, Grandma and Grandpa come from Sayville, New York, and Dad makes a fire in the fireplace and drinks sherry in crystal glasses with them and catches up, since he's their son, while Mom is in the kitchen with Rachel and me. Usually we sing along to the radio while we make stuffing from the Pepperidge Farm bag but add in extra ingredients, like fresh parsley and celery and mushrooms. We make mashed potatoes with *schmaltz,* which is Yiddish for "chicken fat," and we brown onions in it and then whip the potatoes until they're fluffy. We make cranberry sauce from cranberries that grow right here on the Cape, and after you add sugar and water and turn the burner on high, the cranberries pop and then you know it's done. Usually Grandma and Grandpa bring New York cheesecake from Zabar's, and when we're finished eating the turkey and stuffing and potatoes and cranberry sauce and peas and salad and listening to family stories, we go into the living room and talk about how great all the food was and eat dessert.

Usually, when dessert is over, Rachel and I put on a show. Usually we do a dance number and Mom makes a special guest appearance at the end that blows Grandma's socks off, which is a good thing, because there's tension between Mom and Grandma that has to do with Mom being a poor kid from the Bronx. I don't really understand what the problem is, but I know that whenever Mom thinks Grandma and Grandpa have brought us too many presents, her mouth gets tight and she takes Dad into the kitchen, where they whisper-shout until Mom runs upstairs and Dad follows her and they stay in their bedroom for a long time with the door closed, and Grandma says things like "Your mother is quite sensitive, isn't she?" which makes Rachel and me mad, but we can't show it, because we're supposed to be respectful to adults, especially old ones who love us.

"What are Grandma and Grandpa doing for Thanksgiving?" I ask Dad.

133

"They'll have dinner with friends. They've offered to come anytime just to help out while Mom's away, but I told them that we're holding down the fort beautifully, the three of us. It sounds like they'll probably come visit for Hanukkah, though."

"Uh-oh," I say. "I bet they'll bring too many presents."

"If Mom is even home by then," Rachel mumbles, quietly enough that Dad can't hear her from the front seat.

"Will Mom be home by Hanukkah?" I ask Dad.

"I certainly expect so," Dad says.

"See," I say to Rachel.

"See what?" Rachel says, still quietly. "*I expect so* isn't *yes*."

"Well, it's almost *yes*."

"*Almost yes* is like *almost pregnant*. It doesn't mean anything."

"Yes, it does."

"No, it doesn't."

"Uh-huh."

"No way."

"It *does*."

"Fine. Live in your fantasy world."

"Are you girls bickering back there?" Dad asks.

"Almost yes," Rachel says.

"What?" Dad says.

"Nothing, Dad. Don't sweat it," Rachel says. She turns away from me and keeps on peacing.

The lady at Friendly's is very friendly. Her name is Patty, and she has a little plastic turkey pinned to her collar right near her name tag and pink lipstick and makeup that's supposed to hide her wrinkles but doesn't and a fancy blond hairdo with curls and twists.

"Well, you're quite a cutie," she says to me. "And what a pretty young lady," she says to Rachel. "Off on a Thanksgiving adventure?"

Rachel nods.

"And your mom must be waiting in the car?" She looks at Dad. "Giving her a moment of peace, huh?" She winks. "I know how it is. I have four of my own."

"Three hot chocolates with whipped cream to go, please," Dad says.

"No," Rachel says, "I don't want any whipped cream." She rolls her eyes as if Dad should have known, even though she likes whipped cream.

"No whipped cream for you, honey?" Dad asks.

"That's what I said," Rachel says. "No whipped cream. *Nooo whiiiipped creeeeam.*" She says it really loud and slow like Dad has bad hearing.

"Rachel," Dad says, "enough."

"So where are you off to?" Patty says.

"We're going to Boston," Dad says.

"Ohhh?" Patty says, like he said *We're hunting elephants in Africa.* "Now, what's in Bos—"

"We're actually in a bit of a hurry," Dad says before Patty can ask any more questions that he doesn't want to answer.

"Oh, of course you are," Patty says in a dried-out voice, and then she gives our hot chocolates the puniest squirts of whipped cream from the can. "Happy trails," she says to Dad, and pretty much grabs his money and shoves his change at him.

On the way out the door, I turn around and peace her. She doesn't peace back.

"We should have told her Mom is an astronaut and on her way into orbit," Rachel says.

"Freeze-dried turkey," Dad says.

"And pumpkin pie capsules with vanilla ice cream powder," I say.

Rachel smiles.

"Right, Chirp," Dad says, rumpling my hair. "All the vanilla ice cream powder she can eat."

The closer we get to Boston, the worse the traffic is. *Bumpa ta bumpa,* Mom would say, like a genuine Bronx girl, if she were here. Mostly Mom talks regular, but sometimes her accent sneaks in, like *Chirp, honey, can you pass me my cwaw-fee?* I always ask Mom if she's doing that on purpose, and she always says *Doing what on purpose?* so I figure she's not.

"It's going to be a long haul, girls," Dad says, flicking on the classical radio station. Rachel and I are tired of playing peace. We're tired of looking out the window. We're tired of singing all the songs from *Hair* and saying *bleep* for the sex and drug words. I let Rachel use Eggie, my white stuffed duck, as a pillow, and she leans against the car door. She lets me lie down and put my head in her lap. Dad turns off the radio. Rachel starts to sit up so she can argue with him, but he starts singing "All the Pretty Little Horses," which is a lullaby he used to sing to us when we were babies, and she settles back down. Then he sings *"Oyfn Pripetshok,"* which is a Yiddish lullaby his mother used to sing to him. Then he sings my favorite, "Annabel Lee," about a man whose true love is killed by the wind and locked up in a grave in the ocean because the angels in heaven are jealous of their love. By the time Dad sings

> *And this was the reason that, long ago,*
> *In this kingdom by the sea,*
> *A wind blew out of a cloud, chilling*
> *My Annabel Lee*

his voice is so sweet-sad and I'm so drifty-tired that I close my eyes and hear the highway like the sea and feel warm waves of sleep rocking me away.

I open my eyes. Through the car window, I see a little slice of orange roof.

"C'mon, Chirp, we're here!" Rachel says. She hands me Eggie, and I sit up. Dad is walking through the door of Howard Johnson's Motor Lodge. We race to catch up with him.

The office is smoky. Dad's standing at the counter, talking to a man with pimples on his face, who's writing things down.

"Do Rachel and I get our own key?" I ask Dad.

"Is there a soda machine?" Rachel asks.

"And an inside pool? Can we go swimming later?"

Dad looks at us and smiles a tired smile.

"They haven't stayed in many motels," Dad says to the pimple man. "It's a big treat."

Rachel turns red and shakes her head, like Dad's just given away her deepest, darkest secret.

The man says to us, "Are you visiting relatives for the holiday?"

"No," I say.

"Yes," Rachel says.

"She isn't a relative," I whisper to Rachel. "She's our *mom.*"

"That's a relative, Chirp," Rachel whispers, and rolls her eyes, like I have no brain between my ears.

"I *know* that, Rachel," I whisper, "but when people say *relatives,* they mean like grandparents or aunts and uncles or—"

"Girls," the man interrupts, "if it's okay with your father, I hereby present you with your very own copy of the room key. Don't lose it." He smiles and hands Rachel a gold key with a plastic tag on it that says 228.

"Can we find the room and open the door ourselves?" I ask Dad.

"Just this once your pack mule will deliver your personal belongings," Dad says. "Have at it, girls," and he heads off to the car to schlep our stuff.

We run upstairs. There are so many doors. I know that the room numbers go in order, with evens on one side of the hall and odds on the other, but I want to see if I can find our room by intuition, like a fortune-teller. I close my eyes, just in case I can feel something, a vibration maybe, when Rachel yells, "Here it is, Chirp!" She's standing in front of the second-to-last room at the end of the hallway.

Rachel puts the key in the lock.

"One. Two. Three!" We push open the door together. The room is perfect. It has two perfect beds with orange flowered bedspreads. It has two perfect water glasses in two perfect wax-paper bags to keep the glasses sanitary. In the bathroom, there are perfect white bath towels and perfect white hand towels and perfect white washcloths and perfect white soap.

"I love this place."

"It's perfect," Rachel says.

"A TV!" I turn the dial, and we watch the spot of light spread out on the screen and then change into black-and-white static.

"Check the channels," Rachel says.

I turn the dial and keep count. "Seven."

"That's two more than we get at home," she says.

"We'll watch in bed," I say. "We'll rot our brains!"

"Perfect," she says, laughing.

Rachel opens and closes every drawer in the dresser. I turn the fan from low to medium to high. She pulls back the orange bedspread to see what kind of blankets there are. I open the drawer in the nightstand.

"Hey," I say, "someone forgot their book."

"It's a Bible," Rachel says. "A Christian Bible. They put them in every hotel room."

"Who does?"

"The Christians."

"Why?"

"So all of us will see the light, I guess," she says.

"The holy light of Cheez Whiz," I say.

"That's right," she says, giggling. "Hallelujah." Rachel starts tickling me under my arms. I squirm away and the Bible drops on the floor with a loud thump. I rush and pick it up and dust it off, even though it's not dusty. I don't believe in the Christian Bible, but still it makes me nervous to drop it on the ground. I put it back in the drawer.

"Let's open up the curtains," Rachel says. We each take a plastic rod and push back the heavy green curtains. We stand at the window together and look out at the parking lot.

"There's Dad," I say. He's got my knapsack over one shoulder, and he's carrying Rachel's pink suitcase in one hand and a canvas duffel bag in the other. He's walking slowly past car after car, the only person out there. He stops and shifts my knapsack to his other shoulder. Then he just stands and does nothing.

"Wow," Rachel says, "he looks so . . ." She doesn't finish, but I know what she's thinking. Seeing Dad so alone gives me rocks in my chest. We watch Dad walk until he's close enough to the building that we can't see him anymore.

"I bet he really misses Mom," I say. "I bet it's really weird for him to be without her."

Rachel nods.

"Maybe we shouldn't hosey a bed. Maybe we should let Dad choose his bed first," I say.

"Yeah, I guess," Rachel says. She looks really sad, and I think maybe she feels guilty that she's been so mean to Dad. "I wonder if Mom's been able to sleep in the hospital," she says quietly. "She was so, so tired when she left."

"I bet she's been sleeping fine, but probably last night she was too excited about seeing us to sleep," I say. "I bet she can't wait to see us. I bet she's plotzing."

Rachel smiles, because that's Mom's word, left over from her childhood. She says it when she really, really needs to pee and one of us is in the bathroom, or when she's dying for the first bite of her Fudgsicle in the summer and the wrapper is sticky and she can't get it off, or when Rach and I are taking too long with all our talky explanations before we just show her our new dance move. Suddenly I remember so many things about Mom all at once, like how she wraps her arms around me and sniffs the top of my head and smells like lavender and lemons and calls me Snap Pea, and I'm plotzing, plotzing, plotzing to see her, too.

When Dad opens the door, I see him standing there with all our bags, and suddenly there are tears in my throat.

"Honey?" he says.

I just shake my head, because I don't have any words.

"She's okay, Dad," Rachel says. "She just really needs to see Mom."

Dad looks at me. I nod.

"So what are we waiting for?" Dad says. Rachel helps me clip my new purple barrettes into my hair, Dad brushes his teeth, Rachel grabs her lime-green poncho that Mom knit her for her birthday, and we hurry out the door.

Downstairs in the restaurant, Dad says we can order anything we want from the menu, since this is Thanksgiving, but he recommends that we make up our minds soon so we can get to Mom before next Thanksgiving.

I decide to order grilled cheese, because I'm afraid if I order the turkey it will make me too homesick for our usual Thanksgiving, with Dad sharpening the knife and standing at the head of the table and all of us excited because it smells so good and Mom saying not to forget the dark meat because that's the best part and finally the platter piled up high and passed around with the bowls of mashed potatoes and stuffing and cranberry sauce and peas and salad.

"I was thinking of the Thanksgiving special," Rachel says, "but the turkey doesn't really look like turkey." She looks over at the plate of a skinny man in a jean jacket, sitting alone, reading the newspaper. The turkey looks like white bologna and is covered with gloppy brown sauce.

"You might want to steer clear of the turkey," Dad says, "but I bet the mashed potatoes will be good. We can get a side of mashed potatoes."

"Nah, I don't really feel like mashed potatoes," Rachel says, just because Dad's suggested them. Rachel always feels like mashed potatoes.

"Can we order clam strips for Mom? She loves clam strips. We can surprise her," I say.

Dad shakes his head. "Mom is having her Thanksgiving meal at the hospital. She'll have already eaten by the time we get there."

"But what if the turkey looks like *that*?" I ask, pointing to the man's plate. "What if it tastes like bologna? Mom hates bologna."

"Honey," Dad says, "we can't bring Mom clam strips. First of all, they're fried and they'll be all cold and greasy by the time we get there. Second of all, it's important that Mom participate as fully as possible in the program at McLean, and her therapist said that she needs to have her Thanksgiving meal with the other patients."

"But, Dad—" My voice is tight and squeaky. "Mom hates bologna. She says she'd rather eat pink rubber bands. She says—" My throat hurts. I can't think of what else Mom says.

Rachel puts her hand on my leg under the table. She pats my leg. She calms me down.

When the waitress comes over, Dad says, "What the heck. I'll have a grilled-in-butter frankfort," which is just HoJo's fancy way of saying hot dog. Rachel orders macaroni and cheese. I order clam strips.

"I think I'll give them a try," I say.

Rachel smiles just a little. She knows I have a plan.

"Beverages?" the waitress says. She's wearing an orange uniform the color of a Creamsicle.

"Chocolate milk shakes all around?" Dad says. We never get milk shakes. He must be feeling sorry for us.

When the food comes, we clink our milk shake glasses.

"L'chaim," Dad says.

"L'chaim," we say.

"Happy Thanksgiving," Dad says. "Even though this is a tough time, there's still a lot to be thankful for."

What I'm thankful for is that Dad is busy putting mustard on his grilled-in-butter frankfort, so that when I slip two clam strips off my plate and wrap them in my napkin and stick it into my pants pocket, he doesn't even notice.

I'm carrying the lemon meringue pie into a brick building that has a café in the middle of it. The lady at the desk in the Admissions Building told us that a mental health specialist is walking Mom from her room in South Belknap over to the café and by the time we get there, she'll be waiting for us.

"Slow down, honey," Dad says, because my legs keep going faster and faster. They want to be running. They want to be doing attitude leaps on the shiny linoleum floor until they land me right in front of Mommy, who'll laugh and cry and take the pie and say *Wow, my girls, lemon meringue! My favorite!* and *Oh, my sweet chickens!* and then she'll wrap her arms around me first, even before Dad, and sniff the top of my head and whisper in my ear that she couldn't wait even one more second to see me. She'll say *What beautiful new barrettes!* and her hair will be twisted up in her dancer bun and maybe she'll be wearing her cashmere sweater the color of dried sea lavender that she saves for special occasions.

"Be careful with the pie," Rachel says, but she doesn't need to worry. I'm holding it tight.

There's a lady in a bright pink dress, and she's walking in the same direction we are. She might be a nutbar, but I don't know how to tell. She looks regular, with matching pink shoes and curly brown hair.

"Mmmm," she says, "that pie looks delicious."

"It's for our mom," I say. "She's waiting for us."

"Well, I'm sure she'll love it," the lady says, smiling.

"I also brought her—" But then I remember that the clam strips are a secret. "Nothing," I say, but the lady's already passed us and turned down another hallway.

There's a snack bar in a big, open space, and people are sitting around laughing and talking. It's not dark and gloomy. It's not gray, like I expected. I look around at all of the people. Where's Mom? A man in a cowboy hat and a red-checked shirt waves like he wants us to come over. I shake my head. I don't feel friendly. Mr. Cowboy waves again. Where's Mom? I want Mom. Then Dad points and smiles and I'm running past the people and through a doorway into a small room in the back.

Mom doesn't jump up from her chair to hug me. She doesn't laugh and cry and reach out for the pie.

"Hi, Chirp," she says in a quiet, sad voice. She

opens up her arms. Dad takes the pie and sticks it on a table, and I bend down to hug her. She smells like bleach. Her hand rubs my back, like windshield wipers swiping side to side.

"Rachel," Mom says, so I stand up and Rachel takes my place. She gives Mom a hug. I watch Mom's hand rub back and forth, back and forth, on Rachel's poncho.

"You must be Sy." There's a woman with blond hair sitting next to Mom, and she stands up and shakes Dad's hand. "I'm Marcy. I'm the mental health specialist working with Hannah."

Dad says hello, but he's looking at Mom.

"Sweetheart," he says. He smiles and leans in to give Mom a kiss, but she turns her head away and Marcy says, very quietly, "I think Hannah would prefer if you gave her just a little space at first. This is a lot for her."

Dad nods and pulls up a chair next to Mom. He looks at the paintings on the walls, of ships in the ocean. He looks at the floor. He clears his throat.

Marcy looks at Mom.

"So, girls," Mom finally says, "how was the drive?" She already sounds worn out, and we just got here. She has purple circles under her eyes. Her eyelids are pink and puffy, like she got bitten by mosquitoes, but there aren't any mosquitoes in Massachusetts in November.

"Fine," we say at the same time.

"We're staying at the HoJo's tonight," I say.

"Oh," Mom says. "That's nice." She takes a quick peek over at Marcy, who smiles at her.

I want Marcy to go away. If Marcy wasn't here, then Mommy would remember who we are and how much she loves us. She'd notice the pie on the table and say *Let's dive in,* and the four of us would eat it right out of the dish and get white meringue on our faces and laugh.

"So how was your Thanksgiving, Mom?" Rachel asks.

"Fine," Mom says. "It was just fine."

She isn't wearing her cashmere sweater. She's wearing a blue cotton turtleneck with greasy stains on it and brown corduroy pants.

"Chirp, why don't you tell Mom about your play?" Dad says.

Marcy bobs her head up and down like a sandpiper. I wonder if she's going to sit here the whole time or if she has other people's Thanksgiving visits to mess up.

"Well," I say, "I was the turkey. Joey was supposed to be the turkey, but he was absent. I got to dance."

"That's nice, honey," Mom says. She licks her lips like they're chapped. There's white gunk in the corners of her mouth.

"She did a great job," Dad says.

"I bet," Mom says, but she doesn't look at Dad.

"Rachel aced her last math test. She had a perfect score," Dad says.

"Good job, honey," Mom says, and stretches her lips into a smile, but her eyes aren't smiling along.

We're all quiet. I can hear people laughing in the other room. Mom runs her hand through her hair, which isn't in a dancer bun. Her hair is down. Mom's hair is never down. And it's scraggly. If my hair looked like hers, she'd tell me to go brush it and pull it back into a ponytail.

"Well . . . ," Mom says. She reaches out and pats my hand. Pat. Pat. Pat.

Rachel gets the pie from the table.

"Look, Mom. We made this for you." Rachel holds the pie out to her.

"Oh," Mom says, "thank you very much. That was nice of you." She takes the pie and plunks it in her lap, like it's her brown everyday purse. She doesn't look at it. She doesn't see the perfect waves. "You made it yourselves?"

"Yes," we say, and I'm about to tell Mom how I had to stir and stir the lemony stuff to get it thick enough, but Mom's eyes are filling up with tears and she's looking at Marcy and tapping her wrist with two fingers where her watch would be if she had it on.

Marcy stands up. "I think Hannah is ready to head back to her room now," she says, then turns to Mom. "Should I give you a moment to say good-bye to your family in private?"

Mom starts to shake her head, but Marcy is already walking away. She's waiting for Mom by the door.

"Thanks for coming," Mom says, like we're guests at one of the dinner parties she and Dad have a couple of times a year.

"Sweetie?" Dad says. "Is there anything you need? Is there anything we can do for you?"

"I'm sorry. I'm just so sorry," Mom says, and her voice is tiny and scared and so little-girly that I want to block my ears hard enough to hear ocean. Mom hands Dad the pie and pushes herself out of the chair like she's an old lady, like it's the toughest thing she's ever done. She hugs Rachel. She hugs me. I press my face into her neck. Bleach. I need to smell lemon and lavender. I need to smell Mom.

"Okay, honey," Mom says, and starts to pull away.

"No," I whisper, "no, Mom," and hold on tight and sniff, sniff, sniff. I'm going to sniff her back to life. I'm going to sniff her back into my mother with a dancer bun who walks with long dancer steps and laughs like a northern flicker and knows what I'm thinking.

"Marcy," I hear Mom say. "Marcy, please . . ." Her voice is gurgly and wet, like she's talking underwater.

"You need to let your mother go now," Marcy says in a principal voice, a crossing-guard voice, a man-working-at-the-bank voice. I feel her cold hands on my shoulders. This lady who I've never seen before puts her hands on my shoulders and tugs me backward, away from Mom. She rescues Mom from me.

"Happy Thanksgiving. Thanks for coming," Marcy says, really fast, like she doesn't mean it. She takes Mom's hand and leads her away. Mom's crying, wet strangly sobs. She doesn't turn around and wave to us. She doesn't curtsy or sashay or twirl. She doesn't say *See you soon, my sweeties.* She just holds on to Marcy's hand and tucks her head down low, like she's afraid something might bean her as she walks with her draggy leg past Mr. Cowboy with his stupid hat and stupid red-checked shirt and disappears down the hall.

We just stand here, watching where she was. *Tick-a-tick-a-tick-a.* It's my teeth. They're chattering. They won't stop. My bones are icicles.

"Get me out of here," Rachel whispers, and she grabs Dad's hand. Dad grabs my hand. The three of us just stand still, holding hands, stuck frozen. Then Dad says, "My girls," and Rachel cries, "Daddy!" He squeezes my hand hard, my hand feels warm, and then he starts walking. He's walking fast, pulling us along, towing us past all of the nutbars, fast, fast, fast, out of this place, away from here, away from Mom and our lemon meringue pie that's still sitting on the table.

In the car, none of us says anything. Rachel stares out the window. The quiet hurts my ears, but there are no words in my mouth, no words in my head.

"Okay," Dad says when we pull up at HoJo's, but his word flutters and bumps like a sparrow against our front picture window at home. I don't know what word he should have picked, but *okay* isn't the right one.

When we get to the room, Rachel lies on her stomach on our bed and pretends to fall asleep. Dad sits in the armchair with his book open, but he isn't reading. He's just staring all squinty-eyed at the green curtains, like maybe there's a secret message written there that will make everything make sense. I go into the bathroom, change into my black one-piece swimsuit, and put my clothes back on.

"I'm going to the pool," I say.

"Okay," Dad says, not looking at me.

"The rule is, you're supposed to be fourteen or else you need to be accompanied by an adult," I say.

"You'll be fine," Dad says. "You're my Cape Cod girl. You're my quahog. Just get out if anyone tells you to." He looks at me, smiles, and then goes back to trying to read the curtains.

In the pool, I puff my belly up and float on my back like a dead fish.

The water's warm. It fills my ears. My breath goes in and out, in and out. My heart thumps. If I were really dead, I wouldn't hear my breath. I wouldn't

hear my heart. I could float right on the surface without having to move my arms around to stay up. Since
I wouldn't be moving my arms around, I wouldn't
make waves that slosh against the side of the pool. I
would stay absolutely, positively still. No breath, no
thump, no slosh.

When I flip over, the chlorine burns my eyes, but
I like the way everything looks fuzzy and green. I
like how nothing is clear. I surface-dive down, down,
down. With my belly on the bottom of the pool, I'm a
beautiful mermaid. I take my hair out of its ponytail
and put the elastic on my wrist. I swim around with
my long, flowy hair and slithery body. Tiny bubbles
float off my skin. The golden hairs on my arms wave
around. A mermaid never needs to come up for air.
She opens her mouth and tasty minnows drift in. She
drinks seawater. She swims for as long as she wants,
and no one sees her unless she wants them to. No one
sees her and no one talks to her and no one touches
her and says stupid things. No one even thinks about
her. And she doesn't think about anyone.

I want to stay down here in the fuzzy green, not
thinking about anyone, especially Marcy, with her
hands on my shoulders and her ugly voice telling me
to leave Mom alone, but my lungs ache and my head
hurts and I can't help pulling myself up through the
water and gulping in air.

Getting out of the pool, I'm dizzy. I know about
putting my head lower than my heart, so I sit on a

white plastic chair and bend over. When I'm better,
I get my pants. I fish the napkin out of the pocket.
It's hard to unroll it, because it's all stuck together.
Even though I bet it's against the rules, I squat down
by the edge of the pool and dunk the clam strips in,
dunk, dunk, dunk, and sing my song:

> *Cape Cod girls ain't got no combs,*
> *Heave away, haul away!*
> *They comb their hair with codfish*
> *bones,*
> *Heave away, haul away!*

Little pieces of napkin stick to the clam strips like
wet snowflakes. Tiny bits of gold stuff float off the
clam strips and sink.

> *Heave away, my bully, bully boys,*
> *Heave away, haul away!*
> *Heave away, why don't you make*
> *some noise?*
> *We're bound for South Australia.*

CHAPTER EIGHT

JOEY'S SITTING ON OUR front porch reading when we pull up. I can tell he's at a good part, because he's hunched over and doesn't look up until we slam our car doors.

"Hey," he says, and waves. He's wearing a red sweatshirt and no hat and no gloves or mittens.

"What's he doing?" Rachel says.

"He's reading," I say.

"Duh," she says. "Why's he on our porch?"

I look over at Joey. He's sitting in a sun patch, and his hair looks white in all the light. I start to head over to him but Dad says, "Hey, my stint as your pack mule's over. Come get your knapsack," and by the time I pull it out of the trunk, Joey's gone.

Inside, our house feels empty, like no one has lived in it for an eternity, which is longer than a lifetime. I go into my room and close my door. Rachel goes into her room and closes her door. Dad yells up for us to unpack our stuff and put our dirty clothes in the hamper, and Rachel yells down, "You know, you don't have to nag me about every little thing," and Dad yells back, "This is NOT the time," and I hear his study door shut loud, not exactly a slam, since Dad doesn't believe in slamming, but a good, hard, angry shut.

Once I've got my knapsack unpacked, I pack it right back up again with my binocs, *The Secret Garden,* and a wool blanket the color of reindeer moss that I took naps with in kindergarten. In the kitchen, I pack Wheat Thins and five boxes of raisins, since they're full of nutrition, like iron, potassium, and calcium, in case I run into an emergency and can't get back home in the foreseeable future.

I knock on Dad's study door. He says, "Yes?" but not "Come in," which means I shouldn't open the door, because he's thinking hard about something important and probably wearing his black beret that helps him concentrate.

"I'm going out," I say through the door.

"Okay, honey," Dad says.

I'm nervous ringing the bell at Joey's, and not just because of his brothers. There's a dark feeling that creeps out of his house. No one is answering the door, even though I hear footsteps clomping around inside. I count to three really fast, and then I fly down the stairs and along the front path. I'm almost to the street when I hear the door open. Part of me wants to pretend that I didn't hear it and just keep walking, but when nobody calls to me, when there's only a floating balloon of quiet, I'm too curious not to turn around. Joey is standing at the door. He doesn't say anything. He just looks at me, nods, and shuts the door.

I run all the way to my tree, so that once I get there, my body's nice and warm. Most people would say it's too cold now to hang out in a salt marsh, even with the sun and even with a baby blanket wrapped around me, but I'm not most people; I'm a quahog. The marsh lady might be a quahog, too, which means that I shouldn't have to tell her that late November is a particularly good time for seeing red-throated loons. I'm not in the mood to talk to her anyway. She needs to make a little effort if she wants to get to know me. Relationships are not something you can just take for granted, Dad says. They require both people to put energy in.

I lean against my tree and watch and watch but don't see any loons. Maybe when I blink I'm missing them when they pop up to the surface, so I try not blinking. The cold burns my eyeballs. It looks like I'm crying. There's nothing to cry about. Mom is going to keep resting at McLean's, and Dad says she'll probably give electroconvulsive therapy a try, which is a safe and effective treatment for an anxious depression and should make a big difference. She'll be home before too long, and everything will settle back to normal.

"Hey."

I nearly jump out of my skin. It's Joey. He must have followed me here.

"You scared me!"

"Boo," he says in a gentle, quiet voice, so I know he didn't mean to.

I wipe my drippy eyes with the back of my mitten. "I'm not crying," I say.

"I know," he says. He has a pink mark on his cheek, like someone slapped him or maybe a fat branch snapped back on him. He still isn't wearing any hat or gloves or mittens.

"If it wasn't so cold, I'd climb that tree," he says, pointing to the beech, the tallest tree around. "I bet I could climb all the way to the top."

"Maybe," I say.

"I could," he says. "I'd climb all the way to the top. I'd be able to see everything from up there."

"P-town?"

"Yup."

"Boston?"

"Yup."

"Italy?"

Joey looks at me. His eyes are squinty and his mouth is a short, straight line. I think he thinks I'm being mean to him.

"I bet Italy is a really cool place," I say.

Joey still looks suspicious.

"Pizza," I say. "And lasagna."

"Spaghetti," he says.

"Meatball subs," I say, and Joey smiles.

He walks down to the water and scoops up sand with his hands held together like a bowl. When he tosses the sand in, it makes black dots in the dark water. He's moving in slow motion—scoop, toss, scoop, toss—and I think maybe he's never going to stop, but then he does. He comes over to me and he's shivering and the spot on his cheek looks like it's glowing. I stay really still and don't say anything, and Joey sits down right next to me, and I wrap part of my blanket around him and keep my arm there, around his shoulder. His body's shaking, and it makes my body shake, too.

Joey tips backward and I tip with him until we're lying on our backs on the blanket. Cold blue sky. Cold white sun.

"We need the blanket on top," I say, so we squirm around and pull the blanket out from under us. Joey stands up and shakes the sand off, and then he lies down and covers us from our knees to our necks. Joey's arm is against my arm, and I move my leg so it's touching him, too. If I keep my eyes closed, maybe nothing will change. Cold sand. Cold air. Joey's arm and leg against me, warm.

"Okay?" he whispers.

"Okay."

The water sounds like someone slurping soup.

Joey whistles really soft, and I think he's trying to copy the wind. I start whistling, too, but I'm not so good at it and can't help being loud and drowning out Joey, so I stop. Joey stops, and then I feel his breath in my ear.

"You know," he says, "Thanksgiving wasn't all fun and games."

I nod, but my eyes are still closed, so I don't know if Joey's looking at me.

"Open your eyes and look at me," he says in an angry voice. "Look at me when I'm talking to you!"

When I open my eyes and turn my head to look at him, his face is so close to mine, our noses are almost touching.

"You know, I really hate germs." His voice isn't mad anymore.

"You do?"

"Snot keeps germs from getting in your body. That's one of the reasons noses are important."

I have to work hard to keep his two eyes separate instead of one gigantic gray-blue eye right above his nose.

"You have sand on your face," Joey says, and he reaches out like he's going to brush it off, but then he just puts his cold hand on my cheek.

I look at his pink mark.

"Don't touch it," he says.

"I wasn't going to."

"Well, just don't."

I put my hand on his cheek right below the pink mark. We stay put, our hands on each other's cheeks.

"Hear that?" I ask Joey.

"A frog?"

"It's a great blue heron. It croaks like a big fat bull-frog."

"You know what?"

"What?"

"I like your name," Joey says.

"Naomi?"

"Chirp."

I want to give something nice back to Joey. "Thanksgiving sucked." Now he'll know he wasn't the only one who had a lousy Turkey Day.

"Not a grand ol' time," he says.

"Not a barrel of monkeys," I say.

"Not a run for your money."

"Not a fine how-d'ya-do."

"Not a bowl of cherries."

I can't think of any more, so I sit up, take off my mitten, and reach into my pocket.

"What are you doing?" Joey asks, sitting up, too.

"That's for me to know and you to find out." When I hand him some clam strip, he doesn't say anything, even though it looks gross. Even though it's gray and rubbery and probably has tons of germs swimming around on it, he just smiles and puts it in his pocket. While I watch the water just in case a loon decides to surprise me, Joey shakes the sand out of my blanket and folds it into a perfect neat square. He puts the perfect square over one leg, smoothes the wrinkles out, and hands it to me. I put it in my knapsack. Then we walk home.

⇆

When us kids complain that the classroom is too hot, Miss Gallagher says it's *toasty* and *cozy* and we should be grateful that the school has a good furnace now that Thanksgiving is over and winter is upon us. I guess she's forgotten that President Nixon has asked us all to do our part during this oil crisis and turn our thermostats down. My family hates Nixon, but saving energy seems like a smart idea, just like paying attention to the owl in the commercials who says *Give a hoot, don't pollute!*

How am I supposed to put my very best effort into writing my book report when my head hurts and my yellow blouse is sticking to my skin? I roll my long sleeves up. I roll my brown kneesocks down.

No one in *The Secret Garden* is happy when they're all cooped up inside, not Mary and not Colin and especially not Dickon, who's my favorite, because he believes in fresh air and everything that's wick, which means alive and green and growing. The book says he smells like "heather and grass and leaves . . . as if he were made of them," and animals follow him around, and I bet anything that he wouldn't just sit here sweating at his desk in this stuffy classroom because Miss Gallagher has decided that it's cozy. He'd open the windows and sniff the air and play his wooden pipe and lead us all outside, where we'd run around and play tag with the squirrels. He'd know the names of all the birds, just like I do.

I raise my hand. There's a wet spot under my arm, like I'm a teenager who forgot to put on her Ban Roll-On.

It takes a while, but finally Miss Gallagher looks up from her desk and raises her eyebrows at me.

"Please, Miss Gallagher, could we open the windows just a crack, since it's really hot in here?"

"Hot?" she says. "Open the windows?" She looks at me like I'm Oliver, asking for more gruel.

I nod.

"What you need to do, Naomi, is focus on your work, not on the temperature."

"That's *not* what I need," I say, before I've even realized that I've said it.

"Oooohh," Sean says. "Naomi is in trouble."

Now my face is even hotter.

"Sean, you stay out of this," Miss Gallagher says.

"Oooohh," Joey says. "Sean is in trouble."

"Oooohh," Lori says. "Joey is—"

"That's enough out of all of you!" Miss Gallagher is getting up from her desk. She's trying to stomp over to me in her red high heels, but it isn't easy. She has to bend her knees so she doesn't lose her balance and fall down and crack her head open on the speckled linoleum floor.

"Sorry," I say.

"Naomi Orenstein," Miss Gallagher says from in front of Lisa B.'s desk, because she's given up on making it all the way over to me, "I expect much better from you. If I have to speak to you again, you're going to the office."

"I'm really sorry." My forehead is wet, and my neck has the prickles.

Miss Gallagher shakes her head and gives me a what-am-I-going-to-do-with-you fake smile, but I can tell that she's mad, because her eyes are squinty. She has pink lipstick on two of her front teeth. It looks a lot like Bazooka bubble gum.

Sean's wagging his finger at me, but I pretend I don't see. A little square of my blouse is stuck to my upper arm, like the wrinkly paper on a temporary tattoo before you lift it off and leave a splotchy red heart or a yellow smiley face behind. I look at my book report. Not even one word yet. I haven't written one word. I want to scribble like a baby, I'm so cranky hot. In *The Secret Garden,* Mary's cranky all the time, because her parents abandoned her and died, but then she discovers a secret garden and starts working in it and her mood gets much better, especially after she meets Dickon, who teaches her all about "friendly wild things."

Maybe at McLean, Mom looks for frogs in the frog pond. Maybe she walks into the courtyard and stares up through the branches of the maple tree and watches the birds and wonders what they're thinking about. Maybe there's a male cardinal that's so perfectly red she says *oy* out loud. Maybe when it gets stuffy in her room, she opens her window and leans out and sniffs the air and feels better, because she remembers all the stuff we do outside together—for example, clip armfuls of purple lilacs in May that smell so sweet we pretend to get dizzy and fall down laughing in the grass and just lie there until Dad opens the screen door and says *Oh, my crazy ladies,* and even then we keep laughing and just stay put, with the lilacs on top of us and the damp grass underneath us. I hope the employees at McLean let Mom open the windows whenever she wants to because they know that it makes her happy. Or maybe they at least understand that getting overheated is bad for her multiple sclerosis, so they have a special rule that she can open the windows if she really needs to.

But what if they don't? What if she's stuck inside with no fresh air, day after day after day until I don't know when?

Suddenly I'm just too hot. Miss Gallagher is wrong. I don't need to focus on my book report. I stand up from my desk without raising my hand and asking permission. I walk right past Sean and Debbie and Lori and don't care that everyone's looking at me.

"Naomi," Miss Gallagher says, "what do you think you're doing?"

"I'm getting some fresh air."

It takes all of my strength, but I lift the window open.

"Go for it, Chirp!" someone says.

I stick my head out.

"Naomi!" Miss Gallagher says.

Cold, cold, cold in my nose and in my ears and down my yellow blouse.

"Shut the window right now," Miss Gallagher says.

"What if she doesn't?" Sean whispers.

My eyes are closed. I can't stop giggling.

"*Now,* Naomi," Miss Gallagher says.

I open my mouth and the cold rushes in. It tastes like ice.

"Are you listening, Naomi? Do you understand?"

What I understand is my hands on the windowsill and my eyes squeezed shut and my mouth wide open and my body leaning way far out into the winter's-coming, wick-fresh air.

Miss Gallagher said to march myself right down to Mrs. Mitchell's office. I don't think I'm really supposed to march, but I'm not sure, since I've never been sent to the principal's office before. I figure walking fast and swinging my arms is a good compromise. It's nice and cool out here but a little strange being in

166

the empty hall with all the classroom doors closed. It's a perfect place for practicing my leaps, but I'm already in enough trouble without adding inappropriate leaping to the list. Miss Gallagher said I'm to explain to Mrs. Mitchell exactly what I did wrong in my own words, and that I can rest assured that she'll be checking with her to make sure I got it right.

"What do you need, sweetie pie?" Mrs. Angoff leans down and talks in a high voice, like I'm still a little kid. She smells like peppermint.

"I'm supposed to see Mrs. Mitchell. Miss Gallagher sent me."

"Oh, really?" She's surprised, since she's known me as a good girl since kindergarten. "I see," she says, straightening up and talking normal. She knocks on Mrs. Mitchell's door and then pushes it open. "Naomi Orenstein," she says in a serious voice.

The first thing I notice is that Mrs. Mitchell's window is cracked open. A good sign.

"Hello, Naomi," Mrs. Mitchell says. She's sitting at a desk with stacks of papers in messy piles. Her hair is gray and pulled back in a ponytail. "What brings you here?"

"Miss Gallagher."

She smiles, like I've said something funny.

"Why did Miss Gallagher send you to see me?" she asks. "I assume this isn't just a friendly visit."

I look over at the window. I'm really hoping that she'll understand.

"Well," I say, "I like air, too."

Mrs. Mitchell puts her hand over her mouth to hide her smile, but I can still see it in her eyes.

"It wasn't cozy or toasty, like Miss Gallagher said. It was . . ." I kind of want to tell Mrs. Mitchell everything, but I don't think I'm supposed to.

"Naomi," she says, staring right at me, "I need you to explain to me why you were sent to the principal's office."

"I opened the window. It was really hot in the classroom. I didn't have permission."

"So you opened the window without permission?"

"Yes."

"Do you understand that your job as a student is to follow the rules of the classroom and be respectful to your teacher?"

"Yes."

"Can you imagine what it would be like if everyone just did whatever they wanted to all the time?"

This is one of those trick questions where yes and no are both the right answer. I don't say anything.

"Naomi?"

"I'm sorry," I say. "I didn't mean to be bad. It was just so hot, and I was supposed to be writing about *The Secret Garden,* which is all about fresh air and being wick, which means alive, and I couldn't breathe." She's looking at me. Her brown eyes are gentle.

"Anything else?" she says.

Yes, I want to say. *Yes. My mom is stuck at McLean Hospital with all of the nutbars, and I don't think she gets enough air.*

I shake my head.

"Listen," Mrs. Mitchell says, "I'm going to have to call your parents. I'm going to have to tell them that you were disrespectful to your teacher. Can I tell them that you'll promise to do better in the future? Will you give me your word?"

"My mom is away, but you can tell my dad," I say.

"Away?" she says. "Is everything all right? I heard from Miss Gallagher that your mother was having some health issues at back-to-school night. But I haven't heard an update."

If I tell Mrs. Mitchell about Mom, maybe she'll let me stay in her office for a little while and sit by her window and sniff her fresh air. Maybe she'll say *It's okay to cry,* and so I will, and she'll hand me a Kleenex and pat my head.

"Naomi?" Mrs. Mitchell says.

"Just fine," I whisper, which is how Dad says everything will be after they figure out how best to treat Mom's depression.

"You're sure?" Mrs. Mitchell asks.

I nod. If she asks me one more time, I'll tell her the whole story, even though it's private.

Mrs. Mitchell looks like she's trying to figure something out. She's staring at me with her head tipped to the side. "Okay, then," she finally says. "You've made a promise. Come shake my hand."

Mrs. Mitchell stands up and sticks her hand out. It's warm and dry, and I want to keep holding it. I want to sit in her lap at her desk. I want to share a bag of potato chips with her and ask *What bird is always out of breath?* and when she says *I give up,* then I want to say *A puffin* and listen to her laugh.

"Okay, Naomi," Mrs. Mitchell says. "We've got a deal. I expect not to see you here again." She pulls her hand away and smiles at me. "Now get going and get smart."

Since Mrs. Mitchell didn't tell me to march, I guess I can walk back however I feel like it. First I take baby steps, and then I take two steps forward, one step back, and by the time I get to the classroom, Miss Gallagher is making her speech about straightening up our work areas and pushing in our chairs and treating our classroom like we would our own homes so that we'll feel proud when we return in the morning. Everyone is scurrying around, and the room is so noisy with squeaks and thumps and talking that no one pays any attention to me.

⇌

When I sit in the bus seat next to Dawn, she says, "Want me to open the window?" and then she pinches the locks and pushes the window down. She turns around and says to Sally, really excited, "Open your window for Chirp. Pass it on." Sally passes it on to Tommy, who passes it on to Sean, et cetera, et cetera, and soon the whole bus is filled with the *eeeeee* of everyone shoving down their windows. Mr. Bob, the bus driver, doesn't say anything; he never does. He just reaches for his blue wool cap on the dashboard and puts it on while the wind whips everybody's hair around.

"Heck no, we won't go! Heck no, we won't go! Yay, Chirp!" Joey yells from the back of the bus.

I know I'm in big trouble, because I got sent to the principal's office, but I feel happy with everyone's windows open for me.

"Here, Chirp." Dawn hands me a whole packet of SweeTARTS.

I should be worried, since Dad will be receiving a phone call from Mrs. Mitchell this evening and he'll be very disappointed, since he's proud that both of his daughters have their heads screwed on straight and never have problems at school, but I don't feel worried. I don't feel worried, and it's a great ride home, all tangy-sweet and cold-wind-blowy with so many windows open just for me.

＝＝

When Dad comes home from work, I've already got the spaghetti water boiling and the table set.

"Good job, Chirp," Dad says. "I appreciate your taking up the slack." He's sorting through the mail, which is the first thing he always does when he comes home, after he puts his briefcase in its spot by the front hall closet.

"We all need to pitch in, I guess," I say. I'm thinking that Mrs. Mitchell won't call during dinner, and maybe after dinner I can make a really long phone call, so she'll get a busy signal and eventually give up. The trouble is, I'm not a big phone talker.

I put the spaghetti in the pot and go upstairs to talk to Rachel while Dad changes out of his work clothes.

Rachel's sitting on her floor, working on a macramé belt for Bruce for Christmas, just in case he decides to give her a Hanukkah present.

"Are you going to call Bruce tonight?" I ask.

"I don't know," she says.

"Well, are you going to call Genevieve? Or Evie?"

"What's wrong, Chirp?" She puts down the belt.

Even though she acts like a jerk sometimes, Rachel usually knows what's up with me.

"Mrs. Mitchell's going to call Dad."

"Mrs. Mitchell? Really? Wow."

"I needed air, so I opened the window when Miss Gallagher told me not to, and before that I talked back to her, so she sent me to Mrs. Mitchell."

"I always wondered what it would be like to be sent to the principal. What did she do?" Rachel asks.

"She just talked to me a little and said I had to

promise to be better and that she was going to call Mom and Dad."

"She didn't yell?"

"Nope."

"Well, you know Dad won't yell, either," she says.

"I know."

"He'll just talk you to death."

"I know."

Rachel's got her forehead all wrinkled up, and she's nodding just like Dad does. "I'm concerned, Naomi, that this behavior might be an expression of some other upset, such as the fact that your mother is trapped in a nuthouse with an old lemon meringue pie. Do you have anything you'd like to say about this?" she says, and leans in close to me.

"Stop it," I say, giggling.

"Are you sure that you don't have feelings you'd like to share?" Rachel's nose is almost touching mine. She's talking in a deep voice. She's trying not to laugh.

"Yes," I say, giggling harder. She sounds so much like Dad I can't stand it.

"Uh-huh. That's interesting. *Yes.* Can you say a bit more about what *yes* means to you?"

I lean forward and rub her nose with my nose and she says *gross,* but I can tell that she likes it, and then she grabs my knee, which tickles like crazy, and I go for her armpits. We're rolling around on top of all the stuff on her floor, notebooks and pencils and the macramé belt, and it's crunchy. I'm cracking up and Rachel's cracking up and yelling *Stop stop stop,* but she doesn't mean it and I don't stop until she finally flops onto her back and takes a fluttery breath and gives me a peace sign.

"Peace," I say, and flop down next to her. We just lie there. My heart's beating hard. Rachel smells like coconut.

"Hey," she says, "I suddenly feel like I have a lot to say on the phone tonight."

I look over at her. She's smiling at me.

"Thanks."

"No sweat."

The spaghetti I made is overdone, but Dad and Rachel don't complain. Rachel and I eat super fast so she can get on the phone.

"Whoa," Dad says. "You girls are hungry!"

"Uh-huh," we say at the same time.

"Have some more salad," Dad says, passing the bowl across to us.

We each take some and wolf it down.

"And you're in luck tonight," Dad says. "Annie dropped off an apple pie for dessert!"

Rachel races to the cabinet and gets plates.

Normally we'd have a who-can-eat-her-dessert-slower-and-still-have-some-left-while-her-sister-doesn't contest, but tonight we both eat up our pie and don't ask for more.

"May I be excused?" Rachel asks. "I have stuff to do." She gives me the quickest wink, like just one flap of a butterfly's wing.

"Actually, honey," Dad says, "there's something I want to talk to you two about." Maybe Mrs. Mitchell already reached him at work and now Dad wants to tell us how upset he is with me. Rachel looks at me and shrugs.

"I just wanted to let you know that I've been talking with the people who are caring for Mom," Dad says. "We've made the decision to begin treating Mom with electroconvulsive therapy. Like I told you before, medication hasn't been working, and this should really help Mom feel better."

"WHAT?" Rachel yells. She lets her fork fall onto the table.

"Mom is going to begin ECT tomorrow," Dad says calmly.

Dad's already explained to me that ECT will only help, not hurt, Mom, but it still creeps me out to think of electricity going into her brain.

Rachel puts her elbows on the table and stands up partway, like maybe she's going to jump over the dirty dishes and land on Dad and bite his neck like a predator, which is an animal that needs to kill and eat other animals to stay alive.

"You're going to let them electrocute my mother?" she shrieks.

"Rachel," Dad says.

"Dad!" Rachel yells.

"You're overreacting, honey. ECT is a safe and effective treatment for an anxious depression like Mom's. Mom will be under anesthesia and won't feel any pain. There can sometimes be some side effects, like a bit of memory loss, but they're temporary." He reaches toward Rachel, but she shrinks away like his hand is oozing with a contagious skin rash.

"Overreacting?" Rachel yells. "They're going to electrocute Mom and you're trying to tell us it's a good thing!"

"Given the severity of Mom's symptoms, it *is* a good thing," Dad says. "Medication hasn't helped her. I'm confident Mom will learn to manage her MS. It's the depression that we've got to get under control."

"Unbelievable!" Rachel smacks the table and the milk in my glass ripples.

"I know that this is a lot for you to absorb," Dad says, "but you need to trust me that this is a step in the right direction."

"Do you believe in lobotomies, too?" Rachel asks. "Do you think maybe they should give that a try?"

"What's a lobotomy?" I ask.

"It's when they cut out—"

"Rachel!" Dad says. "You are *not* helping here at all. If you can't be reasonable, we're going to end this conversation." Dad's lips are clenched together, like he doesn't trust the words that might tumble out.

Rachel shakes her head. "I'm not the one being unreasonable. They're going to zap her with electricity. Why won't you just admit it?"

"I still want to know what a lobotomy is," I say, but no one's listening.

"I'm not going to keep discussing this with you, since you seem determined to be impossible," Dad says. "My point is simply that it's a safe and effective treatment that should help Mom, not some barbaric torture out of a science fiction movie." Dad shakes his head, as if he's trying to loosen up that crazy idea.

"Well, if you care what I think, which you obviously don't, I think Mom just needs a little more rest and—"

The phone rings.

"She's *been* resting," Dad says. "You saw yourself how troubled Mom still is."

"Well, you could try being a little more patient," Rachel says. "You tell us patience is a good thing, but it doesn't seem like *you* have any." She's so mad that she's spitting out each word.

"Rachel," Dad says, "if you had any idea what I've been up against—" I think maybe he's going to ignore the phone, but he pushes himself up from the table. He's so mad the muscle in his jaw is twitching. "I'll be right back." He stomps to his office.

"Well, I won't be here!" Rachel yells after him. She stands up. Her face is red. Her chin is quivering.

"Sorry, Chirp," she mumbles, and runs out the front door. She definitely—*bam*—does not believe in not slamming.

First, I pick up all of the silverware and put it on my plate. Second, I get Dad's plate and Rachel's plate and stack them under my plate and carry them to the counter. Third, I clear our glasses. Fourth, I use a damp sponge, not a sopping-wet one, and wipe the table until it's clean, which means not just smearing the spaghetti sauce around. Fifth, I go to the living room and get the wooden antelope that Dad gave Mom for their first anniversary and put it in the middle of the table as a centerpiece. Mom says that little things make a big difference, and I figure we need a big difference around here.

Dad walks back into the kitchen.

"Oh, Chirp," he says, but he doesn't sound angry, just tired. He rubs his face. He doesn't notice the clean table. He doesn't notice the antelope.

"Dad." Should I apologize for opening the window in our classroom? Should I be mad at him like Rachel?

"Should I be worried about your sister?" Dad asks in a worn-out voice.

"No. She probably just went to Genevieve's house."

"And you? Should I be worried about you, honey?" Dad asks. "That was Mrs. Mitchell."

"No."

"Good." He looks at me like he's going to ask another question, but then he just takes a slow, loud breath. "Let's have some ice cream."

So I get up and come back to the table with two bowls of Butter Brickle. I bring the Hershey's Syrup because maybe it will make a big difference. We eat without saying one more word, and when we're done, Dad gets us seconds and I don't even have to ask.

PART TWO

CHAPTER NINE

"OWABUNGA!" JOEY YELLS.

"Bowacunga!" I yell.

We're jumping in the slush. We're clomping through the water. We've got our winter boots on, but our jackets are tied around our waists. On the walk to the bus this morning, the world was still gray and frozen winter-quiet, like it's been for months. Now, walking home from the bus, there's strong sun, warm air, everything suddenly so wet and bright and drippy. March thaw.

"A shower, lady?" Joey says, grabbing a branch above my head and shaking it. Drops of cold water sprinkle down on me, along with a few clumps of wet snow that stick in my tangly hair.

"A bath, mister?" I say, and kick icy water at him from the little river that's running along the side of our road. Joey dodges it.

"Missed me, missed me, now you gotta kiss me!" he yells, but I know he doesn't mean it, because he hates germs, and anyway I'm pretty sure that kissing doesn't really start until seventh grade. At Dawn's holiday party, we played spin the bottle in her basement while the grown-ups drank eggnog upstairs, but everyone just kept arguing about where the bottle was pointing, and the one time that it was really obvious who was supposed to kiss who, Tommy reached around Lisa B.'s head like in the movies, and we all shut up because it looked like he was going to pull her in and really give her a good one, but he covered her mouth with his hand and kissed that instead.

My mittens are sopping wet. My tights are sopping wet. My hair is sopping wet.

"We're a little damp," I say, giggling.

"Crap," Joey says, as if he just noticed. He runs his fingers through his hair, surprised that it's drenched. He starts wringing out the cuffs of his brown corduroy pants. He shakes really hard, like a dog after a bath. "My mother's going to kill me." He flaps his arms, as if that will get the water off. "Crap," he says again. "My mother's going to tell my father, and my father's going to kill me."

"It's just water."

"Try telling that to my dad," Joey says. "It's a rule. I'm supposed to be careful with my school clothes."

"But it's just water. It'll dry."

"No messing around in school clothes. That's the

rule. When I came home with grass stains, he said the next time I decided that his hard-earned money meant nothing, he'd . . ." Joey stops talking. His eyes are darting all around like he's watching a hummingbird.

"But, Joey, can't you just tell him that the water will dry?"

Joey's not listening. "This isn't good. This isn't good. This isn't good," he keeps whispering to himself.

"Joey."

"This isn't good. This isn't good."

"Joey!" I yell.

He stops whispering, but he doesn't look at me.

"It's not a big deal. You can just put your clothes in the dryer," I say. "And you can hang your jacket up and it'll be dry in the morning."

"Maybe she'll be watching her program." He's still looking at the ground. "If it's on, maybe I can sneak into my room and change into my play clothes without her noticing. She doesn't know what I wore to school today. She was still sleeping when I got up. Maybe I can sneak past her on the couch. Maybe she won't see me." He's shuffling his feet around like he needs to pee, but I think he's just worried. "Maybe she won't see me."

"Or you could put your clothes in our dryer. No one's home at my house. My dad doesn't get home from work until at least six, and Rachel always goes to her friend's house after school."

Joey stops shuffling. "Your house?"

"Right."

Joey bites his lip. He's thinking about it. He looks at me. "You just want me to take my clothes off," he says, smiling. "You just want me to strip like the weirdos in *Hair.*"

"Gross!"

"Let's go, you sicko!" he yells, and takes off. This time he leaps over the puddles, ducks under the wet branches, dodges the melting hunks of snow, and I follow behind him. He stops in front of my house.

"Hold everything," he says.

"Dick Tracy calling Joe Jitsu."

"No. I mean it. I'm not kidding. Both cars are in your driveway."

Even though it's still sunny afternoon, there it is, Dad's green Dodge Dart, parked in front of the station wagon. Dad's home, and it's nowhere near six o'clock. Dad never comes home from work early. If Dad's home, then something special's going on.

I'm running up the front walk. Water's sloshing in my boots, but I don't care. I can't believe it.

"Chirp!" Joey yells.

Dad said that he'd be picking her up sometime in March, but he just couldn't say when. This must be when. She's here. She's home. I fly up the staircase two steps at a time.

"Wait! What about me?" Joey yells. "You're forgetting about me!" but I can't slow down long enough to even turn around.

Lemon. That's what I smell when I shove open the front door. She's in the dining room, spraying Lemon Pledge on the table. She's wearing her cashmere sweater the color of dried sea lavender, and blue jeans, and green wool socks. Her hair is in a dancer bun.

"Mom!" I yell.

"Snap Pea," she says. Mom puts down the spray can and cloth and opens up her arms. "I'm home, my girl. I'm here, honey," she says, squeezing me tight. "You're soaking wet," she says into my neck. "You should go change your clothes," but she doesn't let me go. I sniff and sniff. She smells like her.

"Let me take a look at you," she says, pushing me back and holding me by my shoulders. She looks at me. I look at her. Dad stands in the hallway and looks at both of us.

What I see is that she still looks tired but just normal-tired, like she stayed up too late at a dinner party drinking white-wine spritzers and talking about Merce Cunningham and bringing the troops home. She seems nervous, because her eyes are kind of flitty, but maybe she thinks I'm mad at her for not sending a thank-you note for the lemon meringue pie, and for not answering my letter that asked for her recipe for latkes, and for not sending Hanukkah presents or even just calling or sending a card with a picture of a menorah lit up bright with candles and some message like *Hope your Hanukkah is filled with light* or *Wishing you a year of miracles.*

"I'm glad, not mad, Mom," I say. She tips her head to the side like a robin.

"Oh, Chirp," she says. Her head's still tilted, like she's trying to figure something out, but I don't know what. People think that when robins tilt their heads, they're listening for worms underground, but actually they're looking for mud bumps that are signs of wormholes so they can know where to poke their beaks in to get food.

No one's saying anything. The quiet feels too loud, so I say, "What kind of bird is always out of breath?"

Mom smiles a little and shakes her head, *I give up.*

"A puffin!"

Mom grabs my hand and pulls me close. "There's a lot that's bumbling around in my brain right now," she whispers in my ear, "but one thing I know for sure is that I'm very happy to see you."

Dad takes a few steps into the room. He stands apart from us and shifts around like a little kid who wants to be asked to come and play. He smiles when I look at him.

"Mommy's home," he says. "She's not going anywhere. She'll still be here after you change out of your wet things."

When I come back in my snuggy-dry clothes, Mom's stretched out on the couch. I sit down near her feet. I hear Dad's study door close.

"I've been gone a long time, haven't I?" Mom says.

A trick question. If I say yes, she'll feel bad for being gone so long. If I say no, she'll feel bad that I didn't feel like she's been gone for so long.

"I'm glad you're home, Mom."

"Yes."

She's looking all around. She's checking out the room like she's in someone else's house. *Those ferns need water. A fireplace! I like that bookcase jammed with books!* is probably what she's thinking.

"It's been a long day," Mom says. "An enormous, gigantic day." Her eyes start to close, but then they pop back open. "Wow," she says, and gives me a tired smile.

"Hi, Mom."

"Hi, honey."

A car door slams. Maybe it's Mr. Morell getting home from work. I hope he doesn't kill Joey.

"I'm doing fine, you know," Mom says. "There's nothing to worry about."

"I know," I say.

I want to cuddle with Mom, but I feel shy. I reach out and hold her foot in her green wool sock.

"You have to tell me everything about everything," she says, but her eyes are fluttery.

"It's okay, Mom. You can sleep."

"Just for a few minutes, honey." She lets her eyes stay closed. "Wake me up when Rachel gets home."

I hold her warm foot and hum songs from *Hair* while the daylight slides out of the room. When the streetlight comes on, it makes a square the color of frozen pond on the wall above the couch. Mom's breath is loud, *iiiiiiinn-out, iiiiiiinn-out, iiiiiiinn-out.* I wonder if they had a good-bye party for her in the café with speeches and balloons. Maybe there were special treats, like brownies and root beer floats, and then the nutbars and the staff lined up and everyone gave her a hug good-bye and said *Good luck,* except the cowboy in the checkered shirt, who waved his straw hat and said *Adios, amigo.*

My hand's tired of holding Mom's foot, and this is way too much sitting still for me, but if I squirm around, I might wake up Mom, which isn't something I should do after her enormous, gigantic day. I wish she'd wake up on her own and ask me again to tell her everything about everything. I squeeze her foot just a tiny bit. I count to six. I whisper every verse to "Frank Mills." Before I can decide what to do next, I hear Rachel clomp up the front stairs.

"Too much homework," Rachel says when she shoves open the front door and sees me standing right there in the hallway, looking at her. Rachel doesn't get the Dad's-car-is-in-the-driveway clue, like I did, since it's almost dinnertime when she gets home and Dad's car would have been there anyway.

"Chirp, I can't hang out. Stop bugging me," she says, even though I haven't said a word. I grab her cold hand and she squawks like a starling.

"Come on." I start pulling her along.

"I said I have stuff to do. Let me go!"

"Trust me."

"Can't I even take my jacket off?" she says, but I keep pulling her arm, like we're playing damsel in distress and she's fainted dead away on the blue raft in Heron Pond and I'm towing her ashore.

We're standing in the middle of the living room. Rachel smells like cold air and watermelon lip gloss.

"So?"

"Ahoy." I point to the couch.

Rachel gasps and puts her hand on her cheek like an actress in a movie. "Mom?" she whispers. Even though it's kind of hard to see without the lights on, who else would it be, lying on our couch?

Rachel leans forward and pushes her face in Mom's direction. She almost tips me over, since we're still holding hands.

"She looks fine. She looks like her," Rachel says. "I was worried that—"

And suddenly I realize that maybe the electricity could have turned Mom's hair frizzy or her skin hot pink like sunburn or her teeth black and witchy, but I don't know, because I never asked. I'm shivery-scared of what could have happened, of the answers to the questions still inside me, even though Mom is right here sleeping, looking just fine.

I don't want to be, but I'm crying. Rachel starts crying, too.

"We're such dorks," she says, squeezing my hand.

"I mean, she's home. We should be laughing, not crying."

"Dumb dorks. *Cock-a-doodle-doo!*" I stick my thumb in my armpit and flap my wing.

Rachel giggles. I'm flapping my wing, and Rachel's shaking her head and laughing, and suddenly Dad's hand is warm on my shoulder. The three of us are in a huddle, snuffling and giggling and sighing, when Mom opens her eyes and looks up at us.

"Wow," she says, "I guess I really am home."

"Hi, Mom." Rachel's voice is slow and shaky, like she's afraid she has the wrong answer to a math problem. She reaches down just as Mom reaches up. Their thin, long arms and thin, long hands stretching toward each other in the icy-blue light, it's beautiful, like dancing.

"C'mon, Chirp. Come help me with dinner," Dad says. "Let's give Mom and Rachel a minute alone together."

The kitchen is summery warm because Dad's been heating up the stuffed clams from Flanagan's Market, which are the best thing in the world, because you eat the hot, buttery clam stuffing right out of the clamshells with your fork.

"Whew! It's a scorcher," I say, fanning myself with my hand, and Dad laughs like I'm the funniest quahog on the Cape. While he makes a salad, I finally get to set the table with four of everything. I put the last glass on the table, and then I yell, "Mom, time for dinner!" much louder than I need to. The words feel round and full and perfect in my mouth.

⇌

Joey needs a pencil. I'm holding one out to him, but he's ignoring me.

"Hey, guys, a pencil? C'mon, please?"

He's talking quietly so Miss Gallagher won't hear him and give him a lecture about the importance of coming to school prepared with all of your supplies, because what grown-up would go to work without his briefcase or tape measure or what-have-you?

"Joey, here!" I wave the pencil right in front of his face. He has a purple bruise the size of a quarter below his eye. He turns away from me and then twists around in his seat to catch a pencil from Tommy, who tosses it from the very last row.

"Thanks, Tommy, my man," Joey says.

My face is burning hot, and I want to write Joey a note and explain what happened yesterday, but Miss Gallagher is walking through the rows of seats, handing out lined paper for our spelling test.

"Eyes on your own paper. I'm ready to begin," Miss Gallagher says, and suddenly everyone has ants in their pants and you can hear the rustle of clothes and the thump of books and the squeak of chairs being shifted around in. The test is as easy as always, with words that I could spell in first grade, like *blanket* and *brook*.

Joey does fine for a while, but when we get to *jewel,* he hunches over his paper and sighs really loud. Then his ears turn red. Then he starts erasing so hard that bits of eraser fluff drift to the floor like pink snow and I bet he's going to erase right through the paper. I stare at him until he looks up.

"Cowabunga," I whisper. He doesn't whisper back *Bowacunga.* He just glares at me like he wishes I would melt away like the wicked witch in *The Wizard of Oz.*

At lunch I wait until he's alone by the trash can in the multipurpose room, which is where we're *still* eating, because the grown-ups think it's too cold to eat outside, even though all the snow is melted and you can't see your breath except first thing in the morning.

"Hey," I say.

"Eww," he says, looking around. "What's that smell? And I'm not talking about the garbage." Then he walks away really fast, like he's scared the stink will kill him.

"Why won't you let me just tell you what happened?" I yell after him.

"Did someone say something?" he yells back. "Nope. I guess not," and then he sits back down at his table and laughs his head off with Sean.

Even though Joey's put a cold rock in my chest,

it's not the worst afternoon, because (a) I get 100 per-
cent on the spelling test, which Miss Gallagher hands
back after lunch, and (b) I can pick any living creature I want for my science report, and in addition to
a brief written description, Miss Gallagher expects us
to use our creative talents and show her how we can
reach for the sky, so I think I might choose the red-
throated loon and choreograph a dance that shows
how they leap into flight from land or water, which is
a unique characteristic.

The bad news is that on the bus ride home, Joey
yells, "Whoever thinks people who don't celebrate
Christmas are big fat Scrooges, raise your hand," and
almost everyone does, except Dawn, who looks confused.

"Why's Joey talking about Christmas when it's not
that long after Valentine's Day?" she whispers to me,
and I want to tell her that he's just trying to be mean
to me, since he knows I'm Jewish and don't celebrate
Christmas, but there's way too much to explain. The
good news is that I'm on my way home, and home is
a whole new barrel of fish now that Mom's there and
waiting for me.

Two Oreos and a glass of milk at my place at the
kitchen table, just like the olden days, but where's
Mom? I want her to be sitting by the window with
the sun on her cheek. I want her to say *Tell me about*

your day, honey, and I'll list all the mean things that Joey did, and she'll cluck her tongue and say something funny like *Let's put peanut butter on his head and see what the squirrels do.* I gulp down the milk, grab the cookies, and follow the thumping noise upstairs. The attic steps are pulled down in the middle of the hallway.

"Mom?" I call up into the rectangle hole in the hallway ceiling.

"Come on up, honey," Mom calls down.

The attic smells great, like old record jackets. I climb the stairs carefully. I don't know how Mom managed it with her draggy leg and tired body. She's kneeling in front of the black steamer trunk. I want to hug her, but she isn't standing up. I want to look at her face to make sure it still looks normal, but her back is to me, and there's no room to walk in front of her because of all of our stuff that's piled up.

"There's so much to do, Chirp," Mom says. "I've got an awful lot to catch up on. Annie spent the morning visiting, because Dad thinks I shouldn't be alone, but I really could have used that time to organize." She turns around and gives me a blink of a smile that's more nervous than happy. Her face is sweaty. She opens the lid of the trunk. "Usually I would have brought all of the winter clothes down between Halloween and Thanksgiving. Usually I would have made sure we had plenty of warm things." She looks into the trunk and sighs. "I guess Dad must have taken care of that."

Mom pulls out a hat I've never seen. It's the color of canned peas with a scraggly yellow pom-pom that reminds me of a cat toy.

"Do you need a warm hat?" she asks, lifting it in the air.

"I've been wearing my purple one," I say.

"Right. Of course you have. You're all set."

She closes the trunk lid. She pulls over a cardboard box.

"Do we need anything in here?" she mumbles to herself, staring at the box like she has X-ray vision. "There must be something that we need."

I wonder if she's going to ask me about my day. I wonder if she's going to ask me about my last 106 days, which is how long she's been gone.

"Extra scarves," she says, lifting a flap on the box and peeking in. "Actually, *extra* extra scarves." She pulls out a red-and-orange-striped scarf and a green plaid scarf. "I guess you couldn't use either of these? It's a little late in the season to be bringing down more clothes. You've been warm enough?"

"I've been fine."

Mom dangles the scarves in the air. "I guess I have to face the fact that this winter has pretty much come and gone while I've been holed up at that place." She looks around at all our stuff, the stack of suitcases, the pile of *National Geographic*s, the picnic basket on the shelf next to the butterfly box, as if she thinks maybe she'll find this winter if she just looks hard enough. Then she shakes her head like she's disappointed and stuffs the scarves back in the box. "Okay," she says, "I guess we should just head down. I guess there's not much for me to do up here at this point."

I go down the steps first. I have to go backward, since they're so steep and narrow. It's Mom's turn after me, and I watch her have a hard time with her draggy leg. She gives it a little push with her hand to keep it moving along. I try not to watch, since it seems kind of private, like adjusting your underpants when they get stuck in your crack.

"I've got to get back into shape," Mom says when she's all the way down the steps. "I've got to do better. I've just been sitting around doing nothing." Mom's talking too fast. She's squeezing her hands together. "Just sitting around, day after day."

"Dad says you've been working on your mental health."

Mom's not listening. "I've got to do better. I've got to do much better."

"But, Mom," I say, "Dad says you've been trying hard. You even let them give you electricity treatments so you could come home and settle back in with us."

"Oh, Chirp," Mom says, turning to look at me. "Oh, my girl." She tucks my hair behind my ear. She kisses my cheek. "I'm going to make good changes, Snap Pea."

"I know, Mom," I say, but I'm not really sure what she means.

"If I can't dance anymore, I'll figure out something else to do. Marcy told me yesterday that I have to start off slow. She said it would be a big adjustment. The first step is to make a list of things I know I can accomplish." Mom is talking too fast again. "Marcy said to cross things off my list so I can notice my progress."

I don't want to hear about Marcy.

"Marcy said to make a list. Cross things off. Marcy thinks—"

"I'm choreographing a dance for my science project," I butt in. "I want to demonstrate how the red-throated loon is able to take off from land *or* water."

"Oh, that sounds terrific, Chirp," Mom says, but her voice is thick and heavy, and I feel stupid for talking about dancing. I feel stupid, but still I say, "You know, Rachel said you'd die if you couldn't keep dancing." It just pops out.

Mom looks surprised. She shakes her head. "No, sweetie. That's not my plan." She smiles with just her mouth, not with her brown-earth eyes, not with her whole pretty face. "This is my plan. First, I'm going to take a little rest. Then I'm going to tackle cleaning the refrigerator. Then I'll make a list so I can cross things off of it. There's an awful lot to do."

Mom's never cared about polishing with Lemon Pledge or having a clean refrigerator. She's never talked about making a list. Or let someone dumb like Marcy tell her what to do.

"Make sure you don't forget to fold up the stairs," I say to Mom, even though she's already almost done doing it. She doesn't notice that I sound snotty like Rachel. She doesn't notice that I'm tapping my foot just like the bossy girls who think I'm a dork because I can't serve the ball over the net in volleyball. Mom smiles her just-mouth smile at me and holds the string and lets the rectangle of wood float up and cover the hole in the ceiling. Unless you pay attention to the string hanging down, you'd never even know that there's a whole slice of room filled with all kinds of stuff, right above our heads.

"Mom, I'm home!" Rachel yells, bursting through the front door. I'm sitting in the hallway, waiting for her. Her cheeks are pink, so I can tell that she's been rushing. She's carrying a bunch of pine branches in her arms. She's got her peacoat buttoned over her notebook.

"Shhhh, she's sleeping, Rach," I say.

"Oh," she says, dropping the branches on the front

hall rug. "I came straight home so I could see her. I didn't even go to Genevieve's house. I mean, I didn't think she'd be sleeping."

"When she gets up, she wants to clean the fridge."

"Clean the fridge? Why?"

"She says she has a lot to do. She says she has to accomplish things."

Rachel unbuttons her peacoat, tosses it down, sits on it.

"Did she hang out with you when you came home?"

"Sort of. Not really. A little," I say. "I mean, she was up in the attic. She was worrying about winter clothes."

"Winter clothes? Winter's almost over," Rachel says.

"I know."

Rachel picks up a pine branch. She shakes her head. She starts to pluck the needles off.

"Maybe we can help her clean the fridge," I say. "We can be the entertainment. We can put on music and show her our moves." I start doing the hitchhike with a little twist mixed in.

Rachel stands up like she's going to dance with me. Then she says, "I don't know," and plops back down.

"You don't know what?"

"Nothing," Rachel says. She's playing with the beads on her macramé choker.

"What?"

"Couldn't she have stayed up until I came home? I mean, she's been gone *forever.*"

"She was tired. Yesterday was an enormous day. An enormous, gigantic day."

Rachel shakes her head. She plucks the last few needles off the branch.

"I think maybe I'll just take off." She stands up again.

"You just got home."

"I think I'll head over to Genevieve's house."

"Joey was a jerk today."

"Tell Mom I'll be home for dinner."

Rachel stands up and puts her peacoat back on.

"We can dance in your room, Rach. We can make popcorn with tons of salt."

"Go ahead and give Mom the branches if you want," Rachel says. "Put them in the blue vase. You don't have to say it was my idea." She looks up the stairs like maybe Mom will suddenly appear right before her very eyes. "I'm out of here," she says. She steps over the branches, opens the door, and *poof,* she's gone.

When Dad gets home, he has two surprises: pepperoni pizza for all of us and a bunch of roses the color of butter, just for Mom.

"I thought we'd make all of our lives a bit easier this evening," Dad says, handing me the pizza box. "Put it in the oven to stay warm, Chirp. You can just leave it in the box, since we're not actually heating it."

"Two hundred degrees," Mom says, walking into

the front hall from the living room. She's got lines in her forehead like she's trying hard to figure something out.

"I can't tell you how good it felt, driving home, to know that when I opened the door, you'd be here," Dad says quietly to Mom, standing close and handing her the roses.

"Oh," Mom says, "thank you, Sy." She holds the roses in her arms like they're someone else's baby with a dirty diaper.

"They're pretty," Rachel says.

"Wow," I say.

Mom just stands there.

"They're really, really pretty," I say.

Mom stares at the roses, but she doesn't say anything.

"Here," Dad says, lifting the roses out of Mom's arms and giving them to Rachel, "go and put these in water for your mother."

"No!" Mom says, way too loud. "I need to take care of things myself!" She snatches the roses back from Rachel, who flinches like she's just been creamed by a snowball. Mom hurries to the kitchen, holding the roses out in front of her, like she's worried someone's going to steal them back.

"Dad?" Rachel says in a small scared voice.

"Just give her a little time," Dad says. "Mom needs some time to settle back in."

I'm still holding the pizza box. I'm supposed to put

it in the oven at 200 degrees. "Oh, honey," Dad says. "It's fine. You can go into the kitchen."

I do my heel-toe Pocahontas walk so I won't bother Mom. I don't leap and I don't sing and I don't whistle. I just carry the pizza right to the oven, stick it in, and turn the temperature to 200 degrees.

Mom's got two vases out, the bumpy orange glass one and the white ceramic one. "Hmmm," she says, "I wonder which vase they'll look best in." She smiles at the vases. She smiles at the roses. She smiles at me, as if nothing just happened.

"To having Mom home," Dad says, lifting his wine-glass.

We all clink.

Dad smiles. Mom smiles. Rachel smiles. I smile.

"Great pizza," Mom says.

"Really great," Rachel says.

"There's plenty," Dad says.

"Good," Mom says.

"Great," Rachel says.

I pile my pepperoni up in a stack. I like to save it for last.

"So?" Mom says.

"Well," Rachel says. She's staring at her plate.

"Really good pizza," Dad says.

"Delicious," Mom says.

If we put music on, it would feel more like a pizza party. If we put music on, I could listen to it and not have to figure out what the right thing is to say to Mom at our second dinner together in 106 days.

"Okay," Mom says.

We're all very busy chewing and swallowing. Mom's smiling at her plate. Rachel's smiling at her plate. Dad must be jiggling his foot, because if you watch really closely, you can see the table shake.

"Okay," Mom finally says, "catch me up. I want to know everything."

Last night we just talked about stuffed clams and how tired Mom was.

"Well," Rachel says, "I don't really know. Everything's fine, I guess."

"Tell me about school," Mom says. "How are your teachers?"

"Okay," Rachel says.

"Just okay?" Mom asks.

"Fine, they're fine," Rachel says. She's running her hands through her hair, and no one tells her to stop, even though she's probably getting pizza juice in it.

"Tell Mom about what Mr. Henderson said," Dad says.

"Mr. Henderson?" Rachel says.

"About your math ability," Dad says.

"That was, like, forever ago, Dad," Rachel says, rolling her eyes. "I don't even remember."

Mom looks at her plate. Her face is red. "I'm so sorry, honey," she says. "I was gone too long, and I'm—"

"Oh, wait," Rachel says, "I just remembered." She's red, too, because she didn't really not remember, she was just giving Dad a hard time, and now she's made Mom feel bad for being gone. "He said I have a great sense of numbers and a head for the big concepts."

"Wow," Mom says. "That's terrific."

"Isn't it?" Dad says.

Mom nods. She turns to me.

I don't want to talk about Miss Gallagher.

"Mom," I say, thinking fast, "did they have a party for you?"

"A party?" Mom looks confused.

"To say good-bye and good luck. You know, with treats and stuff."

"No, honey, there wasn't a party," Mom says.

"C'mon, Chirp," Rachel says, all whispery-mad. "Maybe Mom doesn't want to talk about—"

"No," Dad interrupts in a strong voice. "It's very important that you girls feel like you can ask Mom about her experience away."

"Yes, you can ask me anything," Mom says quietly. She looks at Dad, like she's a little girl. He nods and smiles at her like *Good job.*

"I'm cool," Rachel says.

"No questions at all?" Dad asks.

"No questions at all," Rachel says. She's holding on

to the table with both hands, like maybe she might just float up to the ceiling and drift out of the room on invisible air currents like a red-tailed hawk.

Mom looks at me. "I know *you* have questions, Chirpie." She smiles a tired smile. "Ask away."

"It's good to have questions," Dad says.

They're waiting. I'm supposed to have questions. I close my eyes and remember the pink lady and the long hallway with shining floors and the café filled with nutbars.

"Were you and the cowboy friends?" I ask.

Mom smiles. Dad smiles, too. "No, not friends," Mom says, "but friendly enough."

"Did he always wear that hat?" I ask.

"I think he probably slept in it," Mom says.

Everyone laughs, even Rachel.

"What else?" Mom asks.

"Did you like the pie?" I ask.

"Pie?"

"The lemon meringue pie," I say.

"That we made for you," Rachel says.

"For Thanksgiving," I say.

"You made me a pie?" Mom is teasing us.

"Mom," I say, giggling, "just tell us if you liked the pie."

Mom looks at me. She keeps her serious face on.

I stare back at her. I wait for her to start laughing and tell us that it was the best pie she ever tasted in her whole life and she licked the pie dish when no one was looking and didn't share any with anyone, not even one crumb with Marcy.

"It's okay, Hannah," Dad says.

"Oh, my God," Mom says. She covers her face with her hands.

Rachel glares at Dad. Her hand is in a fist.

Mom's shaking her head.

She doesn't remember. Mom doesn't remember us giving her the pie.

"Some memory loss isn't uncommon after all Mom has been through," Dad says.

"I'm so sorry, girls," Mom says. Now she's crying.

"It's okay, Mom," I say, but it's not. My mouth feels gross, like I've been swallowing marsh water. All through dinner I've been waiting to eat my pepperoni, but now I wish we had a dog so I could drop the pepperoni under the table and watch him chomp it down and whisper to him *Good fella, that's a good boy.*

⇆

"Today is our first lesson in our new unit on health and hygiene," Miss Gallagher says. "Next year you'll be learning more, but it's time for you to have an introduction to this topic now." Miss Gallagher looks like she's trying not to do the fifty-yard dash right out of the classroom. She's pink and twitchy and keeps twirling a clump of her thin, straight hair around her finger. "Can anyone tell me what *hygiene* means?" She gives us a smile, as if it might trick us into not noticing how wigged-out she is.

"It's what you say to your friend Jean when you see her," Lisa B. says. "Hi, Jean!" she says to Debbie, waving her hand and giggling her head off.

"Hi, Jean!" Debbie says, waving back. She's laughing even harder than Lisa B.

"Girls!" Miss Gallagher says.

"Hi, Gene!" Joey says, waving to Sean.

"Hi, Gene!" Sean says, waving to Joey.

"Boys!" Miss Gallagher says. She takes a deep breath. She closes her eyes for just a second. When she opens them, she says, "Let's see," in her sugary voice, looking around the classroom. "Claire, will you please look up the word *hygiene* in the dictionary?"

We all whisper, "Hi, Jean!" as Claire walks by our desks on her way to the bookshelf, but Miss Gallagher pretends that she can't hear us. While Claire is looking up the definition, Sean raises his hand.

"Yes, Sean."

"Isn't this when you teach us about—"

"Stop it, Sean," Lori says. "You're so disgusting."

"—doing it?" Sean says, cracking up.

"Doing what?" Dawn asks.

"Oh, my gosh. She isn't serious, is she?" Lori whispers to Debbie, loud enough for everyone to hear.

"Claire, please read us the definition," Miss Gallagher says, as if nothing is going on.

"*Hygiene: conditions or practices conducive to health,*" Claire reads.

"So," Miss Gallagher explains, "hygiene is what you do to take good care of your body. Does anyone have any examples?"

Joey starts humming the tune to *The worms crawl in, the worms crawl out, the worms play pinochle on your snout, your body turns to ghastly green and pus comes out like thick whipped cream.*

"Gross!" Lori and Debbie say at the same time, but they're giggling.

"And I forgot my spoooooon," Joey sings under his breath.

"Joey, enough!" Miss Gallagher says. "Let's try this again," she says. "Who can tell me one practice of good hygiene?"

Sean raises his hand. Miss Gallagher pretends she doesn't see him. She looks around at all of us, hoping one of us has an answer. No other hands go up.

"Okay, Sean," she says quietly. She's staring at the clock above the blackboard as if she wishes she could fast-forward it to three o'clock.

"One practice of good hygiene is not to eat your booger snots," he says.

"Or anyone else's," Tommy whispers.

"Gross!" Debbie says. "That's so unbelievably disgusting."

"Enough!" Miss Gallagher *whump*s her hand down

on her hip, and her stomach jiggles under her tight red jersey.

"Ooh! Ooh!" Joey's raising his hand, waving it around. "I have something important to add."

"Joey," Miss Gallagher says in a mean voice to shut him up.

"No, really," Joey says. "It's about snot, I mean *mucus,* and hygiene." Joey isn't fooling around. He wants to tell everyone what he already told me about how snot keeps germs from entering your body.

"One more word and you're all going to put your heads down on the desks," Miss Gallagher says. "If you're going to behave like kindergarteners, I'm going to treat you like kindergartners."

"But it's about germs and—"

"Okay," Miss Gallagher says. "Thanks to Joey it's now officially nap time. Heads down on the desks like you're in kindergarten. I had hoped that you could behave like sixth graders, but obviously you can't."

"There's a fungus among us," Joey mumbles, which is funny, but Miss Gallagher doesn't think so, and she smacks her attendance book down on her desk really hard to prove it.

Actually, this doesn't feel like punishment. My arms on the desk make a little nest for my face, and it's snuggy warm when I breathe. I'm wearing my purple Danskin shirt, and it's smooth and soft against my cheek. Gulls just lay their eggs right on rocks or the bare ground. Woodpeckers make their nests in rotten tree trunks or limbs. Kingfishers dig nests into the sand.

"Hey, Chirp," Joey whispers.

It's the first time he's said my name since Mom came home.

"Hey," I whisper back.

"Nice move, bowels," he says.

"What?"

"It's your fault."

Miss Gallagher stands up from her desk. "I'm *not* hearing any talking during nap time, am I?"

I don't trust Joey not to get me into trouble, so I try closing my eyes. What I see behind my eyelids is mostly fuzzy gray with blurry bits of white, like stars poking their light through a hazy night sky. Eagles, hawks, and owls have three eyelids. An upper lid. A lower lid. And a third lid called a nictitating membrane that's like a thin skin they can pull over their eyeballs so the wind and the sun don't bug them when they fly.

"Hey, stinky," Joey whispers.

I don't open my eyes, but that doesn't mean I can't hear him.

"I gave it back," he whispers.

I know I should ignore him.

"Gave what back?"

"Figure it out."

Miss Gallagher is walking around the classroom. I

can hear her heels *plick plick* on the floor. When the sound stops, I open my eyes.

Joey's staring at me. He won't stop staring. I close my eyes again, but I can still feel him, like a water pistol aimed right at my face.

"Cut it out," I whisper.

"You stinker," he whispers. "She who dealt 'em . . ."

Something smells bad, but I know I'm just imagining it. I bury my face in my sleeve and try to imagine that my purple shirt smells like damson plum jam. Mom likes damson plum jam even better than marmalade.

"The road to hell is paved with good intentions," Joey says.

He's freaking me out. I need to get away from him, but I don't know if we're allowed to go to the girls' room during nap time. I raise my hand. Miss Gallagher is correcting papers at her desk and doesn't see me.

"She who seeks shall find."

Joey just won't stop. And the smell's getting worse. I want to stand up and walk away before I start crying, but I don't have permission, and the last thing Mom and Dad need now is to have me sent to Mrs. Mitchell's office again. Last night while I was brushing my teeth, I heard Mom say to Dad, "I guess we wasted our money putting me up at McLean's. I'm just a hint of who I was, and I don't have a clue how I'm going to get better. I'm in worse shape than you realize. Much worse." And Dad said, "Sweetheart, you've gone through periods of depression before and always pulled through. You'll start to feel . . ." But Mom wasn't listening to him. She just kept saying, "Much worse. Much worse. Much worse."

"She who seeks shall find," Joey whispers again.

I lift my head up. He's smiling at me, but like an enemy, not a friend.

"I'm sorry, Joey. I didn't know that my mom was coming—"

"Heads down," Miss Gallagher says.

I put my head back down and raise my hand, but she's back to correcting papers and doesn't notice me.

"Foiled again," Joey whispers.

"Joey, please. Just leave me alone."

"Mercy upon you," he whispers. "In your desk."

I don't know what he's talking about, but I reach my hand into the opening in my desk. I feel around and find my pencil box, my headband, my social studies book. My hand keeps roaming around like a hermit crab. At the very back of my desk, there's something crinkly. I pinch it and slowly drag it forward so I can see. A wax-paper bag. I push it open with my finger, and the smell clobbers me. At the bottom of the bag, something gray and green and slimy.

"Under the circumstances, I can no longer accept your generosity," Joey whispers.

The clam strip. He's giving it back to me, which means he's definitely made up his mind not to be my friend.

CHAPTER TEN

"How's this, Mom?"

She's sitting on the back porch steps, watching me.

I already know that I'm doing a good job clearing the wet leaves away from the purple crocuses that are blooming in the garden. This year Mom didn't rush out as soon as she saw the first bulbs poking their green noses up through the ground. She didn't get down on her knees on a folded-up towel, like she always does, and say *I've got to give these babies a little elbow room.*

"Mom?"

She looks like a kid in her puffy green down jacket with her arms wrapped around her knees.

"Am I doing this right?" I ask.

She nods.

"These purple ones are so pretty," I say. "And aren't

there still some yellow crocuses out here somewhere?" I put my hand above my eyes like I'm a sea captain, trying to spot land. I look all around the ocean of my muddy yard. I try to make it seem fun so that maybe, maybe, Mom will cheer up and be a sea captain, too. But she doesn't look up. She doesn't stop hugging her knees.

"You can supervise me," I say. "Maybe you should show me what to do, since you're the one who knows how to garden. Maybe I'm not doing such a good job."

Mom shakes her head.

"Maybe I need your help," I tell her. Dad says it's important for us to encourage Mom to feel useful. It's not easy for her to cope with the reality that not only does she have multiple sclerosis but she fell apart after the diagnosis and had to live on a psych ward for more than three months. Dad says picking up those pieces is no easy feat, no easy feat at all.

My fingers are freezing. I go and sit next to Mom and stick both of my hands in her jacket pocket.

"Chirp," she says, like she wants to prove that she still knows who I am.

"So what new stuff are you going to plant in the garden, Mom?" I ask.

"Plant?" Mom says. She looks out at the yard and shrugs.

"How about if we make a list? Marcy said it was good for you to make lists and cross things off. When you first got home, you made lists." I stand up to go get some paper and a pencil. I want Mom thinking *violets, daffodils, tulips,* bright colors flashing in her brain.

"Thinking about spring tires me out, Chirp," Mom says.

"But in May we can pick lilacs!" I say. "We love picking lilacs."

Mom reaches for my hand. "Just sit with me, honey."

I sit back down.

I need to stay patient with Mom, especially since her new psychiatrist just told her that he thinks her depression is chronic, which means it will never completely go away. She's been depressed at different times in her life and will probably always struggle with it. That's news she needed like a hole in the head just two weeks after getting home.

Three black-capped chickadees play follow-the-leader around the rhododendron bush. I can't tell if Mom's watching them.

"You don't have to pick lilacs," I say. "You can just keep me company when I pick them."

Mom puts her arm around me and squeezes tight. When I look at her face, tears are streaming down.

"Listen, Chirpie," she says, brushing the tears away like they're pesty no-see-ums. "I need to tell you something important, okay?"

"Okay."

"You're a really special girl. A beautiful, strong, special, special girl. You know that, right?" She's gripping my arm.

"Uh-huh."

"Good," she says. "It's important." She lets go of my arm. She rests her hand on my knee. "When I was a girl, my mother loved to tell me what was wrong with me. I made no sense to her at all." Mom stares out at nothing. *"Luftmensch."*

"Luftmensch?"

"It's a Yiddish word. It means a dreamer. From my mother, the worst thing a person could be."

"But didn't she like some things about you?"

Mom doesn't answer for a long time. Finally she says, "My hair. My mother liked my hair."

Wind whips across the yard. The grass shivers.

I touch Mom's hair, but she doesn't look at me.

"She didn't love me," Mom says quietly. "That's just the simple, hard truth."

A crow screeches, and all three chickadees take off into the air at the exact same time.

"Wow!" I say.

Please, Mom. Please, Mom. Notice.

"Wow," Mom says, with a little smile.

We watch the chickadees until they disappear into the trees.

"Lilacs are my favorite flower," Mom says.

"I love them," I say.

"Me too," she says.

"They smell so good."

"Like sweetness and light, Chirpie."

I put my hand in Mom's pocket. She reaches in and holds my hand. It's sweetness and light, our hands together in her warm pocket.

⇌

"Krispies, Chirp," Rachel says, even though the cereal box is practically touching Dad's arm. Dad hands Rachel the box, but she won't take it. She waits until he puts it down on the table. Dad nods *You're welcome* as if Rachel said *Thank you.* I guess Dad's plan is to act like she's nice to him, even though she's pretty much stopped talking to him since we found out that Mom forgot about the lemon meringue pie.

"So, do you girls have anything special happening in school today?" Dad asks.

"Dad!" He knows that I have my red-throated loon report. He was my audience last night and the night before, because Mom went to bed right after supper, since she's still so blue.

"Oh, right," Dad says. "You'll do a terrific job with your presentation. I'm sure you'll nail all of the leaps."

"Not to make you nervous or anything," Rachel mutters into her Krispies.

She turns everything Dad says into something else.

"Thanks, Dad," I say, extra cheery so he doesn't feel bad.

"Of course," he says, getting up from the table. As he walks behind Rachel, he reaches out his hand. He lets it hover above her shoulder like a bird about to land, but then he keeps walking.

I hear him in his office, talking on the phone.

"Hi, Clara. She's still sleeping. I'm feeling a bit concerned. Maybe you could stop by again today and—

"Lunch? That would be great.

"Just so she won't be alone for very long. It's been an awfully tough transition for her.

"And can you stay until the girls get home from school?

"Great.

"Yes, Annie said she'd come again tomorrow.

"Thanks. Yes. Thanks. Of course. Hannah will find her way through this. I appreciate it."

"Okay, girls," Dad says at the front door. "Have a good day. Don't forget to clear the breakfast dishes, and make sure you don't slam the front door when you leave so you don't wake up Mom."

"We will. We won't," I say. "See you tonight."

"Adios, amigo," Rachel says as soon as Dad closes the front door. She pulls her big silver hoop earrings out of the pocket of her bell-bottoms and puts them on. She's wearing her red bandana blouse, and it's so cool.

"Maybe you could help me make one like it?" I say, touching her angel-wing sleeve.

"Sure, Chirpie," she says. "It's pretty easy. You just sew a bunch of bandanas together. You'll look far-out. Just like a full-fledged teenager."

"We started 'hygiene' in school. Sean asked Miss Gallagher if she was going to teach us about 'doing it,' and Lori and Debbie couldn't believe that Dawn didn't know what it was."

Rach laughs. She shakes her head. "You already know the important stuff. Your amazing big sister has told you the basics."

"I know. And Mom's given me a few talks about—"

"Men-" Rachel pops up from her chair and grabs it before it tips over and wakes Mom. She sticks her arms up in the air like she's a cheerleader.

"-stroo-" I pop up, too.

"-aaaay-" Rachel waves her pretend pom-poms.

"-shun." I clap my hands, but quietly.

Milk is dribbling out of our mouths, we're laughing so hard.

"I can't stand the way that word sounds," Rachel says.

"It's so incredibly gross," I say.

"Why can't Mom just say *period*? A normal word, like *comma* or *question mark*."

"When mine comes, I'm going to tell her I got my comma."

"Good idea, Chirp," Rachel says.

Rachel grabs her bowl and glass and starts walking to the sink, but then she turns around and sits down next to me.

"So, what do you think about Mom?" she says.

"She told me that spring coming makes her tired."

"She's always loved spring. I really don't want her to go back to the hospital."

"Did Dad tell you that she's going to?"

"No, I'm just kind of worried about it."

"Maybe Clara will make her feel better. I heard Dad talking on the phone. She's coming for lunch again, so Mom won't be alone today. Mom really likes Clara. Maybe she can help."

"Yeah, maybe."

"And Annie's coming over again tomorrow."

We clear the table together. Even though Rachel usually leaves for school ten minutes before me and three tardies in junior high means detention, she waits while I grab an index card from the telephone table and draw a dancer with curly hair. I write, *To Mom, Feel better, xoxo, your Leaping Loon,* and put it by her place at the table. Then Rachel and I head out the door and close it, *shhhhhh,* behind us.

Dawn chose the chipmunk for her report. So far, she's told us that chipmunks are smaller than squirrels and run around on the ground, which everybody already knows.

"Another interesting fact," she says, "is that they eat seeds from bird feeders. Also, they sometimes eat vegetables out of people's gardens, like our tomatoes in the summer."

"Wow, fascinating!" Debbie says, and Dawn smiles, because she doesn't know what sarcasm is.

"The best part of my report is coming up," Dawn says. She looks over at the record player on Miss Gallagher's desk and jumps up and down. Maybe she choreographed something, too, which is a little disappointing, since I want my report to be special.

"Before you move on," Miss Gallagher says, "I'd like to ask you a question."

I want Dawn to move on, because after Dawn comes Tommy and after Tommy comes me.

"Where do chipmunks make their homes? What is their *habitat*?" Miss Gallagher asks Dawn.

"Outside," Dawn answers.

Everyone giggles, and Dawn looks confused.

"Well, yes, outside, but where outside? Can you be more specific?"

Dawn isn't having fun anymore. She's staring at the floor. "In our backyard?" she asks in a tiny voice.

Everyone laughs. I feel bad for her, but I'm not sure what to do.

"I don't know. I don't know." Dawn's ears turn pink. She's twisting her hands together.

"Class?" Miss Gallagher says.

"In burrows underground," Lisa B. says. "They dig tunnels."

"I knew that," Dawn says. Her eyes are watery. "I *did*." One more second and she'll be crying.

"It's easy to forget things when we're on the spot, Dawn," Miss Gallagher says. "Why don't you please finish up your report?"

Dawn drags herself over to the record player like she's been poisoned and is waiting to die. "And now for my grand finale, I'm going to play for you an example of singing chipmunks," Dawn whispers. She puts the record on and just stands up in front of everyone while Alvin and the Chipmunks sing their squeaky Chipmunk song.

"Please sing along," Dawn says, all miserable, and then she walks to her desk, picks up a pink Easter basket filled with dry-roasted peanuts, and hands them out, three peanuts each. Nobody sings, but I kind of hum along so Dawn won't feel so bad.

"Thank you for your report, Dawn," Miss Gallagher says. "Tommy?"

Tommy always hates standing up in front of the class, so I know he'll keep it short and sweet. Hopefully we can skip Miss Gallagher's habitat question, too, since Tommy made a diorama in a shoe box he passes around that demonstrates cougars in the plains in Argentina, and he's labeled everything very neatly, like the grass made out of broom straws painted green and the rabbits made out of cotton balls, which is exactly the kind of thoroughness that Miss Gallagher appreciates. I point my toes as hard as I can and then flex them, to warm them up for leaping.

Tommy takes a deep breath and starts reading his report, which he's actually typed on a typewriter. Just like I thought, he reads super fast and includes all kinds of interesting facts, like cougars have different names—*mountain devil, sneak cat, silver lion*—and they have territories they stay in that are usually in the shape of a circle or an oval. Tommy's almost at the end of his report. I can tell, since he's speeding up like a runner right before the finish line. As soon as he's done, he starts walking back to his seat, so I pop up.

"Whoa, Naomi," Miss Gallagher says, "let's give the class the opportunity to ask Tommy questions about his excellent report. Class?" Tommy looks terrified, but he walks back to the front of the class. I have to sit down. I hope we don't run out of time before the end of school.

"If a cougar and a lion got in a fight, who do you think would win?" Sean asks.

"I don't know much about lions," Tommy mumbles.

"How long did it take you to make your diorama?"

Claire asks. She just wants to talk to Tommy, since she has a crush on him.

"I don't know," Tommy says. He looks at Miss Gallagher. "Can I sit down now, please?"

I'm already up out of my seat and Tommy's halfway back to his, so Miss Gallagher just smiles and says, "Wonderful job, Tommy. You taught all of us new things that we didn't know about cougars."

Finally it's my turn. "Just one minute, please," I say to everyone in a very polite voice. Then I run to the back of the classroom and pull my wings out from behind the bookshelf. They're still kind of dented from when Joey and I sat on them on Halloween, but I've added flecks of white paint to change them from gull wings to loon wings, and they look pretty good. Miss Gallagher asks Joey and Sean to please push her desk back against the blackboard while she ties my wings on, just like we planned.

I take a deep breath and imagine warm honey pouring on my head and running over my shoulders, which Mom says you should always do before any kind of performance. I pull my index card out from the waistband of my black Danskin pants.

"What you're about to see is my interpretation of a red-throated loon taking flight, first from land, then from water. Being able to take off from both is a unique characteristic. I'll also do an interpretation of a loon swimming underwater. When my dance is done, I'll share some interesting facts about this very special bird. Thank you." Everybody claps, which seems like a great beginning.

I start out on the floor, with my head tucked under my wing.

"Dead," Joey whispers.

"Sleeping," Dawn hisses.

Slowly, I raise my head and blink my eyes. Then I do a couple of hops on my knees, to show that a loon can't really walk very well on land. I flap just a little. Then harder and harder. I lean forward and tip my toes underneath me. A few more flaps, and then I'm on my feet and pushing off fast into my first attitude leap, which stands for the loon launching into flight.

"Cool," Lori says. Miss Gallagher is smiling.

I fly in a little circle, and then I flap down the aisle. Everyone ducks so I don't smack them with my wings.

"Go, bird, go! Go, bird, go!" the class yells while I fly around the room, and Miss Gallagher doesn't even shush them. I'm heading back to the front of the room so I can demonstrate liftoff from the water when suddenly—Dad! He's peeking through the window in the door with Mrs. Mitchell. I can't believe he decided to surprise me by coming to my report! I'm a little bit embarrassed, because no other parents are here, but I'm really happy to see him. I want to wave to him, but it's too hard with my wings on. *The show must go on,* so I get in position at the front of the room and sway and bob, a loon in water, waiting for Dad to come in and sit down. I don't want him walking in right as I'm demonstrating the water takeoff. *Sway, bob, sway, bob, sway, bob* . . . I wish Dad would hurry up. *Sway, bob, sway, bob, sway, bob* . . . Is my dance getting boring? Just as I decide to start flapping my wings in preparation for takeoff, the door opens.

"Excuse me," Mrs. Mitchell says, "I hate to interrupt you, Naomi, but your father is here to see you. Will you come out into the hallway?"

"Could I please just take off from the water and then—"

"I'm sorry. It's important, dear," Mrs. Mitchell says. I look at Miss Gallagher, and she nods.

"I'll be right back," I tell the class. I start to flap out of the room. Everyone claps. "It's not over," I say. "I'll be right back."

"What is it, Dad?" I say as soon as the door's closed.

"Honey," he says, "you need to take your wings off." His voice is shaking.

"But, Dad, I'm right in the middle of my presentation!"

"Chirp." He reaches out and starts untying a wing. Mrs. Mitchell is untying the other one.

"Why?"

"We need to go, honey," Dad says.

"Go?"

"Leave now," Dad says. His hands are shaking. "We need to leave, honey, I'm sorry to say."

Mrs. Mitchell takes my wing off and leans it against

the lockers. "Here," she says, and helps Dad untie his strap.

"Where are we going?"

Dad hands my other wing to Mrs. Mitchell. "Okay," she says, looking at the ground. She hands me my jacket and lunch box. Somehow she already got them out of my locker.

Dad grabs my hand and pulls me through the hall. He's walking so fast I have to run to keep up with him. As soon as we're outside, he kneels right down on the pavement and looks into my face.

"It's Mom," he says. "I have terrible news."

"You took her back to the hospital."

"Oh, God," Dad says. He rubs his face with his hands.

"I want to finish my dance," I say. "I was just about to take off from the water."

"Listen, honey. Mom isn't in the hospital. She died. Mommy died."

"No, she didn't," I say. "She's just really sad. There's a chance she'll have to go back to the hospital again."

Dad holds my shoulders. He puts his face so close to me that his words make wind in my eyes and he says that Mom died, she really did die, this morning after we left for school, and he knows this because Clara went to the house and Mom wasn't there, but there was a note on the table that said she was very sorry but she just wasn't able to go on this way and she loves us very much and she didn't want to make this harder on us, so she wanted us to know that she went to Hutchins Pond.

"Is that where we're going, Dad?"

"No, honey," Dad says. "I've already been there. With the police."

"Police?" I say.

"Mommy drowned, honey."

Dad tries to hold me, but I'm flapping my wings.

Oh, my baby girl. Oh, my poor baby.

I'm diving underwater. I'm kicking my feet.

Dad picks me up and puts me in the backseat. He closes the door.

"We're driving to the junior high school. We're going to go get Rachel now," Dad says in a loud voice. "We're turning left here on Herring Drive, and soon we'll come to the light. At the light, we'll make a right. Main Street."

The water's sparkly green. Cold and green. I'm speeding through it.

"Then just another mile and we'll be there. We'll go get Rachel. We'll get Rachel, and we'll all go home."

Flap, flap, flap. Down, down, down.

"Okay," Dad says. "Okay, we're almost there."

I'm swimming through the sparkle. Bursts of blue-green light.

"We're here," Dad says. "Chirp." He takes my hand and pulls. "Chirp." He pulls and pulls me across the parking lot. Rachel's in the office, waiting. She jumps up when she sees us. She runs out to the car. She looks at Dad. She looks at me. "It's the worst news, isn't it, Dad? It's the worst thing that could happen, right?"

Dad nods.

"Aiiiiiihhhhh!" she screams. "Aiiiiiihhhhh! Aiiiiiihhhh! Aiiiiiihhhhh!"

Hands on my back. Breath in my ears. *Oh, my girls! Oh, my girls!*

I dive back under, swim and swim into cold black quiet, wet deep black.

CHAPTER ELEVEN

DAD AND RACHEL MAKE too much noise. Cry and moan and yell. Talk and talk and talk. *Chirp?* They knock on my door. *Chirpie?* They push my door open. *Can we come in and be with you? We need each other.*

There's nothing to say.

I pull my pink rug into the corner. I shove my desk over to make a triangle with the wall with just enough space for me to crawl in.

I guess we should just let her be. I guess she needs some time alone. Pssssss. Whisshhh. Pssssss. Their whispering is cold air blowing.

I get my pillow and red wool blanket and white quilt and yellow Therma-Weave off my bed. Eggie. All of my Danskin shirts and pants out of my drawer, the purple ones and yellow ones and green ones. I drag everything in. My pillow goes in the middle. Then all of my clothes in a circle. I roll each of the blankets up and push them against the wall and desk.

A nest should be well constructed. It should keep you warm even when there are strong gusts or a downpour. It can't just fall apart. It should be as safe as possible from predators.

I'm finally done. Nest building isn't easy. It takes most birds a minimum of three days. I'm so, so tired. I've never been so tired. I curl up. My nest is warm and snuggy. *Loooooolooooooloooooooloooooo.* I sing myself to sleep.

The phone rings. Sun on my face. *The rabbi is coming.* Knock on my door. The front door slams. *Ten o'clock tomorrow.* The phone rings. *Clompclompclomp.* The phone rings. *She must be hungry.* My door opens. A dog barks. They pat my leg. *Come eat, Chirp. Come out of there now.* The phone rings. *Chocolate doughnuts.* The doorbell rings. My door closes. Smell of coffee. *Yes, it's a long drive. The Jewish cemetery.*

"Here, honey, put these on," Grandma says.

The tights are too small. They won't pull all the way up.

"They fit okay?"

I nod.

Grandma hands me a dress. I put it on.

You didn't even like her, I think. But I don't say it. I don't say anything.

Rachel and Dad are talking outside my door. They're always, always talking now. Their words fill up all the space, so I stay quiet to balance things out.

"Off we go!" Grandma says, like it's going to be fun.

I'm in the middle. The seats are leather. The glass is dark, I guess so that no one can look in and see Dad and Rachel with their red eyes and drippy noses.

"How are you, Chirp?" Rachel says.

"It's a very sad time," Dad says.

"Oh, Daddy," Rachel says, and starts to sob again, so I lean back and Dad reaches across me to hold her and his jacket sleeve is in my face.

If I were sitting up front with the driver, I could just look out the window and have no questions asked at me and no sobbing sister and no sleeves in my face.

"I can't believe she's in a coffin in that hearse," Rachel says. "I can't believe we're going to Mom's funeral."

> *Deep blue sea, baby.*
> *Deep blue sea.*

Rachel looks at me.

> *Deep blue sea, baby.*
> *Deep blue sea.*

I keep humming. It's a song Mommy loves.

"Daddy," Rachel says.

> *Deep blue sea, baby.*
> *Deep blue sea.*
> *It was Willy*
> *What got drown-ded*
> *In the deep blue sea.*

"Dad!"

"Be patient with her, honey," Dad says to Rachel, as if I'm not there.

"Well, she could at least talk to us," Rachel says. "And she doesn't even cry."

Dad sits back. Without his sleeve in my face, I can see out the window.

Pitch pines.

Dad puts his hand on my leg.

If I squint, all the trees melt into dark green ocean. Pretty.

There's a clump of people standing on a hill. Grandma, Grandpa, Clara, Mrs. Mitchell, Sally's mom. Some other grown-ups. I wave and they wave back.

Dad says that Rabbi Greenbaum needs just a minute with us, the *mourners,* which is only Dad and Rachel and me. If Mom's parents were alive, they would count. So would her sister, but she didn't come, because she and Mom didn't talk to each other and she lives in Mississippi with her goyish husband.

Rabbi Greenbaum is standing under a tree, away from everyone else. When he sees us, he flaps his arms like a giant black bird and rushes over. He reaches up like he's going to put his arm around Dad, but he just slips a yarmulke on Dad's head.

"Naomi, I'm so sorry for your loss." Now he's crouched down right in front of me. He smells like oatmeal cookies.

"Yes," I say.

He has something in his hand. An oatmeal cookie for me?

He pins a black button with a black ribbon on my jacket and stands up. "An ancient tradition of our people," he says. Suddenly he's reaching for me. I step back, but he grabs at me. He rips the ribbon. *Owwww.* I know that all he's done is ripped the ribbon, but it hurts it hurts it hurts, like my heart's tearing in two. *Noooooo!* Rabbi Greenbaum's hand is warm on my head. He's talking in Hebrew. "It helps us feel our grief," he says, and then he rips Rachel's heart and Daddy's heart and now, finally, all three of us are crying. We cry as we walk over to everyone else, with our ripped black ribbons fluttering in the breeze.

The rabbi is talking.

In that box is Mommy. In that box is Mommy. In that box is Mommy. In that box is Mommy. In that box is Mommy. In that box is Mommy. In that box is Mommy. In that box is Mommy.

The box is disappearing. Four men with four straps are lowering it into the hole. *Stop it. No. Stop it.*

Dad has a shovelful of dirt. He's going to dump it in the hole. I grab his arm.

Hands hold me back. "Shhh, honey. No, sweetie." *Thud. Thud. Thud.*

Now they're pushing me closer to the hole.

"Take the shovel, sweetheart."

"It's your turn, Chirpie."

"It's okay, honey."

The shovel is cold. I stick it into the pile of dirt. I hold it over the hole.

> *Deep blue sea, baby.*
> *Deep blue sea.*

I turn the shovel over.

My dirt hits Mommy. *Thud. Thud. Thud.*

> *It was Willie what got drown-ded*
> *In the deep blue sea.*

I throw the shovel down and run.

I run past Rabbi Greenbaum's tree, down a concrete path, across wet grass. My tights are too small, and they rub against the tops of my legs. The short white fence is easy to climb over.

Plenty of trees, but I like this maple best. I sit down and look up. What I see is lots of branches chopping the gray sky up into little pieces. Two black-capped chickadees. One house finch. It's rare to spot a purple finch until it's warmer outside. House finches are common. They have stubby wings, which makes their tails seem long by comparison. What's best is their funny twittery song that goes on and on and on.

Are there more rolls? We need a fresh pot of— I'll put out more fruit salad. Yes, yes. Napkins? In the cupboard over the sink.

The ladies are bustling around the kitchen. Ladies from the synagogue where we never go. Ladies from Mom's dance brigade. Ladies from town. Watching all the ladies makes me even more tired, and I'm already so tired I want to curl up in my nest and sleep forever, except that I have to be here for all of the company that wants to stop by so they can tell me how awful they feel for me and what a terrible tragedy this is. I'm glad we're not traditional Jews, since they sit shiva for seven whole days. I just have to try to be a trooper for the rest of today and for three hours tomorrow and the day after.

"Honey, have you eaten? You have to eat something." Clara hands me a plate with a hard-boiled egg and some noodle kugel.

"She's never been a big kugel fan," Grandma says, rushing over.

"Oh. Oh, sorry. I didn't know that," Clara says, and her eyes fill up with tears. She walks away.

While Grandma watches, I eat the kugel and leave the egg.

Grandma frowns but doesn't say anything.

"Chirp." It's Mrs. Paganelli. She's got a plate full of food. She holds it out in the air while she hugs me with one arm. "I'm so sorry for your loss," she says.

What I want to say is *She's not lost. I know right where she is. And you do, too.*

"Thanks," I say.

"If you need anything, anything at all, you just let me know," she says. "Will you promise me that? I need you to make me a promise."

I nod.

"Promise?"

I nod again.

"Say it," she says.

"Promise," I say.

"Oh, good!" she says, and starts wolfing down her potato salad.

I want to eat chocolate bubke in my nest.

The dining room's too crowded. *Excuse me excuse me* is what I'll have to say to get to the bubke, and I don't feel like talking, which I heard Dad tell Rachel is a symptom of my overwhelming grief. There are too many people blocking the bubke. I lean against the wall and wait.

Delicious, I'll have to get the recipe. Right. Imagine doing this to those two young girls! Yes, yes. No. We'll go visit my in-laws in Maine, as always. A note on the table. Really? Half the calories. Well, that's something I'll never understand. I guess a little sherry can't hurt. I know. I saw her swimming last summer. A bit of a sweet tooth. Of course, he will. Absolutely. Hopefully her suicide won't be front-page news.

"Chirp."

Daddy touches my arm.

"Honey, you remember Marcy from the hospital? She drove all the way here to see us when she heard about Mommy."

Does he want me to say thank you? I can't say thank you. I don't even want to look at her.

I look at Joey instead. He's wearing a suit and blue-striped tie. He must have tied the tie himself, because the knot's all lumpy. He's leaning against the wall like I am. He's by himself. He's eating fruit salad. He waves. I wave back.

"Marcy wants to talk with you, honey," Daddy says, poking my arm. Marcy's crying. She kneels down in front of me.

"I'm so sorry, Chirp," she says. Her nose is pink and swollen, and she keeps swiping at it with a crumpled-up Kleenex. She's looking right into my face. I really, really want to close my eyes. "You know, your mother loved you very much."

I shake my head. I don't want her talking about Mom. I don't want her telling me anything about her.

"Yes. Yes, she did, Chirp."

I shake my head harder to get her to stop.

Marcy grabs my hand. "It's very important that you understand how much your mother loved you," she says. "You know that, don't you?"

Daddy's looking at me, too.

A little space has opened up at the table between where Mrs. Bonazoli and Mrs. Mitchell are standing. Just three pieces of bubke left on the plate.

I jerk my hand away from Marcy. She tries to grab it again. She's a greenhead fly, and I'm a flyswatter. Smack! I miss.

"Naomi!" Dad says.

I run to the table and snatch a piece of bubke. Suddenly Joey's right beside me. He snatches the other two pieces.

"Here," he says, shoving the bubke into my hands. I fly out of the room and up the stairs as fast as I can. I slam my door. I crawl into my nest.

First, I tear the bubke into lots of pieces. Then I roll the pieces into balls.

Downstairs it's silverware clanging. It's the smack of ice in glasses. Noisy stupid questions. Noisy stupid answers. Noisy stupid nothing.

In my nest, suppertime. With my eyes closed, I open up wide. *Plop.* The first bubke ball. *Chew. Chew. Swallow. Next. Chew. Chew. Swallow. Next. Chew. Chew. Swallow.* I take it nice and slow. Hopefully, by the time I'm finished with my sweet supper, everyone will have put their long, dark coats back on, taken their noisy stupid nothing, and gone home.

Early morning and Daddy's in his office. He's not going to work for five more days. Rachel's wearing Mommy's red flannel bathrobe. She knocks on Daddy's door. She doesn't wait for him to give permission. She just goes right on in.

I pour myself another bowl of Grape-Nuts. When I eat them, I can't hear Dad and Rachel talk. *Crunch* is all I hear.

"Give Grandma and Grandpa a hug good-bye," Daddy says. We're all standing in the front hall. It's our last day of sitting shiva, but Grandma and Grandpa aren't going to stick around, since they have a long drive ahead of them back to New York.

"I'll write you letters," Grandma says. "And call you on the phone." She pats my head. She opens up her purse and hands me a whole box of peppermint Chiclets.

"What do you say, Chirp?" Rachel says, like I'm a little kid, and before I can open my mouth she says, "Thank Grandma, Chirp."

I can't believe her. I want to pull her hair, but I just turn around so I don't have to see her dumb face.

"What is it, Chirpie?" Rachel says, all gooey sweet and touching my hand, and I can't help it, I'm so mad that she's pretending to be Mom, I start to cry.

"It's hard to say good-bye, isn't it, sweetheart?" Dad says.

"We understand," Grandpa says. "Let's just say, 'See you later, sweet potater,'" and he touches the side of his plaid driving cap with two fingers. Before I can hug him or Grandma, he takes Grandma's hand and pulls her out the door.

"We'll talk soon," Grandma says, blowing kisses.

"Freda, you're just making this harder on the children," Grandpa says in a loud whisper. "Let's go." And suddenly they're in their blue Dodge Dart, driving away.

"Well," Dad says.

"Well," Rachel says, putting her head on Dad's shoulder.

"I'd hoped they'd feel like more of a comfort," Dad says in a sad voice, and Rachel looks up at him, but

I don't hear what just-right thing she says, because I'm walking past them and out the door, even though I've got my slippers on.

It's good to fly the coop. It's good to not say thank you. It's good to have cold air in my face. It's good to see the gray sky. It's good to run so fast down to the salt marsh in my wet slippers that my feet sting.

I touch my tree. *Tag, you're it.*

I touch the water. *Tag, you're it.*

There's no point searching. The red-winged black-bird nest that I left for the marsh lady is gone. Maybe she took it. Maybe it's the one precious thing that she has to call her own.

If I head back home right now, I'll get there before our guests start showing up again with more chicken soup and more meat loaf and more sponge cake.

I touch the sand. *Tag, you're it.*

I touch my tree again. *Tag, you're it.*

If I don't leave right now and run fast, I won't get home before all the people do.

I pick three pieces of marsh grass. Mom taught me how to braid my hair when I was in first grade. I sit in the wet sand and braid. I put the marsh-grass braid where the nest was. I pick nine more pieces of marsh grass. I braid and braid. I leave three more marsh-grass braids next to the first one.

I don't feel like running, so I don't. I walk in my wet, sandy slippers, slow and steady, like I'm Nettie in *Carousel,* which is the play the high school did two years ago and I got the record for Hanukkah last year:

> *When you walk through a storm*
> *Hold your head up high*

I squint my eyes like there's rain blowing in my face. Everything turns blurry-edged and gentle. I sing the whole song six times, and when I get back to the house, cars are parked out front. It looks like a party. I can see people through the window, holding white paper plates. I pretend I'm not me. I pretend that I'm just a regular not-me person walking by.

Wow! I wonder what the Orensteins are celebrating on a Tuesday morning. Maybe it's the youngest girl's birthday. Maybe they let her stay home from school and invited her friends over. There's probably chocolate birthday cake and chocolate ice cream. I hear she loves chocolate. She's supposed to be a nice girl.

I stand on the front porch like I'm a guest who's waiting for the door to open. I watch all the people inside eating and talking. Rachel waves to me through the living room window like *Hurry up and get in here!* I smile and wave back. *Thanks for asking! I'd love to come in.*

CHAPTER TWELVE

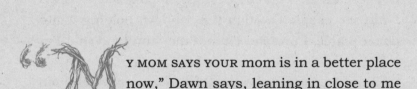

"MY MOM SAYS YOUR mom is in a better place now," Dawn says, leaning in close to me with her toothpaste breath.

I pretend that I don't hear her over the grumble of the bus.

"She says that just because your mom didn't welcome Jesus into her heart doesn't mean God won't welcome her into heaven."

Dawn pats my arm. She's looking at me with her watery blue eyes. She's waiting for me to say something.

"SweeTARTS?" I ask.

Dawn hands me a whole pack.

"You know, we made you a class card. Miss Gallagher said it was important for us to show you our support. It's called a sympathy card. We're going to give it to you during morning announcements today."

I need her to stop talking. I try to look out the window, but Dawn's head is in the way.

"Don't worry," she says. "Nobody's going to ask you questions about how your mother died. Nobody's going to ask you any questions at all, because Miss Gallagher said we're not allowed to. Sean said, 'Well, how *did* she die?' but Miss Gallagher said that was none of his business. It's none of my business either, I guess, is it?"

I shake my head.

"That's what I thought. So I'm not going to ask you. I'm not supposed to, anyway. That's what Miss Gallagher said."

I want to get off the bus. I want to run all the way home. I want to crawl back into my nest, but my nest isn't there anymore, because Dad said that now that I'm going back to school, I need to sleep in my bed, not in a nest on the floor, and, no, he's not saying that my grieving is over, but it *is* time for me to face the world again and take on my normal activities and responsibilities. Then he pushed my desk back against the wall and carried my blankets back to my bed and spread them out and kept smoothing them and patting them and smiling at me as if getting all the wrinkles out was a fun game we were playing together, even though it wasn't.

"I was sad when you weren't on the bus," Dawn says.

"What?"

"I had to sit all by myself on the bus, because you weren't here. Eight days. I counted."

She sounds mad.

"No one else would sit with me." Dawn folds her arms across her chest. She pushes her bottom lip out like a little kid.

"You were gone a long time," she says. "A really long time."

I think she wants me to feel sorry for her.

"Eternity is a long time," I say.

Dawn stares at me.

"Eternity is forever," I say.

Dawn nods slowly, like she knows what I mean, but I can tell she doesn't.

"Are you taking the bus home after school?" she asks. "Can we sit together?"

I don't answer her, even though I heard her loud and clear.

"Chirp?" She tugs on my sleeve. "Are you taking the bus home after school? Will you sit with me?"

I make her wait a long time. I make her wait until the bus stops. I make her wait even a little bit more, until she's all squirmy and uncomfortable. "I'm not sure what my plans are," I finally say, and stand up. "Do you even know what *eternity* means?" I ask, and then I walk off the bus.

The classroom looks the same. The classroom smells the same. The only thing that's different is that everyone keeps saying "Hi, Chirp" and "Welcome back, Chirp" and "We missed you, Chirp" in quiet little voices, like they're scared of me. Even Sean says, "Oh, you can go first," and jumps out of the way when I'm standing behind him at the pencil sharpener.

"Well," Miss Gallagher says during morning announcements, "we're all very pleased to have you back in class with us today, Naomi." Her eyes are as flitty as they were the first day of school. I guess I scare her, too. "Your classmates would like to express their sympathies," she says. "Sally, will you please get the card?"

Sally pops out of her chair and scurries to the bulletin board and unpins a card and rushes over to me, all nervous like a wild rabbit.

"We're very sorry for your loss," she whispers. Someone else must have told her what to say. She drops the card on my desk and disappears.

I don't know what I'm supposed to do. With birthday cards you open them up right away and read them and say thank you. I've never had a sympathy card before. I can feel everyone staring at me.

The front has a pink heart, like a Valentine.

I don't want to read the inside with everyone's eyeballs on me.

"It's pretty," I say, which sounds so dumb. I put the card in my desk.

Miss Gallagher tells us to please take out our phonics workbooks and get started on chapter five, which should be easy, since she reviewed prefixes in some detail last week. I haven't finished chapter four, so I'm raising my hand to ask her what I should do when she magically appears at my desk.

"How can I help you, dear?" she asks. Miss Gallagher never says *dear* or just shows up at your desk to help. You have to keep your hand raised until all the blood drains out of your fingertips and they start to tingle. And even then she might not come if she's doing more important things at her desk.

"Should I finish chapter four or start working on chapter five?"

"Oh, don't you worry, dear," Miss Gallagher says. "You just do your best, and don't you worry about a thing." And then she pats my head and walks away.

I'm not worried. I just need to know what to do.

"She didn't even read the card," I hear Debbie whisper. "We worked hard on that card."

"Yeah, she just stuck it in her desk, like she didn't care," Claire whispers back.

I open up my workbook to chapter five. *Prefix.* Like fixing something before it's even broken? That makes no sense. Everybody else already knows what a prefix is. I'm the only one without a clue.

I'm glad I have a bedroom door that closes. I'm glad that I'm on this side of my bedroom door and Dad and Rachel are on the other side and down the stairs and in the living room, where they're talking. I'm glad I can't hear what they're talking about. I'm glad that in my room no one is talking, except me to myself, playing the glad game. I'm glad that Passover only comes once a year. I'm glad that our Passover seder is over for this year so I don't have to sit at the table again with just Dad and Rachel and miss Mommy's matzo balls and miss Mommy's *day-dayenu, day-dayenu* singing and miss Mommy's *Whew! Is the horseradish hotter this year than usual?*

I'm glad I have Mommy's sea lavender sweater. I'm glad it's soft. I'm glad I have a face that I can hold it against. I'm glad that on my face is a nose that knows how to sniff. I'm glad that when my nose sniffs, it can still smell Mommy.

"I'm in the kitchen!" Rachel yells when she hears me drop my school stuff down in the front hall.

The house smells like onions.

"Hang your jacket up," she yells. "Don't just drop your stuff down."

I leave everything right where it is and walk into the kitchen.

She's wearing Mom's green-checked apron. Her hair is in a dancer bun.

"I'm making meat loaf," she says, smiling at me. "And mashed potatoes and onions."

I pour myself a glass of milk and sit down.

"Why's your hair like that?" I ask.

"Like what?" she says, as if she always wears her hair exactly like Mom's.

"Never mind."

"How was your day?"

"Fine," I say.

"Dad loves mashed potatoes and onions. I'm surprising him."

Rachel's melting margarine in a pan.

"What's that for?"

"To fry up the onions."

"That's not how Mom did it, you know."

Rachel turns and looks at me like I'm crazy.

"Of course it is," she says.

"No, it isn't," I say. "She used *schmaltz*. That's what made it special."

"She used margarine."

"Nope. Don't you remember? She cooked down chicken fat into *schmaltz* and kept a jar of it in the fridge. Then she'd always fry the onions in the *schmaltz* when she made mashed potatoes."

Rachel knows I'm right.

"I think you're wrong," she says. "Maybe you

just don't remember right." Her lips are tight like a stretched balloon.

"I remember just fine," I say. "There's nothing wrong with the way I remember." I remember the way Mom would tap the wooden spoon on the edge of the pot like she was a drummer when she was waiting for water to boil. I remember the way she'd give me a spoonful of spaghetti sauce she was simmering and say *Your opinion, madam taste tester?*

"Okay, okay," Rachel says. "Don't get yourself all worked up."

"I'm not all worked up. Just don't tell me that I don't remember right."

"Fine. Whatever you say," Rachel says. She turns her back to me. "Oh, great," she says, "now the margarine's burned!" as if it's my fault. She throws the pan into the sink, and it smacks into the other dirty dishes, hissing.

I drink my milk. I try not to say anything. I stare at my drawing of a purple-and-green-striped tiger that Mom magneted to the fridge when I was in kindergarten. Whenever I'd say, "Mom, it's faded. Take it down," she'd say, "Faded? It's perfect, honey. It's my beautiful tiger."

"Take two," Rachel says. She walks to the fridge and gets out the margarine. I try not to say anything, but the words bubble up out of my mouth before I can stop them. "I remember a ton of things," I mumble.

"Right," Rachel says, with an awful little laugh in her voice.

"I do!"

Rachel ignores me. She starts humming "I'll Be There" by the Jackson 5 while she gets out another pan.

"I pretty much remember *everything*," I say.

Rachel starts singing, like I haven't said anything.

"You're the one who doesn't remember!" I say.

She keeps on singing, and suddenly I'm so mad that I'm yelling.

"I bet you don't even remember that that's exactly the way Mommy wore her hair. That's *her* dancer bun, not yours!"

Rachel looks surprised. She touches her bun. Then she shakes her head and says, "Okay, that's got to be the stupidest thing I've ever heard," and walks out of the room. I follow her. In the front hall, she stops and puts her hands on her hips.

"Naomi," she says. She points at my stuff on the floor.

"What?"

"I asked you to pick your stuff up."

I just stare at her.

"Naomi?"

I start to walk past her.

"What are you doing?"

"I'm going to my room," I say, nice and calm, even though my heart is pounding.

"But I asked you to pick your stuff up," she says.

"And I'm not listening to you," I say.

"Chirp!" Rachel grabs my arm, but I jerk it away.

"You're trying to look like Mom! You're trying to cook like Mom!" I yell.

Rachel's mouth makes a little O. She just stands there.

"You aren't Mom!" I scream.

Rachel grabs me again. Her fingers are digging into my arm. "You think I like this?" she screeches at me. "You think I like taking care of you all the time? Making you dinner and telling you to pick your stuff up over and over again? You think I like listening to Dad tell me how sad he is, so sad that I think he sometimes wishes he was the one who was dead?"

She screeches and screeches like a stellar jay, but I can't hear her, since my hands are covering my ears and making the sound of the ocean and my feet are running out the door.

Joey's standing in the road, like he's been waiting for me. He's not even throwing rocks. He's just standing there.

"C'mon," I say.

"Where?"

"Away."

"Away?"

"Yes, we're going away," I say, and suddenly it sounds like a really good idea.

Joey doesn't say anything. He just looks at me like he's giving me the chance to punch him in the arm and say, "Just kidding!" and when I don't, he nods.

"Okay," he says. "We need to be smart here. We have to have money. And warm clothes. Bring extra socks. And a flashlight."

"And don't forget your toothbrush," I say, because I don't want him to be the only one who knows how to do this.

"If we're taking off today, we have to hurry up. My dad will be home soon, and then I won't be going anywhere," Joey says. "I'm grounded for spilling my orange juice this morning."

"Five minutes," I say.

"Five minutes," Joey says. "Behind your rhododendron bush."

We both have our stuff spread out in front of us so we can see what we've brought, except for our underpants, which we agreed we don't have to show each other, and Mom's sea lavender sweater, which I keep in my knapsack, since it's my private business.

Everything I have with me is mine, except for the twenty dollars Dad keeps under his handkerchiefs in his top drawer in case of an emergency.

"This *is* an emergency," Joey says. "Or at least,

it will turn into one if we don't have that money." I guess he's right, but I still feel really bad about taking it. Joey has nine dollars. I don't know where he got so much money.

"Binoculars? You need binoculars?" Joey says.

"They could come in handy for scouting," I say.

"You just want to watch birds."

"So, what's wrong with that? I like birds."

"Fine," Joey says.

"Soap *and* shampoo *and* conditioner?" I ask.

"Yes," Joey says. "Non-negotiable."

I guess he cares a lot more than me about hygiene.

Joey didn't think to bring food. I have six carrots, a hunk of cheddar cheese, and a whole pack of pita bread. And my canteen with water.

Joey brought *From the Mixed-Up Files of Mrs. Basil E. Frankweiler,* which was really smart, since it's about a brother and sister who run away and maybe we can get some pointers.

"Time to amscray," Joey says. He's already got most of his stuff neatly packed back up in his brown duffel bag. I'm trying to shove my baby blanket into my knapsack. It doesn't fit. I already have on my winter coat, but I put the blanket over my shoulders like I've just come off the boat at Ellis Island like my ancestors escaping persecution in the old country. Then I lead the way from the rhododendron bush, across our yard, to the sandy path that will take us to the fire road and out to Route 6.

CHAPTER THIRTEEN

I T TAKES MUCH, MUCH longer to walk to the glass house than it did to ride our bikes, and by the time we get there, my feet are aching and it's starting to get dark.

"First, we need to clean up," Joey says. "Then we can eat supper."

"Okay," I say.

"Find a pine branch that you can sweep with. I'll try and open the door."

"Okay."

I'm glad Joey's telling me what to do. All by myself, I'd just curl up in the woods in my winter jacket with my baby blanket around me and listen to the birds and maybe never get up again.

It takes a while to find a good sweeper branch and even longer to get it off the tree. I have to twist it around and around before it finally breaks. When I get back to the house, Joey's inside. He's standing in the middle of the floor.

"Cool, huh?" he says, smiling.

The floor's twinkling like the starriest night. It's the broken mad glass, some mine, mostly Joey's, catching light from the sun as it goes down. White and yellow and violet sparks.

"Cool," I say.

"Wicked cool," Joey says. "I guess it's been doing this every night for years and years and I've never seen it before."

"It's too pretty to sweep up."

"Don't," he whispers. "It's almost over. The sun's almost down."

We stand and watch until the last flash of sunlight slides over the glass.

"Maybe it's an omen," Joey says.

"An omen?"

"Like a sign that everything will be okay," he says.

Nothing will ever be okay again. I already know that.

"Maybe," I say to Joey.

I get my sweeper branch and start sweeping the glass into the corner. Joey follows behind me, dusting the floor with a red T-shirt.

"We'd better sweep it again," he says. "Maybe two more times."

"I'm tired," I say.

"Yeah, but mostly you're sad," he says. He doesn't

stare at me with big bug eyes. He doesn't ask me stupid questions.

I nod. All I want is to sit on the floor and listen to the mourning doves.

"Just sit down," Joey says, like he's read my mind. He takes the sweeper branch from me.

I sit down and look around. With all the broken windows, our glass house is like being inside and outside at the same time. I can see the sky and the pitch pines. I can smell the night air. The mourning doves make the saddest sound, and I can't help it, I close my eyes and moan along with them, *oh, oh, oh,* while Joey keeps sweeping. He gives me my privacy and doesn't say anything at all, just sweeps, even when my moans turn into a little bit of crying. I cry while Joey sweeps while the mourning doves moan.

When I finally open my eyes, Joey's taken off his winter coat, because he's working so hard.

"When I was a little kid, I thought they were *morning* doves, because they were up early in the morning," I say.

"I used to say *chickmumps*," Joey says. "I still think it sounds better."

"You're a good sweeper," I say.

Joey smiles.

I wonder how long we'll stay here. I wonder what my plan is.

"Joey?"

"Put your flashlight in your jacket pocket. It'll be really dark soon," he says.

He's spinning in a circle, polishing the floor.

"What are you doing?"

"Our sleeping spot," he says. "Bring me your blanket." Joey spreads my blanket out, then runs his hands over it, smoothing out the wrinkles. He pulls all of his neatly folded clothes out of his duffel bag— his blue wool sweater and his blue jeans and his green flannel shirt and four pairs of socks. He takes everything and carefully arranges it in a circle.

"Your turn," he says. "Add your stuff to my stuff."

I put my blue jeans and gray sweatshirt and green turtleneck and three pairs of socks into the circle, everything but the sea lavender sweater.

"When Rachel and I sleep out in the woods or at the salt marsh, we use sleeping bags. I thought about bringing them but figured they'd be too heavy for us to carry."

Joey shifts our stuff around, plumping and poking and pushing until we have a perfect nest of clothes.

"We'll be just fine tonight," he says. "You don't need to worry. We'll eat supper, and we'll sleep in our sleeping spot. And we'll figure out tomorrow, tomorrow."

Suddenly I'm cold. Even in my winter jacket, I've got the shivers. My teeth are chattering, and I can't stop shaking.

"Hey," Joey says. "Don't start freaking out on me."

"I'm cold," I say. "*Really* cold."

"Listen, we're going to be just fine. I told you every-thing's okay, and it is." He walks over to me and touches my hair, and then he starts rooting around in his duffel bag. He pulls out a little packet and rips it open.

"A moistened towelette, free at the Clam Shack with every order of fried clams or oysters!" Joey says, like he's the radio guy on 104.7. I should laugh, but there isn't a laugh inside me. Joey wipes his hands and then gives the towelette to me.

"Sorry, you can't have your own," he says. "I don't have that many. I need to make them last."

I wipe my hands and then get us each a piece of pita bread and some cheese.

"A toast," Joey says, holding up his cheese.

All I can think of is *l'chaim,* and that doesn't seem fair to Joey.

"*Beads, flowers,*" he says.

"*Freedom, happiness,*" I say, glad that Joey knows the songs from *Hair,* too.

We clink cheese.

"This is really good," Joey says. I'm not sure if he means the bread and cheese, or running away and staying in a glass house with me.

"Very," I say.

"Why's it called Peter bread?" he asks.

"Pita," I say. "Pita bread. It's Mediterranean. They eat it in Israel and other places. You can't get it at

Flanagan's. My dad picks it up at the supermarket in Hyannis on his way home from work."

"Well, it tastes amazing. This is the best bread and cheese I've ever had."

He's right. The food tastes really, really good.

"It's good, right?" he says.

"Far-out," I say.

Joey looks at me and smiles. "You're not a bad little squirt," he says. "Not bad at all."

We both get quiet, and for the first time I notice you can hear the ocean, just a soft rumble, like a car driving too fast down a dirt road. A great horned owl calls *hoo-hoo hoooooo hoo-hoo*. I love the sound, but Joey hugs himself, like he's scared. Dad always says we're most frightened of what we don't understand.

"It's a male," I explain to Joey. "They have lower voices than the females. You know what else?"

"What?"

"They don't build their own nests. They use left-over ones from the year before. Usually from great blue herons or red-tailed hawks."

"What else?" Joey asks.

"In parts of England people think owls bring good luck. I think so, too."

"What else?"

"Some people call them winged tigers, since they're such great hunters."

"Flying would be cool," Joey says. "I've always wanted to fly."

Hoo-hoo hoooooo hoo-hoo.

"We could fly to Boston," I say. "We could see the swan boats."

"Swan boats?"

"Haven't you ever been to Boston?"

"Just once. Vinnie went to go stay with our uncle. But then we had to pick him up in the middle of the night."

"Why?"

"Because otherwise my uncle was gonna call the police."

"Oh." I don't give him big bug eyes. I don't ask stupid questions.

"Swan boats?"

"They're boats that look like swans. A driver pedals you around the pond in the Boston Public Garden, and all the ducks and geese swim along. My mom and I—" I remember her blowy hair. I remember the way she laughed and turned pink when the handsome man with the dark hair and green eyes talked to her. I remember how warm her hands were in my hands when we danced up the dock together.

"Hey," Joey says softly, "we'll talk about it tomorrow."

"About what?"

"Going to see your swan boats."

I don't know if Joey can see me in the dark, but I'm nodding *yes.* My plan. *Our* plan. This is it!

"But now we should both do our business before we go to bed," Joey says.

"Our business?"

"You know."

"No, I don't."

Joey shakes his head and walks to the door.

"You go left and I'll go right," he says, and then I get it.

"You can just say *pee*," I say, but he doesn't hear me, because I guess he's already doing his business.

I squat down and try, but I'm so cold, the pee doesn't come. There are lots of crunchy night sounds, rabbits and bobwhites and chipmunks rustling around in the brush.

"All ashore who's going ashore," Joey yells, so I figure he's finished and my coast is clear. It's really hard to see him, since there's only the tiniest slice of moon. I follow his *cheeup cheeup cheeup* raccoon sound back to our nest. He's curled up on his side. I crawl in, right in front of him.

"Cheeup," he says.

"Cheeup," I say.

"Cheeup."

"Cheeup."

It's cold. Joey snuggles in behind me. I think about getting Mom's sea lavender sweater so I can smell her, but the air's chilly and Joey's warm, pressed in behind me. He's breathing slow and steady, and the wind is a quiet shush, telling me to close my eyes and go to sleep.

I wake up with my heart pounding from a bad dream I can't remember. Joey's asleep, and I'm not a baby. I'm not going to wake him. A dream is a dream, and now I'm awake. I'm awake in the dark in our glass house, and everything is okay. Mom isn't here to say *All the bad dreams, go out of this house. Whoosh!* and wave her hands to scare the bad dreams away. All she is now is a cold, dark rock in my chest.

I have to pee, but I'm scared to stand up with my heart beating so hard. I take deep breaths and try to calm down. It's awful, pulling myself away from Joey's warmth and standing up, but I make myself do it.

Outside, it's quieter now. Just the crickets. Just the splash of my pee on the ground.

> *Starlight, star bright, first star I see*
> *   tonight.*
> *Wish I may, wish I might,*
> *Have the wish I wish tonight.*

I close my eyes and make my wish. I wish for the handsome man with the green eyes to take me for a ride on his swan boat.

⇔

A sound wakes me up. It's Joey, right outside the window, brushing his teeth. I'm really thirsty, but he's got the canteen of water jammed between his knees.

"Joey, I need some water."

He doesn't say anything, just keeps brushing.

"Joey!"

He still doesn't say anything, so I make myself get out of our warm nest and go outside. I can tell it's very early morning, because the light is the color of a ripe apricot and the birds are singing their heads off.

"I'm thirsty, Joey."

He pours some water into his mouth, rinses, and spits. He puts more toothpaste on his toothbrush, like he's getting ready to start brushing all over again.

"I'm such an idiot," he says. "A stupid idiot."

"No, you're not," I say. "Can I have some water?"

Joey hands me the canteen. "Pour it in. Don't put your mouth right on it," he says. "I can't believe what an idiot I am." He's walking back and forth, shaking his head.

I take a long drink of water. It's cold and tastes like metal. I drink some more.

"What an idiot! I didn't brush my teeth last night. I ate dinner and then went to bed. Do you know what happens if you don't brush your teeth? The bacteria eat your tooth enamel!"

"Well, you're brushing now," I say. "It's probably okay." I hand the canteen back to Joey.

"No, Chirp, it's not okay," Joey says. "The bacteria multiply, and they stick to your teeth and tongue. It's so disgusting."

"Gross."

"And there are tons of different kinds, sliming away all night long."

I want to go and get my toothbrush, but Joey grabs my arm.

"Don't you get it, Chirp? I know all about bacteria, and *still* I forgot to brush my teeth."

"I'll remind you," I say. I want Joey to let go of me so I can get my toothbrush.

"You don't get it!" Joey's yelling now. "If I'm so stupid, if I can forget something as important as brushing my teeth, how will I make it out here without my parents? You think I can just head home when I feel like it?" He sounds so mad he's scaring me. He's waving his toothbrush around.

"This is it for me. I can't go home. You think I can just walk in and say, 'Hi, Pop! Sorry. I'm home now'? You think he's gonna wrap his arms around me and say, 'Glad to see you, son'?"

Joey's asking me questions, but I know he doesn't want me to answer them.

"Joey?"

"Shut up." He's crying now. He's brushing his teeth really hard and crying really hard, and there's snot dripping out of his nose and toothpaste dribbling out of his mouth.

I don't know what to say. I don't know what to do. I sit down, because even though Joey's acting like he's mad at me, I don't think he wants me to leave him all alone. There's an ant dragging a white hunk of something through the sandy dirt. It's making the tiniest track. I can hear Joey sniffling and coughing and brushing, but I don't look up. I keep watching the ant. One thing I know is that you can keep someone company without ruining their privacy. While Joey rinses and spits, the ant takes a little breather, but then it gets going again. The white hunk it's dragging looks a lot like a grain of rice. I don't know why no other ants are pitching in to help. There are tons of ants just wandering around doing nothing while this guy is working up a sweat.

Ant-watching is okay but not nearly as exciting as bird-watching. I can hear all kinds of birds calling and fluttering and hopping around in the woods. To get a good look at all of the action, I need my binocs. I peek to see what's up with Joey. He's walking back to our house, taking huge steps like he's a giant. I wait until he's inside, and then I take baby steps to give him some more time to pull himself together. When I walk in, he's taking his clothes out of our nest, folding them carefully, and putting them in his duffel bag. His eyes are red, but he must have wiped his nose and mouth, since I can't see any snot or toothpaste anymore.

"Hey," Joey says in a quiet voice, "I'd like us to have a meeting."

"Okay."

"How about by the milkweed," he says. "Two minutes." He's rearranging his clothes in his duffel bag.

I grab my binocs out of my knapsack and run outside.

Tons of chickadees in the bushes. Warblers like to hang out with chickadees. It's still a little early in the season for them—they don't usually get here until May—but I can't help hoping I'll see one. Mom called yellow birds lemon drops. She'd say *Sure do love those lemon drops* when we'd see a warbler or goldfinch flash by. I love the way she'd make up names for things, like—

"Earth to Chirp, come in, Chirp," Joey says.

I put down my binocs.

"I'd like to call our meeting to order." Joey smacks a bunch of milkweed leaves on the ground, like he's the big boss, which is okay with me.

"Okay."

"Well," Joey says, "I think we need a plan. Agreed?"

"Yes."

"You're supposed to say *agreed*," Joey says.

"Agreed."

"I think I have a perfect plan. You like the swan boats, and I've never seen the swan boats. How about if we go see them today?"

"Agreed."

"You only have to say *agreed* when I say *agreed*, okay?"

I nod. I don't want to do anything to jinx our perfect plan.

"How are we going to get to Boston?" I ask.

"Bus. We can take the bus from in front of the general store. That's what Vinnie did."

"But Mrs. McCurdy knows us. She'll ask why we aren't in school. She won't sell us bus tickets."

"Yeah, but she'll probably sell them to just you. Maybe you can go into the store by yourself and buy two tickets."

Joey doesn't say it, but I know what he's thinking. The girl with the dead mother. The girl whose mom *drowned.* Everyone feels sorry for me.

"I guess I can say that they're for me and Rachel. I can say that my dad thinks we need a little break, so we're going to visit our aunt in Boston. You know, *My dad's just getting our suitcases out of the car.*"

"Mrs. McCurdy won't ask you a lot of questions," Joey says. "She won't give you a hard time."

We're all packed up in just a couple of minutes. We've only spent one night, but still, it's kind of sad, leaving our glass house.

"Should we make more sparkle before we go?" Joey asks. He's looking up through the broken windows. The sky isn't apricot now. It's gray blue, like the back and belly feathers of a great blue heron.

"Nah." Crashing glass doesn't feel right.

"What should we do?" Joey asks.

"Spit?"

"Perfect," Joey says. "Meet you in the middle." I walk to one side of the room and Joey walks to the other.

"On your mark, get set, go!" I say, and we both start taking big steps and counting them out loud. When we get to six, our toes are almost touching.

"Okay," Joey says. "About-face!" We turn so we're back-to-back. "One, two, three," and we both huck a nice, wet looey onto the dried-out plywood floor.

"Sayonara," I say, looking around at the broken windows and the cobwebs and our pile of mad glass in the corner and our two hucked looeys.

"Sayonara," Joey says. We pick up our stuff and head out.

It's hard to tell exactly what time it is. I'm pretty sure we're ahead of the school bus, but just to be safe, we follow the dirt paths and side roads and stay off Route 6 as much as we can until we're just about at the general store.

"I'm hungry," Joey says. "We didn't eat any break-fast, and eating breakfast is really important." His forehead is wrinkled, and I don't know if not eating breakfast is like not brushing his teeth and he's going to have another freak-out because he's scared that he doesn't know how to take care of himself.

"Guess what?" I say.

"What?"

272

"Pop-Tarts!"

"What kind should we get?" Joey's really excited.

"Strawberry? I'll get them when I get the bus tickets."

Joey starts singing *"Strawberry Pop-Tarts, here we come, right back where we started from!"* at the top of his lungs. Maybe I should shush him, since we're kind of like fugitives and shouldn't draw attention to ourselves, but I like the sound of his loud voice right next to me. I like that now he's swinging his duffel bag back and forth and kicking up sandy dirt as if he could walk forever.

"We're lucky it's not raining," I say.

Joey looks up at the blue sky.

"We're lucky it's not snowing," he says.

"We're lucky there isn't a meteor speeding right toward us."

"Or an atom bomb that would blow us up into smithereens."

The wind smells like wet grass. All we have to do is walk down a little hill and past the bait shop, and then we're at the general store.

"Maybe you should wait here," I say.

"It's against the law to skip school, you know," Joey says. "We're criminal elements."

"How's that different from just plain old criminals?"

"I have no idea," Joey says.

I get my money and then hand my knapsack to him to hold.

"What if she wants to talk to my dad?"

"She won't want to."

There's no one in the store. Mrs. McCurdy isn't even at the cash register. I walk down the aisles, looking for the Pop-Tarts. It's tricky figuring out how to look old enough that I could be trusted to buy bus tickets to Boston by myself but still sad enough that no one will bug me. I can't stand too straight and tall, because that isn't what sad looks like. It isn't what sad feels like, either. Sad is a huge rock on your head that pushes you down. Sad is wishing you could crawl on the ground like a black beetle.

The Pop-Tarts are near the cereal. I grab Brown Sugar Cinnamon, too, to surprise Joey and help keep his spirits up. Two boxes of Pop-Tarts. And a bottle of apple juice. I hear a door slam in the back, and then footsteps.

By the time I get up to the cash register, there's a man there. He's skinny and has pimples and scraggly black hair, and I don't think I've ever seen him before. He doesn't even say hello or ask if that's everything, like Mrs. McCurdy. He just rings up the Pop-Tarts and apple juice and sticks his hand out for money, so I give him the twenty-dollar bill.

"I'd also like two bus tickets to Boston," I say when he hands me the change.

"Round-trip?" He sounds irritated.

I'm not sure what that means, so I just shake my head.

"Two one-way tickets to Boston," he mumbles to himself, and pulls out a little booklet of tickets and rips two out. "Ten dollars," he says. I hand him a ten-dollar bill. He hands me two tickets. That's all there is to it. Easy-peasy. I'm reaching for the door handle. I want to show Joey the tickets. I want to eat a strawberry Pop-Tart and then a brown sugar–cinnamon Pop-Tart, which is absolutely not the kind of breakfast Orensteins ever eat.

"Hey, kid!" the man yells from behind the counter.

My heart starts racing like it did in my bad dream. Is he going to run over and pin my hands behind my back and call the police? I don't want to not go to Boston. I don't want to not see the swan boats. I don't want to have to come up with another perfect plan.

"Don't get off in Hyannis," he yells. "Just stay on the bus until you get to Boston."

"Okay!" I yell, and let the door slam closed.

"What time's the bus coming?" Joey asks. We've each just eaten two Pop-Tarts. Joey wants another, but I think we should wait, because if there's anything I've learned, it's that you never have a clue what's going to happen next, and I don't want to be caught off guard with not enough Pop-Tarts. The bus could break down on a deserted road, and we could be stranded for days with just our carrots and the tiny bit of pita and cheese that's left.

"Chirp, I asked you a question."

"I don't know."

"You didn't ask what time the bus is coming?" Joey's voice is all squeaky, like he just can't believe it, like I've got to be the stupidest girl on the planet.

"It doesn't matter," I say. "We still have to sit here on this bench until it gets here."

"Well, it would be *helpful* to know what time it's arriving," he says, all snotty.

"We don't even have a watch," I say. I look up at the sky and pretend that Joey isn't here. *Vanished. Poof.* What's here is the bluest sky, with two herring gulls circling and a flock of red-winged blackbirds shooting by and a wind that smells like wet grass and a brown paper bag sitting on my lap that's packed with two almost-full boxes of Pop-Tarts and a bottle of apple juice.

There's not even time for Joey to notice that I've vanished him when the bus roars up. It's much, much louder and bigger than our school bus. The driver just takes our tickets. He doesn't say a word. He must figure that the ticket seller checked out our story. When the door closes behind us, my heart squeezes tight, and I grab Joey's hand before I even realize what I'm doing.

"Cowabunga," he says, and doesn't pull his hand away.

"Bowacunga," I whisper, because suddenly there's a rock in my throat.

The bus is almost empty. Just two guys in the back in hard hats and a lady sleeping with her head against the window, with red lipstick smeared around her mouth and her blond hair all poofed up. There's a dark line from her eye to the middle of her cheek that looks like she cried a big black tear.

Suddenly I'm not sure I can make it to a seat. A rock on my head is pushing me down. My legs are crumpling, like I've landed a leap wrong.

"Joey?"

"C'mon," he says, and shoves me into a seat across the aisle from the black-tear lady. He climbs over me, sits down, and the driver takes off. I don't even ask Joey, I just lean my head against his shoulder. He touches my hair. This should be a big adventure, alone on a bus with Joey, heading to Boston. I should want to pay close attention to everything. I should want to look out the window and not miss a beat. But my rocks are weighing me down. I close my eyes. The noise of the bus is swirling green water, spinning whirlpools of almost-black green.

When I wake up, my face is pressed against Joey's neck. It's soft and warm and smells like hay. I keep my eyes closed an extra minute so I can keep sniffing, and then I sit up.

"I missed Hyannis?"

"We're almost to the Sagamore Bridge. I just saw a sign," Joey says.

There are all kinds of people on the bus now. I look around. Two men with matching black eyeglasses and flabby faces talking to each other. A pretty lady with skin the color of coffee with cream reading a book and chewing gum. An old Chinese lady with wrinkly skin, snoozing with her head against the window.

"Too many people," I say.

Joey looks at me. "What do you mean?" he says. "You've got tons of room."

I can't explain it. Even though Joey's right, I feel crowded. I don't want all of these people on the bus. I don't want them talking and reading and chewing gum and sleeping.

"I wish I could throw them off," I say.

Joey just stares at me.

The bus is pulling onto the bridge.

People on the bus. People on other buses. People in their houses. People in their cars. People going to work. People cooking dinner.

"Wow," Joey says, looking out the window. "The Cape Cod Canal. See the boats?"

What I see is the water. The dark blue stripe of cold water.

"The boats are cool," Joey says.

I nod. I don't tell him what I'm seeing now. All the people pushed into the water. The pretty lady. The two flabby men. The bus driver. The Chinese lady. The black-tear lady. Flapping their arms. Yelling. They make white splash. They scream for help. No one hears them.

"Are you okay?" Joey asks.

They're sinking down. They're disappearing.

"Chirp?"

"No," I say, "I'm not."

Joey hands me a brown sugar–cinnamon Pop-Tart. I scrape the hard white frosting off with my front teeth. The sweet feels good in my throat. As soon as I eat the Pop-Tart, Joey hands me another. Then another. Then another.

CHAPTER FOURTEEN

"Is this where we get off?" Joey asks. "South Station?"

I look out the window. Pavement. Train tracks. Parked buses. Cars whizzing by. Nothing looks familiar.

"I'm not sure," I say. Where's the green grass? The last time we were here, I remember people throwing Frisbees. A pretzel vendor on the corner. A hippie girl in a long purple skirt playing the guitar under a tree next to a man with frizzy red hair who banged on a bongo drum but not to the beat. Mom and I walked through Boston Common and came to a garden with tulips and fluffy pink peonies. And then the pond with the ducks and geese following behind the white swan boats, where we met the handsome boat man with green eyes.

"You *have* to be sure," Joey says. "If this is it, we need to hurry up and get off!"

"Ask somebody," I say. The Chinese lady is in front of me, and the black-tear lady is across the aisle. I just pushed them into the water. I just watched them disappear. I didn't want to help them. I can't ask *them* for help.

"Excuse me," Joey says to the Chinese lady through the space between the seats, but he's too late. The bus has started up again.

"Shoot," Joey says, staring out the window. "What if we just totally screwed up? We should have asked the name of the stop. I just thought we got off in *Boston.* How was I supposed to know that there's more than one stop? I can't believe this! What if—"

"Can I help you kids?" It's the black-tear lady. She's leaning across the aisle. She's smiling at us. Her voice is really deep.

"Is this where we get off for the swan boats?" Joey asks.

"Boston Common," I say. "We're meeting our aunt and uncle in Boston Common."

"Next stop," she says. "You're fine. It'll just be a few more minutes." She's got a bit of a mustache, which looks kind of strange on a lady. And really big hands.

"Thanks a lot," I say.

"I love the swan boats," she says in her deep voice. "I've been riding them since I was little."

"I love them, too," I say. "My mom and I used to ride them together when we'd come to Boston."

She's waiting for me to say something else.

"This time it's just me and my brother, just the two of us, to see our aunt and uncle. We want them to take us on the swan boats," I say.

"Okay," she says. "Just you two this time."

"That's right," I say. I don't like lying to her.

"Okay, honey," she says. "Anything else you want to tell me?" She's playing with her hair, floofing it up with her fingertips and patting it back down again, as if she's not that interested in my answer even though I think she is.

"Did you know that a female swan is called a pen? Most people don't know that," I say.

"Nope, that's new information to me." She's looking right into my eyes, but gently.

"I know a lot about birds," I say. "They're kind of my hobby. I read about them and I watch them."

"That's great," she says. "It's important to pay attention to what's going on around you. Especially when you're traveling without a grown-up."

"Oh, my aunt and uncle will meet us in Boston Common," I say. "They're very excited that we're coming to visit. They have all kinds of special things planned for us. And anyway, I'm pretty mature for my age."

She nods. "Sometimes, when I was a kid, I'd pretend the swan boat was a real swan that could read my thoughts. Being a kid was kind of rough some-times."

I can't tell her everything, but at least I can tell her something. "The last time my mom and I were here, the swan boat driver was super nice, and he said he bet my mom was a beautiful dancer and that we should come back someday and visit him."

She doesn't say anything. She just looks at me like it's still my turn to talk. When I don't say anything, she says, "I've got to ask you something. Is everything okay, little sister? Anything I can do to help?"

I can't think of one thing to say. There's a sad hunk of quiet between us. Finally she says, "Okay, then. If you're not going to tell me something, I'll tell *you* something. When I was a kid, I really wanted to be a swan boat driver when I grew up. I thought ped-aling that boat around the lagoon under the weeping willows, with the ducks and geese swimming along, would be the most wonderful way to spend my days. All of the tourists from around the world asking me questions. And the kids, out on the water, getting just a little bit of peace for a change."

"Well, then, how come you aren't one?" I ask.

She looks at me, shakes her head, and lets out a laugh so low and bubbling I can't help laughing, too.

"Let's just say that life took me in a different direc-tion, honey," she says.

"Life does that, I guess," I say, and she cracks up, like that's the funniest thing she's ever heard.

"You're one smart cookie," she says. "A philosopher. Don't let anyone keep you down, you hear me?"

I nod and smile. She has the nicest smile I've ever seen, even with her messed-up lipstick.

Joey's staring at her. "Are you a—"

"How about you don't ask me the question you want to ask me, and I'll keep my burning question about you two to myself?" she whispers, like we're in a secret club together.

I have no idea what Joey wants to ask her, but I'm pretty sure what she wants to ask us.

"That's fine," I say, poking Joey.

"Absolutely," he says, turning red and looking away.

I don't know if Joey's upset her, but I give her a smile, just in case, and she smiles her beautiful smile and touches her hand to her heart. I want to keep talking with her, but she leans back in her seat and closes her eyes.

"What did you want to ask her?" I ask Joey.

He just shrugs. "Nothing," he says, leaning forward to take another peek at her. He pulls *From the Mixed-Up Files of Mrs. Basil E. Frankweiler* out of his duffel bag. "I think I need to learn more about city life." Joey opens the book. "Pick up some tips and stuff."

"Park Square!" the driver yells. We jump up.

Joey didn't get to read even one sentence.

I feel a hand on my arm.

"Listen, you be careful, little sister," the black-tear lady says. "There are all kinds of crazies out there. You need to take good care of yourself."

"C'mon, hurry up!" Joey's pushing my knapsack, trying to shove me down the aisle.

"Don't worry, lady," I say, and then I surprise myself. I bend down so low that I can see the makeup stuck in the crinkles near her eyes. And I kiss her cheek, right on the black line where her black tear must have rolled down.

"Where's everybody going?" Joey asks.

We're standing on the sidewalk, and people are streaming past us. Ladies with shopping bags from Filene's Basement and Jordan Marsh. Men with brief-cases in one hand and cups of coffee in the other. A guy with no hair, playing tiny cymbals and wearing a twisted-up sheet the color of a Creamsicle. There's a steady wind and lots of hair is blowing.

"This is what it's like here," I say. "Everybody's just doing their thing."

"Well, it's loud and smells bad, and I don't think you know where we are," Joey says.

"Yes, I do. I know exactly where we are." I watch a lady rummaging around in a garbage can. When I realize who it is, my heart starts racing. It's her; it's the marsh lady! She must have taken a bus here, too, or maybe she hitchhiked the whole way. But when she stands up with a wrinkled Burger King bag in her hand, I see that it's just some other wrinkly lady with snarly hair, wearing a lumpy green jacket.

"There's the Pewter Pot," I say to Joey, pointing across the street. I remember Mom bought me a chocolate-chip muffin and a mug of cocoa to warm me up after our swan boat ride. "Now all we have to do is cross *that* street and we're in Boston Common."

"We're not lost?" Joey says. "You know how to get to the swan boats?" He sounds like he's just about to cry.

"Right there is Park Street Station. That's a T stop. Once we cross the street, we're in Boston Common."

"Cross the street?" Joey says. "Here? The cars aren't even stopping."

I look at him. His lip is trembling and his eyes are darting back and forth, watching the cars and the people dashing out in front of them.

"Listen, Joey. I've been to Boston, like, five times. I'm practically a city girl. All we have to do is cross with all of the other people when we get the walk light."

"Yeah, and we can all get killed together. No one's paying attention to the light. This was a stupid idea. I'm not crossing the street. I'm staying here." Joey folds his arms tight in front of himself and looks down at the ground.

"You can't stay here. We didn't come all this way to just stand on the sidewalk."

"Well, I'm not going. You can't make me."

I take a step closer to Joey. I'm so close I can smell the sun in his hair. "Listen to me," I say. "Right across the street is Boston Common. And right across Boston Common is the Boston Public Garden, where the swan boats are. And at the swan boats is this really great guy who asked me and my mom to come visit again. Well, my mom can't do it, she just can't, and you know why, but I can and you can and we're going to!"

Joey takes a deep breath. He looks at me. Then he nods and sticks out his hand. "You win," he says.

"Good." I grab Joey's sweaty hand and steer us right next to a delivery guy who's wheeling three big cardboard boxes. When he steps off the curb, we do, too. We try to stay right next to him so that his boxes are our shield, but he's moving too fast, especially with Joey lugging his duffel bag, and people coming toward us keep bumping us backward.

"Holy mother of God!" Joey shrieks as a car cuts right in front of us.

"Just keep going," I tell him. "We're almost there."

"Like I have a choice," Joey says, just as a lady comes up behind me and whumps me in the leg with a shopping bag and doesn't even say excuse me.

"We made it!" Joey says when we step up on the curb on the other side. "That was nuts! You owe me."

"You're nuts," I say.

"Takes one to know one," Joey says. He smiles at me, and it makes me want to touch his hair. Instead,

I stick my arm out, like I'm Carol Merrill standing in front of the curtain on *Let's Make a Deal*.

"*This* is Boston Common." I know it's crazy, but I want the Common to look exactly the same as the last time I was here.

"See, a pretzel vendor!" I say, pointing. "You can buy a pretzel for fifty cents, and they warm it up for you over a little fire. You squirt mustard on it from a bottle."

"It doesn't seem very clean," Joey says, looking at the pretzels dangling on a metal rod and the greasy spots on the plastic cart.

"Well, they taste really good," I say. "Great, actually." When Mom and I were here, she bought one for us. She held a warm pretzel out to me and said, "Most people don't know that pretzels were the original wishbones!" We both pulled and I got the knot, and Mom laughed and said that she hoped I made a really great wish, because she had a hunch it would come true.

"Definitely not very hygienic," Joey says.

"So that means you won't split one with me?"

"Heck, no, I won't go," Joey says.

I get fifty cents out of my knapsack, since the pretzel vendor looks grumpy and I don't want to make him wait while I fish around for it.

"One pretzel, please," I say, holding out the money.

He grabs it and hands me a pretzel and the mustard squirt bottle without saying anything.

"Gross," Joey says when he sees the crusty brown gunk stuck around the opening of the bottle.

I walk to the nearest bench, take a bite of the warm pretzel, and close my eyes like I'm in heaven, but the truth is that I'm really disappointed that Joey wouldn't split it with me so I could do the wishbone trick just like last time, and my eyes are closed because I'm scared I might cry. I take my sweet time eating the pretzel. With my eyes closed, I hear pigeons cooing. I hear people walking by. I hear wind blowing past my ears. I hear a drum. Maybe it's the man with the red hair who was with the hippie girl in the purple skirt. I want to hear her play her hippie songs. Last time, Mom and I were in a hurry to meet Dad and Rachel and had to rush right by her.

"C'mon," I say, opening my eyes and looking around. Joey pretends he doesn't hear me because he's fascinated by a tree trunk, but I don't care. I'll find the guitar lady. She probably knows all of the cool songs, like "Blowin' in the Wind" and "Where Have All the Flowers Gone?" Hippies don't mind if you sing along. She'll probably like it if I do a dance interpretation with lots of leaps and help her get more money in her hat.

I follow the sound of the drum. Joey's walking behind me, not next to me, which is the perfect place for him to be if he's going to be such a lousy sport. First I'll find the hippie girl, and then I'll find the dark-haired, green-eyed swan boat driver and say *See, I'm back!* and he'll be so happy and Joey can just tag along behind me like a baby.

"Hey, girlie," an old man in a dark jacket sitting on a bench yells, "do you know how to catch a squirrel?"

Why would I want to catch a squirrel?

I shake my head and keep walking.

"Pull down your pants and show him your nuts," he yells. My face is burning hot, even though I don't really get it. Some other man says, "For Christ's sake, Sal, leave the kid alone!" My heart's racing, because there are lots of benches with old men in dark jackets sitting on them, and unless I want to step over the black chain fence and get off the path, I have to walk right in front of them all.

"Joey!" I yell, but I don't need to, because he's already catching up to me.

"Hey," he says.

"Hey."

He does a little hitch step so that our left legs are stepping forward at the same time, which is something that usually only girls do. We walk together, perfectly in step, past a dogwood with its creamy white flowers and two leafy elms, and I start to feel better.

"That'll be my brothers someday," Joey says.

"What?"

"Vinnie and Donny, sitting on a bench, yelling stupid things."

I shake my head, not because he's wrong but because I don't want to think about home.

"*No,* what?" Joey says.

"Talking about you-know-where."

"They're probably really worried about you. They maybe even called the police."

"We're fine," I say. Police? I didn't think of that. Dad having to talk to the police. Again. And Rachel. I wonder if she's a mess.

"We know we're fine, but they don't," Joey says.

"Stop," I say. "Please."

Joey sighs and shrugs, but he doesn't say anything.

A fat gray squirrel runs right in front of us, then stops, like he's playing freeze tag. It's as if he wants to hear whatever we're going to say next.

"Come on. If we find the drum, we'll find the hippie girl playing her guitar. I bet she'll be cool. Last time she was wearing a purple skirt. I bet she can really play."

Joey points to a little hill. We step over the black chain, cut across some grass, and climb it. At the bottom, under a cherry tree just busted out in pink blooms, is the drummer. He doesn't have red hair. He isn't playing a bongo drum.

"It isn't him," I say. My throat hurts. Why isn't anything the same?

"Well, we can listen to him if you want to. He sounds pretty good." Joey starts drumming along on his duffel bag. The drummer is skinny with frizzy black hair. He's hitting a white bucket with drumsticks.

Joey's trying to be nice to me, but he doesn't get it.

"I don't want to listen to any old drummer," I say. "I was looking for a *specific* drummer, because I wanted to hear the hippie girl play her guitar. She had on a pretty purple skirt. I really wanted to see her again."

"Well, that's not why we're here anyway, is it?" Joey says. "That's not why we spent ten dollars and rode a bus all the way from the Cape, is it?"

He's right. The dark-haired driver with green eyes. He'll be so surprised to see me! He'll probably give me a hug and take us out in his swan boat all by ourselves. Just me and Joey and him. I'll watch the ducks and geese with my binocs and maybe even get to see a pair of swans. And when I walk on the dock after the windy ride, my cheeks will be pink like the cherry blooms and everyone will think *What a beautiful girl!*

"Cowabunga!" Joey yells, and starts running down the hill, his duffel bag in front of him thunking him on his knees.

"Bowacunga!" I yell, and run after him.

We run and run all the way across the Common until we get to Charles Street. Before Joey has a chance to freak out, I take his hand and we run across the street together and it's not nearly as bad as last time.

"Wait," I say, stopping in front of the black iron gate. I take off my knapsack and stand still, catching my breath. I don't want to walk into the Boston

Public Garden panting and sweaty. I don't want my dark-haired friend to feel disappointed when he finally sees me after all of this time. I try to run my fingers through my curls to get some of the tangles out. There's a lady with long, shiny, perfect blond hair watching me, and I wonder if she's thinking that I should have used Johnson's No More Tangles to make my hair more manageable.

"Here," Joey says. He's reaching into his duffel bag. "You can have your own." He hands me a moistened towelette still in its wrapper.

Wiping my face feels as good as sticking it in front of a fan on high in the middle of August.

"Ah, a taste of civilization," Joey says, wiping his face, too.

"Ah, civilization."

"Can I have some apple juice?"

I hand Joey the bottle. He pours juice into his mouth without letting his lips touch the rim. His hair's all flattened and wild, like a patch of dried-out weeds after a dog's rolled around in it. I slowly reach my hand toward Joey's head, and he doesn't pull away. His hair is soft and beautiful. I don't even try to get the tangles out. I just run my hand over it really slowly, because it feels so good, and Joey closes his eyes and smiles.

The lady's still staring at us. She's wearing an orange pantsuit the color of Tang. I poke Joey, and he opens his eyes.

"Look," I say, glancing at the lady.

Before I can say anything else, Joey hands me the bottle of apple juice, picks up his duffel bag, grabs my hand, and starts walking fast, tugging me along.

"C'mon, Marcia," he says in a loud voice, just as we pass the lady. "We have to catch up to Aunt Betty. She hates when we make her wait." I scurry to keep up with him as he turns the corner and keeps walking down the sidewalk, dodging all of the people coming toward us with briefcases and baby strollers and shopping bags.

"Don't turn around yet," Joey says.

"Marcia," I say, trying not to giggle.

"Marcia," he says.

When we've rounded the next corner, Joey stops, puts down his duffel bag, and leans against a skinny tree. "I think the coast is clear. But let's just wait here for a few minutes."

"Marcia?" I ask, cracking up.

"It's the first thing I thought of," Joey says, laughing, too. "Maybe because of Marcia in *The Brady Bunch.*"

"I can't stand her," I say. "She's bossy and tattles and—"

"Okay. Next time, I'll call you Scarlett."

"Next time?" I haven't thought about the fact that now we're actually runaways who could get caught.

"Don't worry," Joey says.

I must look worried. Would we have to go to the police station? Would they lock us up in a cell until our dads come to pick us up?

"What do you think will happen if we get caught?"

"I don't want to think about it," Joey says.

"I guess they'd call our parents and tell them that—"

"I don't want to talk about it."

"But, Joey—"

"I mean it, Chirp," Joey says. "Don't talk to me about it!" He picks up his duffel bag and starts walking fast, away from me.

I catch up with him. "I like the name Scarlett."

Joey doesn't say anything.

"A lot."

Still nothing.

"Thanks for the getaway," I say. "It was smart thinking."

Joey looks at me and smiles just a little. "Never fear, Joey's here," he mumbles, and I can tell that he's not mad anymore that I made him think about stuff he doesn't want to think about.

When we get back to the black gate, the Tang lady is gone.

"Time for the swan boats," I say.

"One small step for man," Joey says.

"Quack," I say.

"Wacko," he says.

We walk through the black gate together.

"Wow!" we say at the same time. On our left is a huge rectangle of red tulips. On our right is a huge rectangle of yellow daffodils. They're so bright I want to eat them.

"I guess spring has sprung," Joey says.

"I guess so," I say.

Now that we're almost to the swan boats, I suddenly don't want to get there. The pond is in front of us, and my stomach's all jumpy.

"Hold on," I say, and pull my binocs out of my knapsack. "Do you know the difference between a starling and a grackle?"

"A what and a what?"

"They're both in the blackbird family. People confuse them all the time."

Joey's staring at me. "Don't you want to get to the swan boats? Don't you want to hurry up and see your friend? Maybe after he gives us a ride on the swan boat, we can find a library where we can do research and figure out our next move, which place we want to visit next."

I'm already sitting on a bench under a magnolia tree. The dark red buds are just beginning to open.

"Since I schlepped my binocs all this way, I figure I should use them. I'm offering you a free bird-watching lesson." I look over in the direction of the swan boats. I can't see if he's there.

"I want to ride a swan boat," Joey says. "I want to meet your friend."

"Well, first I'm going to do a little bird-watching," I say. My voice sounds weak, like I'm hiding something.

Joey rolls his eyes, but he plops down on the bench. "My brother says that chicks are crazy," he mumbles.

"Grackles and starlings sometimes hang out together, and they're similar because they're noisy and aggressive. And they walk instead of hop. But the starling has purple and green mixed in on its back. The grackle just has green."

"Okay," Joey says.

"And the grackle is bigger."

"Okay."

"I don't see any right now. Just pigeons and robins."

"Well, take your time," Joey says. "I can sit here all day." He starts whistling.

I keep looking through the binocs. No grackles. No starlings. No sparrows. No chickadees. It's like all the birds are hiding.

"*She* must be going to the swan boats," Joey says. A little girl with curly dark hair and a pink party dress is tugging on her mother's hand and quacking.

"I was about her age when I first came here," I say.

"I was about *my* age when I first came here." Joey

stands up and looks at me. "C'mon," he says, "quit stalling. Let's go." He grabs my hands and pulls me up.

Now that we're on our way, I'm so excited I can't stop talking.

"I don't think we need to bother getting tickets," I say. "My friend will just let us on, I think. I mean, maybe it's against the rules and he can't, but I bet he'll want to."

"Okay," Joey says. "I don't mind saving money. Maybe we'll get ice cream later on our way to the library."

"He reminds me of Bert in *Mary Poppins*. He's really friendly." I could tell Mom really liked him, and he liked her. "He's probably a good dancer. He looked like a good dancer."

"Uh-huh."

"He wanted us to come back. He really wanted to see us again." I don't think I'll have to tell him about Mom. He'll probably just know. Maybe when we're drifting past the weeping willow trees, he'll get a strange feeling. He'll just look at me and know.

"Whoa," Joey says.

Suddenly, out of nowhere, little kids are buzzing past us like a swarm of bees. Grown-ups are racing after them, yelling at them to slow down.

"I guess it's a field trip," I say.

"First graders," Joey says. "Second graders, tops."

I hadn't pictured other people around. Just me and Joey and him.

I hope we won't have to share our boat. I hope we can float along quietly under the willow trees, just the three of us.

"Cool!" Joey says. He's stopped walking. He's staring at the water.

The boats are lined up at the dock. The swans at the back of the boats where the drivers sit are so white and shiny it's like looking at snow in the sun. I squint into all the whiteness. It's so bright I can't see.

"Where is he?" Joey asks.

"I don't know."

"C'mon, let's get closer," Joey says, and since I don't know what else to do, I follow him. We walk past the schoolkids, who are sitting in a circle on the grass getting talked at by their teacher, and down to the water. Two guys in white shirts and blue caps are standing on the dock next to the swan boats with their backs to us. I can see the red beaks of the swans above their heads.

"Swan boat drivers," I whisper. "It's *them*." My heart's thumping in my chest.

"Say hi," Joey says. "They'll turn around, and if one of them is him, you can surprise him."

I shake my head. I don't think I can talk.

"The kids are lining up," Joey says. "I think they're coming over. You should say something before they get here." I look. Joey's right. They're standing in two perfect lines, like the girls in the Madeline books. They must have been yelled at.

"Hi," I say. My voice is just a little squeak. The drivers don't hear me.

"Hurry up," Joey says. "The kids are coming."

"Hi," I say again, louder.

They turn around. The one on the left is blond with crooked teeth, but on the right, it's him! Dark, wavy hair. Light-green eyes. Super handsome.

"You need to buy tickets from the ticket seller," he says, pointing to the booth.

"Hi," I say, smiling. I'm so happy to see him.

"Do you have your tickets?"

"No."

"Okay," he says. "Once you get your tickets, over there, you can get on the boat." He smiles at me, then turns back to the other driver, like he's about to ask him something.

"Wait," I say. "Remember me?"

"Let's see," he says, wrinkling up his forehead, like he's thinking really hard, "did I give you a ride before?"

"Remember?" I say. "It was last spring. I was here with my mother."

"Oh?" he says. "Last spring? Well, welcome back." He takes off his cap and runs his hands through his hair.

"I think you've got another admirer, buddy," the

blond driver says. "And her mother." He laughs. My dark-haired friend punches him in the arm like it's a funny joke and then puts his cap back on and starts to walk away.

"Wait!" I say, following him. "You said we should come back to see you! You said you bet she was a beautiful dancer!"

"Okay," he says, stopping. "Well, I'm glad to see you again. And I'm sure she *is* a beautiful dancer."

"How can you not remember?" My face feels warm.

"Listen, sorry to disappoint you, but I've got to get back to work now." He points at the boat.

"No," I say. "We came all the way from the Cape to see you. You have to remember her!"

He lifts his eyebrows up like *What's her problem?* to the blond driver.

"Hey," he says, "we take tons of people out on rides. Girls and boys and mothers and grandfathers and aunts and—"

"No dogs," the blond driver says.

"Or gorillas," my friend says, grinning.

"This isn't funny," I say. "Look, we were the only ones on the boat except for an old lady. It was windy and our hair was blowing around and you—"

"Okay, kid, maybe you should just calm down." He looks at the blond driver like he needs help.

"No!" I yell. "You can't do this!" My ears are burning hot.

"He's not doing anything," the blond driver says, stepping toward me. "You're the one who's yelling at him. Either get your ticket or leave."

"You can't not remember her! She was beautiful, and you thought so, too!"

Joey puts his hand on my arm, but I shake it off.

"You can't do this! You have to remember her! You have to remember us!"

My dark-haired friend's looking at me like I'm crazy. He's bouncing on his toes like he's about to sprint away.

"You can't forget us! You can't!" I'm screaming so loud it hurts. I'll hit him. I'll throw him in the water and watch him sink.

"Okay, this is insane," he says, and he's walking away from me like *I'm* the bad guy. I try to follow him, but Joey's grabbing both my wrists.

"No! No! No!" I'm kicking Joey's leg. I'm kicking his duffel bag. I'm screaming.

Joey's hands are on my wrists. Joey's voice is in my ears. *Chirp. Stop. Chirp. Come.* He's stronger than me. He's pulling me past the little kids. He's pulling me past the ticket booth. Everyone's watching.

Joey's arms are around me. I'm sobbing on his neck. I can't stop.

I hear a woman ask, "What's going on here, honey?" I hear Joey say, "My sister gets like this sometimes. I'm the only one who can calm her down. Our babysitter's just waiting right over there by the water fountain. But thanks for asking."

Joey pulls me down onto the grass. *Mommy. Mommy. Mom.* Tears on my face. Tears in my mouth. Tears in my ears. She was a beautiful dancer. We loved the swan boats. The wind blew our hair. I'll never stop crying.

We're standing near a pay phone on the street. I cried all the way through the Boston Public Garden and the Common. I'm still crying. I can't stop.

"Listen," Joey says. "A change of plans. We're not going to the library. We're not doing any research about where to go next. You're going to call your father. You need to call him *now*. What's your phone number?"

I tell Joey my phone number.

"We have to add the area code," he says. "Don't worry. I know it. Five. Oh. Eight. We'll call collect." He puts in a dime. He talks to the operator. He hands me the phone.

"Say *hello*," Joey says.

"Chirp? Are you there?"

It's Daddy.

"Chirpie? Honey? Are you there?"

It's hard to breathe. I'm gulping in air. My nose is dripping. My shoulders are shaking.

303

"Chirp?"

Daddy's so worried. I have to say something. Joey's watching me.

"Daddy." My voice is tiny.

"Oh, my God! Honey, are you okay?"

I nod.

"You're crying, honey."

"I'll stop soon," I say. I take a slow, raggedy breath. The air feels good.

Joey taps my shoulder and waves. He walks away and leans against a building to give me my privacy.

"Talk to me, sweetheart. Tell me anything."

I take another slow breath. I'm finally not crying.

"The swan boat driver forgot us," I say.

"Swan boat driver? What do you mean, honey?"

"He didn't remember."

"Remember what?"

"Me and Mom. He forgot us." I start crying again, quiet, sad, worn-out tears.

"Oh, sweetheart, you're not in Boston, are you? How could you be in Boston?"

"We took the bus."

"You took the bus to Boston? You and Joey took the bus to Boston and are there now?"

"Yes."

"Oh, God. Oh, my God. You're okay?"

"I'm tired."

"We were praying you'd come home any minute now, you'd come home in time for dinner."

I picture our dinner table set with just two plates; one for Dad and one for Rachel. No Mom. No me. My heart fills up with wet sand.

"Oh, Daddy!"

"Chirpie, where are you, exactly? Are you near the swan boats?"

"Yes."

"Listen," Daddy says, "I'm going to be there in less than two hours. I'm going to hop in the car the minute we hang up the phone and get there as fast as I can. This is what I want you to do. Are you listening?"

"Yes."

"Do you remember the Pewter Pot, where Mom took you? I want you two to go there now and wait for me, okay? If anyone asks what you're doing, you say you're waiting for your father to come pick you up. That's what you say to anyone at all who asks, that your father will be there very soon to pick you up. Okay?"

"Okay, Dad."

"Do you have any money?"

"I took your emergency money out of your drawer. Sorry, Daddy."

"You buy yourself and Joey a snack at Pewter Pot, anything you want, and I'll be right there."

"Dad?"

"What?"

"Joey's father's going to kill him."

Dad's quiet. I hear him breathe. "No, Chirp. No

one's going to hurt Joey. You tell him that. You tell him that I promise."

"Okay."

"See you very soon, honey. Get yourselves right on over to Pewter Pot, and I'll be there soon."

"Okay."

"Bye, honey."

"Bye, Dad."

When I look back to the spot where Joey was, I don't see him. He's not leaning against the building, waiting for me. He's not facing in my direction, watching to make sure I'm okay. "Joey!" I run over to where he had been standing. But he's not standing; he's crouched down low. It's like his legs crumpled up underneath him and he slid down the wall. He's huddled up in a ball. He isn't moving. He's like a round gray rock. I bend down just as he lifts his head up. "I guess we're going home now," he says, in just about the saddest voice I've ever heard.

Our waitress's name is Sandy Lynn, and she's chubby and old and wearing a yellow dress with puffy sleeves and a white ruffly apron and bonnet, and I wonder how she feels, dressed like a colonial lady and serving people Tab and ham-and-cheese sandwiches in 1973. She already brought us glasses of water with ice and asked us what the heck we're doing alone in the middle of downtown Boston, and I told her, just like I'm supposed to, that we're waiting for my father to pick us up and he's coming very soon. Now she's giving us a minute to take a look at the menu.

"It feels good to be inside," Joey says.

He's right. It's kind of dark in here since they didn't have electricity in colonial days, so Pewter Pot doesn't use bright lightbulbs. It makes it cozy and feels good on my cried-out eyes.

"My dad said we should get anything we want," I say. I already know what I want. Two chocolate-chip muffins and a mug of hot cocoa.

"Spaghetti and meatballs," Joey says.

The wallpaper is flowery, like at Grandma and Grandpa's house. If this was their house, I'd walk into the bedroom at the end of the hall and crawl into the bed with the lavender comforter and all the fluffy pillows and go to sleep for a long, long time.

"Did your dad say anything about my parents?" Joey asks.

"He said your dad isn't going to kill you."

"What?"

"I told him that your dad is going to kill you, but he said that he isn't. He said to tell you that he promises that no one is going to hurt you."

Joey pokes the pink packets of Sweet'N Low with his finger. "Like the headshrinker could stop him," he mumbles.

"What?" I say, even though I heard him.

"Grown-ups just do what they want," Joey says.

"No one can stop them once they decide on something. Like your mother."

I haven't thought about that. I've only thought about Mom alive and thought about her in the hole in the ground but not about the steps in between. I haven't thought about her deciding to drive to the pond or get out of the car or walk into the water. I haven't thought about how it is she could drown if she was such a good swimmer. Or if she stopped to watch blue damselflies or ripples in the water before she went under.

"So do the two adventurers know what they want yet?" Sandy Lynn is back.

"Two chocolate-chip muffins and a hot cocoa for me, please," I say.

"I'd like spaghetti and meatballs," Joey says. "And lots of cheese, please."

"Coming right up," Sandy Lynn says, and then she smiles and walks away while she's still writing our orders down on her pad of paper.

"Can I ask you something?" Joey's never asked me if he can ask me a question before, so I figure it must be important.

I shrug. I don't want to think anymore about Mom's drowning day. I don't want Joey to ask me if she was wearing her bathing suit or if she hung her jacket on a pine tree before she walked into the water. I don't want him to ask me if her shoes were on or off. I look at Joey, and he looks back at me.

"Never mind," he says. He puts his hand on top of my hand. He starts whistling the theme song from *I Dream of Jeannie.*

Sandy Lynn clunks our food down on the table. Some of my hot cocoa sloshes onto the saucer, but I'll slurp it up as soon as she walks away.

"You two should wash up before you eat," Sandy Lynn says. Obviously, she doesn't know Joey. He definitely doesn't need to be reminded to use good hygiene.

"Make like a banana and split," he says, jumping up and running to the men's room. I wait awhile before I head to the ladies' room because I know Joey will take forever. When I get back to the table, he's beaten me. He's already sitting there, his hair wet and combed to the side, his cheeks scrubbed pink. He hasn't started eating, even though I know he's really hungry and loves spaghetti and meatballs. He's been waiting for me.

"Someday I'm going to kiss you," I say, before I even realize it.

"Someday I'm going to let you," Joey says.

I eat my muffins and drink my hot chocolate while Joey eats his spaghetti and meatballs, but I'm so rocks-on-my-head tired, I have to use my hand to prop my head up.

"Go to sleep," Joey says.

"Maybe I'll just rest a little," I say, putting my head down on the paper place mat.

It's cool against my cheek. There are so many sounds: Joey slurping his spaghetti, the *tink-tink* of forks, a door closing, footsteps coming close, then fading away like fog pushed by wind across the salt marsh, puffs of white drifting by, then thinning out into nothing.

"Chirp!" I'm being lifted up, strong arms wrapped tight around me. *Daddy!* I circle his waist with my legs and hold on. I can feel him sobbing, his chest pushing against mine. When he finally puts me down, everyone in the Pewter Pot is staring at us.

"Okay, show's over," Sandy Lynn grumbles. She's like a giant beech tree, planted in front of us, blocking the view. "You just take your time and say your hellos," she says gently. "No need to rush."

"Thank you," Daddy says, not looking at her. He's running his hands over my shoulders, down my arms, across my face, as if he's searching for injuries. "I should have called the police to tell them you were in Boston, after you called me. Anything could have happened to you in this crazy city."

I reach up and touch his wet face.

"Oh, sweetie," he says.

"Oh, Dad."

"Last night I talked to Sergeant Pirelli. We figured you and Joey were probably camped out somewhere close by; you know the woods and salt marsh like the back of your hand. He said if you weren't home by this afternoon, they were going to start searching. I can't believe you were so far from home!"

"I'm sorry, Dad." I feel bad I made him worry.

"My Chirp," he says, touching my cheek.

"Daddy."

"God, if I'd lost you, too . . ." Dad's shaking his head.

"She's not *lost*," I say, "she's *gone*."

"That's right, Chirpie. You're right. She's gone." Daddy's voice sounds like he's got rocks in his throat, just like me. He's holding both of my hands too hard in his, but I don't mind. I think he's trying to feel the blood flowing in my veins.

"Daddy," I say, leaning in and putting my head on his chest. He smells like dry grass. He smells just like him. I want to fall back asleep for a long, long time, right where I am, Daddy's breath in my hair.

"We've got to get you home," he says. "We've got to get you home and tuck you into bed. I'm so sorry, Chirpie. This is all too much."

"I took good care of her, Dr. Orenstein," Joey says quietly. I look at him. He's playing with the Sweet'N Low, stacking the pink packets up on his place mat.

Dad startles, like he's seeing Joey for the first time.

"Of course you did, Joey," Dad says. "Thank you."

"You're welcome."

"You're a good boy," Dad says. He reaches out and pats Joey's head. "You're welcome in our home any-time, Joey. You just come right on over."

"Thank you."

Dad puts ten dollars down on the table, which I think is extra money to reward Sandy Lynn for not being some weirdo who's mean to kids. He lifts me up again like I'm a little girl. I want to tell him to put me down, that I'm way too old to be carried now that I'm a runaway who made it in one piece all the way to Boston, but it just feels too good, my arms around his shoulders, my legs dangling down. Dad and I lead the way, and Joey follows us through Pewter Pot and out the door.

"Wow, it's still not dark," Joey says. The sky is a purplish gray.

"If feels like it should at least be tomorrow by now," I say.

"Or the day after," Joey says.

"You kids must be exhausted," Dad says. "Let's give your parents a quick call, Joey, and then we'll get going."

"My parents?" Joey's voice is trembly.

"Just to let them know that you're fine and we're heading home now."

"But you'll talk to them, not me, right?" Joey asks. "I mean, I'll be home really soon, and I can talk to them then."

Dad's quiet, and I know he's trying to figure out what to do.

"Dr. Orenstein?"

"Right, son," he says gently. "I'll make the call."

Dad puts me down next to our car. We've been gone for a little more than one day, but the car seems unfamiliar.

"In you go," Dad says, unlocking the door. We hop in. "I'm just walking to the pay phone," he says, pointing to the end of the block. "Right there. You see it?"

We look over the front seat and nod.

"I'll be right back. Lock the door," he says. He takes two steps, then looks over his shoulder to make sure we haven't disappeared.

"Wave to him," I say to Joey.

We wave. Dad waves back.

"Your car smells like saltines," Joey says.

"Saltines don't have a smell."

"Yes, they do."

"No, they don't."

"They smell like salt."

"Salt doesn't have a smell."

"Yes, it does."

"What does salt smell like?"

"Like saltines."

I look at Joey, sitting next to me in our car in downtown Boston in the purplish light.

"I'm going to miss you," I say.

"I live across the road," Joey says.

"That's not what I mean."

"I know."

Dad's walking toward us. Now he's jogging.

"Okeydoke," he says when he gets into the car. I'm waiting for him to tell Joey that his parents send their love or at least say hi, but he doesn't.

"Excuse me, Dr. Orenstein," Joey says, after Dad pulls out of the parking space and starts driving, "but what did my parents say?"

"They're glad you're safe. They'll see you when you get home."

"Um, so you talked with them yesterday when you realized Chirp was gone?"

"Yes. When it got dark and Chirp still wasn't home, I went to see if maybe you knew where she was. Your parents said that you weren't home, either, so we figured that the two of you were together. We thought that you were probably sleeping outside like Chirp and Rachel sometimes do in the summer."

"What did they say? I mean, were they . . . ?"

"They were very worried, just like I was," Dad says.

"But were they . . . I mean, what did they say?" Joey's nervous. I want to hold his hand, but I feel shy with Dad right there in the front seat.

"Mostly they were worried, because they care about you," Dad says. I can tell that he's not saying everything. Joey can tell, too. He's squirming around like he can't get comfortable.

"Okay," Joey whispers.

"Don't worry, son," Dad says. "They're going to be very happy to see you."

"Thanks," Joey says, but he doesn't sound thankful. I try to touch his hand, but he jerks it away.

When I wake up, we're parked in our driveway.

"Okay," Dad says, "we're home." There's a soft yellow glow in every one of our windows, and I wonder if Rachel decided it was okay, just this once, to waste energy and purposely turned all the lights on so that I'd feel extra welcome.

Joey doesn't move, but I can't tell in the dark if it's because he's sleeping or because he just doesn't want to get out of the car. Before I can even poke him, Rachel's at my door, trying to pull it open. I lift up my button and she's reaching in, hugging me.

"I'm so sorry, Chirpie." She's crying and laughing at the same time. "I'm so glad you're okay. I can't believe you actually took a bus to Boston! We were so worried about you. Dad and I were frantic. We were *frantic.*" Her words are spilling all over me. She's tugging on my hand.

Joey's just sitting there, not moving. With the car light on, I can see that he's awake. He's staring out the window, into the night.

"Joey?"

"Okay," he whispers, "I *know*." He carefully opens

the car door like he's an old man who isn't sure where he is or where he's going.

"C'mon, Chirpie," Rachel says, grabbing my knapsack from the seat and linking her arm through mine.

Now Joey's out of the car and leaning against the bumper. He's looking at his house. I want to go stand next to him, just the two of us and no one else for just a minute, but I'm attached to Rachel's arm.

"Popcorn," Rachel says. "I'll make us popcorn with lots of salt."

Joey takes a few baby steps down our driveway. Even though he's schlepped his duffel bag everywhere the past two days, it suddenly looks way too heavy for him. I wonder if he's going to make it across the road.

"I'll be right back," I say to Rachel. "Give me a minute."

"But you just got home and—" She starts walking toward the house, forcing me to follow along.

"No." I slip my arm out of hers and stand still in the cool night air. My sister reaches for me, but I step back. "No," I say again.

"Dad?" Rachel says. She sounds worried, like maybe I'm going to slink off into the woods.

"Rach, honey," Dad says, "it's okay. The two of them have just shared a lot together. Give your sister a minute."

Rachel sighs but she catches up with Dad. They walk up our front stairs and go inside.

From the end of our driveway, I watch Joey across the road. He's moving slowly, lugging his duffel bag up his walkway, dragging it across the bricks like it's a stubborn basset hound. I'm worried that his parents might hear the scrapey sound and peek out and get mad at him, since he's probably wearing out the bottom of the bag. When he gets to the steps, he stops and turns around. Is he looking for me? His hair's shining white in the porch light.

"I'm right here," I whisper-shout.

He waves. I wave back, but I'm not sure he can see me in the dark. He's just standing there. He isn't climbing the couple of steps to his front door. He isn't turning the doorknob and disappearing inside.

I want to hear an owl. The ancient Greeks believed that if an owl flew over soldiers before a battle, they wouldn't lose. They wouldn't get slaughtered by the enemy. It's another fact about owls that I could have told Joey, that I should have told Joey, when we were in the glass house and he was scared.

Joey's running back to me. His footsteps sound like a pounding heart.

"Hey," he says.

"Hey." I open up my arms. We're pressed together, holding on tight. His body's shaking.

"I don't want to go—"

"We'll walk to the bus stop every day," I say into his ear. "We'll bike to the glass house after school. We'll hang out in the salt marsh, and when it's warmer, we'll climb to the top of the beech tree and try to see Italy."

Joey looks at me, his face wet, then at his house again. He shakes his head because he knows that all of our plans can't save him.

"I guess I've got to go," he whispers.

"Want me to come?" I ask, but we both know the answer.

Joey walks back to his house, slowly, slowly, since the rocks on his head, the rocks in his heart, are weighing him down. He reaches out and rings his doorbell, which means he knows the door is locked. If I were his parents, I wouldn't lock it if I knew that my runaway son was coming home. I'd leave the door wide open, even if it meant that a bat might fly through and I'd have to shoo it out with a broom, even if it meant that the chilly night air would seep in. If my runaway son was coming home, I'd be standing right there at the open door, waiting to give him a hug and say hello.

The door doesn't open. Joey rings the bell again. I want to hear an owl. I want to hear any old night bird. Nothing, just tons of spring peepers singing their squeaky little song. I can't stand watching Joey on his porch while the door stays shut tight.

"Cowabunga," I whisper, but he can't hear me.

I'm running across the road, because I feel too alone watching Joey so alone, when suddenly the door jerks open. A big, hairy hand reaches out, grabs

Joey's jacket, and yanks him, hard, inside. It happens so fast I almost think I've imagined it. But his duffel bag is sitting there on the porch, still waiting, like a lonely dog.

Before I know what I'm doing, my fist is knocking, knocking, knocking. I hear one of Joey's brothers yell, "Jeez, Dad! Just leave the kid alone!"

Mrs. Morell opens the door, tears streaming down her face.

"Yes?" she says, looking back over her shoulder into the house. Joey is wrapped up in Vinnie's arms. Mr. Morell stomps around them.

"Here," I say, handing Mrs. Morell the duffel bag. "This is Joey's."

"Thank you," she says quietly, and starts to close the door.

"Wait!" I say, in my loudest, clearest voice. Mr. Morell stops and stares at me. "Don't blame Joey. It was *my* idea. He was just being a good friend, a *great* friend, to come along and look out for me. You should be proud of him."

Vinnie nods and pulls Joey into him tighter.

Joey lifts his head off Vinnie's chest. "Yeah, Dad. You're never proud of me," he says, looking right at Mr. Morell. Then he settles his head back against his brother.

No one says anything for a long time.

"Okay. That's all, folks." Mr. Morell claps his hands like it's the end of a performance. "Charlene, close the door." But Mrs. Morell takes her sweet time. She gives me the chance to watch Mr. Morell turn away and slowly climb the stairs. And to hear Vinnie say to Joey, "Next time you decide to piss off Dad, come talk to me first." It's only after Joey lifts his head and gives me a little smile that she finally closes the door.

"I'm in here!" Rachel yells when she hears me come in. What I want is to sit in the dark in the living room and look out the window and see Joey's bedroom light turn on so I'll know he's okay, just unpacking his duffel bag and getting into his pajamas and then brushing his teeth and going to bed like any boy at night.

"I'm making us popcorn," Rachel yells.

"Come on in," Dad yells.

When I walk into the kitchen, Dad and Rachel both rush over to me.

"Here, sit down, honey," Dad says, pulling out a chair for me like he's a waiter at a fancy restaurant.

Rachel's standing so close to me that I bump her with my elbow when I sit down, but I guess she doesn't notice.

"Oh, I think I'm burning the vegetable oil," she says, racing back to the stove. "I thought you'd like some popcorn, lots of salt." She's smiling and nodding like those waggle dolls people put on the dashboards of their cars.

"We're so glad you're home, honey," Dad says.

I know it's just popcorn popping, but when I close my eyes, what I see is handfuls of pebbles dropping onto the road. White stones, gray stones, brown stones, bouncing on the black asphalt.

"Are you okay, Chirpie?" It's Rachel, still looking worried. "We want to hear all about everything."

"If you're ready to talk about it, of course," Dad says.

"Of course. If you're ready to talk about it," Rachel says.

"But we really *do* want to hear."

Rachel's dumping the popcorn into a shiny metal bowl. She's sprinkling tons of salt on it. "Let's go sit in the living room," she says, and starts leading the way, Dad behind her.

I want to sneak out the back door and into the toolshed. I'll listen to the squeaky peepers and the sound of my breath. If the marsh lady is hunkered down in there, I'll tell her that she has to scoot over and let me sit down on the wooden planting bench and get comfortable. She has no choice. Maybe her life has been hard, but mine hasn't been all peaches and roses, either. I just got home from running away, and Mom is still dead and always will be. There's nothing I can do about it. And Joey could be in trouble at this exact second, and there's nothing I can do about that, either, except keep being his friend, since he's right: you can't make grown-ups not do what they're going to do.

"Chirp? Are you coming?" Rachel's back in the hallway.

I want to want the popcorn that's waiting for me in the living room. I want to want to thank Rachel for the extra salt, which is how I like it. I want to want to cuddle on the couch with her and Dad and tell them all about my adventures.

But my legs are stuck like I walked into the salt marsh at low tide and sunk down into the silky mud, where the oysters live.

Rachel's looking at me. Her eyes are deep brown like Mom's.

"I'm tired," I say.

"Too tired," she says. And then I see it, the dark under her eyes like smudges of damson plum jam.

For the first time, I get it. Mom was her mom, too.

"You're tired," I say.

She nods.

I wrap my arms around my sister's waist and squeeze. She's not as thin as she used to be. I remember how it felt to twirl around with her. It's been too long since we've danced together, but I'm not sure if we'll ever do it again.

"I can't hang out and talk with you and Dad tonight," I say. "I just can't."

"I know," she says. She sounds disappointed, but she doesn't let me go.

"Maybe tomorrow."

"Okay," she says. "Or the next day."

The clock ticks in the hallway. Dad clears his throat in the living room.

"You know," I whisper in my sister's ear, "the lilacs will bloom soon."

"Really?"

"I don't want them to," I say. "I don't want them to bloom without Mom here."

"We'll go out and clip them together."

"And then throw them in the trash can," I say.

Rachel lets go of me. She's looking at me, but I can't tell what she's thinking. What if she says *Oh, Chirp! Of course we won't throw the lilacs in the trash can! We'll arrange them in the blue vase and the orange vase and the white vase, just like Mom did, and then put them on the living room table and in the front hallway, where they'll look so pretty, but we'll have to be sure not to put any in the kitchen since they'll smell too sweet for Daddy and he won't be able to eat his meals.*

"We'll set them on fire and watch them burn," my sister says.

I'm so relieved, I throw my arms back around her. "We'll dig a hole and bury them alive!"

"We'll snip them into little pieces and drown them with the hose!"

"Stupid flowers!"

"Idiot lilacs!"

We're laughing, but we could just as easily be crying.

"God, I'm glad you're home," Rachel says, and now she *is* crying.

I squeeze her tighter.

"I don't want to go to school tomorrow," I say. "I really just want to stay home."

"I'll tell Dad we're both staying home. I didn't go to school today in case you came home, but I can miss tomorrow, too. I have a math test, but I'll take a make-up. We can just hang out."

"Girls?" Daddy yells from the living room. "Popcorn's getting cold."

"Tell Dad—" I pull away from Rachel and take a step backward.

"That you've gone to bed and will see him in the morning," Rachel says.

I smile and Rach smiles back.

"Good night," I say.

"Good night, Chirpie."

I start to carry my backpack up the stairs, but I stop when I hear footsteps behind me. It's Dad. He puts his hand, warm, on my head and follows me upstairs.

"You can skip brushing your teeth tonight if you want," he says.

"I don't think so. Joey says—" If I start talking about Joey, I won't be able to stop. Dad will try to convince me that Joey's going to be just fine, that I have nothing to worry about. But I know that Dad doesn't know that. There are plenty of things Dad doesn't know. He sits down on the toilet lid, and I sit on his lap and brush my teeth, just like I did when I was little. We walk to my room, Dad's hand warming the top of my head again. He waits outside my door while I change into my flannel nightgown.

"Ready," I say.

"Okay." Dad comes in. He pulls back my covers, and I get into bed. "We'll talk more tomorrow," he says. "I want to hear everything."

"Okay."

"Great," Dad says.

"Well, maybe not everything." I don't know exactly what I mean, but it feels good to say it.

"Okay, then. Maybe not." His voice is so sad. "Anyway, honey, I'm glad you're home. Good night." He kisses my forehead and turns out my light.

"Good night, Dad."

As soon as Dad's gone, I sit up and look out my window. Joey's light is still off, which might be a bad sign. On the other hand, there's a chance that he already got ready for bed with his light on, then turned his light off, and now he's safely sleeping to the sound of his parents talking through his bedroom wall. *I'm so glad to have him home. He scared us half to death, but he's a good boy.* I lift my window all the way up so I can hear everything that goes on at night.

Mrs. Newlon's sprinkler is on. Someone somewhere

is listening to the radio. And I know that in the salt marsh, the herons and egrets are asleep, standing in the water. If a predator heads toward them, they feel the vibrations in the water and wake up. Ducks and geese have the same built-in alarm system. They fall asleep, floating in the water. But if there's danger paddling toward them, they feel the water move. Smart birds, their instincts say *Wake up, stay safe.* And me? My instinct tells me it's time to lie down, snuggle under my covers, and close my eyes, home.

ACKNOWLEDGMENTS

My deepest thanks and love to my mother, Shelley Ehrlich, who taught me that language is light; *may her memory be for a blessing*. Doris Goldberg, you're right: Mom would have been so proud.

I've been in remarkably good hands throughout the writing of *Nest*. Thank you, Susan Golomb, agent extraordinaire, for your savvy and smarts. Thanks, too, to Krista Ingebretson, for your gentle, patient guidance. Wendy Lamb, I'm grateful to you for so much, including your keen editorial eye and unending enthusiasm, and especially for falling in love with Chirp and Joey! Dana Carey, I appreciate all of your hard work and support. I'd also like to thank Soumeya Bendimerad, Cailean Geary, Candy Gianetti, Colleen Fellingham, Alison Kolani, Tamar Schwartz, Tracy Heydweiller, Kate Gartner, Stephanie Moss, Teagan White, Kathy Chetkovich, and Charles Reilly.

To Dad, my brother and sisters, and all of my family, my love and appreciation. My friends, know that though I'm not listing you here by name, your belief in me has made all the difference. Emma and Riley,

I love you. Thanks for your patience and excitement and for gracefully sharing me with my "other kids" who live in this book. And, finally, to Neal: my muse, my brilliant reader, my true love. I'm grateful to you beyond words.